WHAT CAUSED THE 1692 WITCHCRAFT HYSTERIA?

HYSTERIA AND FORGIVENESS IN EARLYNEW ENGLAND

BY HOWARD KAEPPLEIN
EDITED BY MITCHELL F. BARKER

Howard Kaepplein
Harvard, Massachusetts
kaeppleinpublishing@gmail.com

First Edition 2014

Published by
KMR & Company
Marlborough, MA 01752
kmrco@verizon.net

ISBN 978-0-9907269-1-3
Cover depicts the trial of Abigail Faulkner trial, her accuser pointing
and Richard Barker observing.
Illustration by Kay McGinnis Ritter.

DEDICATION

FOR

BENJAMIN BARKER FULLER
THAT HE MAY KNOW HIS HEROIC ANCESTOR

AND

RUTH KAEPPLEIN POWERS (1922-2009)
WHO BEGAN THE BARKER GENEALOGY RESEARCH

CONTENTS

WHAT CAUSED THE 1692 WITCHCRAFT HYSTERIA?

I have been searching for the answer to this question since I learned that my mother's ancestors were involved in it. I did genealogical and historical research on my Barker ancestors for more than eight years and eventually wrote a novel to tell their story. Now, at last, I believe I have found the answer. I can take you through my long study to the conclusion, but I have decided to make the journey less burdensome for you, by starting at the end and working backwards.

PART I: THE CONCLUSION

First, some clarification of misunderstood aspects of the 'Salem witchcraft.' Salem was the seat of Essex County, and thus, the location of the jail and courthouse. The first 'witchcraft' incidents appear to have taken place in Salem Village, which was the original name of what is today, Danvers, Massachusetts. Charges quickly were made in other Essex County towns, including Salem Town. The largest number of charges were made in Andover – more than fifty.

Most intelligent people know there was no such thing as witchcraft. It was a fantasy in the imagination of a few Puritan zealots to punish those who failed to follow the prescribed norms of behavior.

After decades of wild speculation and more scholarly analysis, we are finally zeroing in on the cause of this sad episode in American history. It is becoming clear that the cause was the unraveling of fundamentalist Puritanism in Massachusetts and the angry backlash against it by the entrenched fundamentalists.

Puritanism was perhaps the strictest and most severe religion ever visited on the American continent. Rules for comportment were unwavering; the basic teaching stressed God's providence (mostly punishment) rather than today's teaching of God's love for all of his people. Puritan preachers instilled a fear of God in their parishioners as well as a love of God. Punishment by the authorities included dismembering of ears or fingers and banishment from the protection of the community.

The first indication of unraveling Puritanism occurred in Andover in 1681 when Pastor Frances Dane significantly reduced his preaching. There is no historical record that specifically explains why he did that, but there are many clues. Because of Dane's reduced preaching, Andover selectmen called a second pastor, Rev. Thomas Barnard.

The selectmen attempted to cancel or greatly reduce Dane's salary, but he appealed to the General Court, who set up a commission to decide the issue. The commission included judge Saltonstall, who later indicated his doubts about witchcraft and resigned from the Court of Oyer and Termina. Also on the commission were revered elders of Ipswich, Haverhill, Rowley, and Newberry. Some of them may have known Dane and Barnard. When they issued their decision regarding Dane's compensation, they also urged him to increase his preaching. For the next eight years Dane and Barnard shared preaching duties, apparently peacefully. It may be that some members of the commission met regularly with Barnard and Dane to check on their level of cooperation.

On June 28, 1689, everything changed. Abenaki Indians attacked Dover, New Hampshire, killing 23 and capturing 29. In August 1689, they over-ran Pemaquid. In the winter/spring of 1690, they burned Salmon Falls and Casco. Finally, on January 24, 1692 they attacked York, Maine, killing more than 100. Cotton Mather published a widely-distributed pamphlet describing the attacks in horrible detail. He ascribed all of the attacks to 'God's Providence' against the colonists for their sins. Actually, many of the attacks were ordered by the French from Quebec, who paid for each white scalp the Indians provided to them.

Nonetheless, many other fundamentalist Puritans took up the claim of God's

Providence. Specific complaints about new preaching were heard and there is evidence that Pastor George Burroughs of Salem Village had changed his preaching. Years after Thomas Barnard completed his service and died, there appears to have been some suggestion that he had provided some of the fundamentalist pushback to Dane's new preaching. Siddeley's Harvard Graduates provides mini-bio's of several listed graduates. In the bio of Rev. John Barnard, son of Thomas Barnard, an excerpt from his letters states "I have read all of my father's sermons and found nothing untoward in any of them." No copy of any of those sermons exists today, nor of any of Pastor Dane's.

Witches were believed to be under a spell, controlled by the devil. One magistrate asked one of the accused, "How long have you been in the devil's snare?" Witches were also believed to inhabit several members of a family. After the hysteria was launched by Cotton Mather's proclamation of Satan's influence, twenty-six of Pastor Francis Dane's extended family were charged with witchcraft. One could clearly conclude that the real target was Francis Dane; his preaching had likely changed in 1680-81 and it was believed to be influenced by the devil.

The highly respected Richard Barker led the reaction, claiming the devil's influence in Dane's new preaching. Barker, the senior member of the Andover selectmen, likely wrote to Cotton Mather when Dane changed his preaching. Since Dane had severely cut back his preaching, Mather took a measured response by recommending a second pastor, Thomas Barnard. Mather knew Barnard from their days together at Harvard.

Cotton Mather invoked the specter of Satanism as the cause of George Burroughs' change. It was the primary reason why Cotton Mather called him "king of hell" when he urged the execution of Burroughs to proceed despite some cries from the crowd to halt it, after Burroughs' stirring prayer on the gallows. Word spread that the devil was actively at work in Massachusetts and was operating through witches.

Many considered Cotton Mather the primary defender of the Puritan faith, as he did, himself.

The general belief was that witches were mostly women, so the conclusion was that Pastor Dane had come under the influence of witches in his extended family. The townspeople responded to Barker's warning, bringing witchcraft charges against twenty-six of Pastor Dane's extended family. Dane's resourceful daughter, Abigail Dane Faulkner, seems to have been a special target, perhaps because she was the most intelligent and influential of his family members.

One wonders whether there was a plan to support the entrenched Puritans when Richard Barker's son, William, was charged with witchcraft. He was prepared with a detailed confession which contained all of the elements of the witchcraft charges the magistrates were pressing the accused to confess to. He also added new anti-Puritan statements which further supported the witchcraft process. When William Barker served his purpose by testifying against Abigail Faulkner, the magistrates apparently failed to return him to his cell and he walked out with his brother John and the rest of the crowd.

PART II: THE RATIONALE

BARKER ANCESTRY

I am not an historian, although I am a history buff. I have many history books, most of which I have studied thoroughly. This is the result of my research into my Barker ancestry, beginning with a most unusual marriage I came across in the Massachusetts Vital Records.

ACTON MASSACHUSETTS MARRIAGES

BARKER,

Jonathan and Nancy Swan,

both of Sudbury, Canada

June 18, 1788

This marriage presented many questions. First, the exact location of Sudbury, Canada. A simple Google search revealed that it was the early name of the town that later became incorporated as Bethel, Maine. Apparently, one of the earliest settlers came from Sudbury, Massachusetts, and people used the term, Sudbury, Canada, to indicate that it was a different Sudbury – one further north, although not really in the country of Canada.

TRAVEL TIME

It seemed quite unusual for two people from this town in the western mountains of Maine to travel all the way to Acton, Massachusetts, to be married. I contacted the director of the Bethel Historical Society and asked how long this journey would have taken in June 1788.

FROM SUDBURY, CANADA TO ACTON, MASSACHUSETTS

- Minimum of Six Days
- 30 mi. on foot, Sudbury, Canada, to Fryeburg, Maine
- Canoe down Saco River to Saco, Maine
- Schooner down coast and up Merrimack River to Methuen
- Horse-drawn coach to Acton, Massachusetts

This was his answer, noting that the trip down the Saco required fording the canoe over three falls on the way. The Saco River is rather shallow, requiring considerable effort to avoid rocks on the journey.

EXPLANATIONS

- In 1692 Timothy Swan accused William Barker of witchcraft
- William then accused Abigail Dane Faulkner of witchcraft
- Abigail was convicted and sentenced to be hanged

The next obvious question and its answer had already occurred to me because I was familiar with the Andover witch hysteria of 1692.

RELATIONSHIPS

- Betrothed were great grand niece and nephew of Timothy and William
- Justice of the Peace was Francis Faulkner, grandson of Abigail Dane Faulkner
- The more important bit of information was the answer to the question, "Why did they travel to Acton, Massachusetts, to be married?"

I visited the Acton Historical Society a few miles east of my home in Harvard, Massachusetts. They immediately told me that the Justice of the Peace at that time was Col. Francis Faulkner, grandson of Abigail Dane Faulkner. Thus, it seems, this was a marriage of reconciliation for the enmity that was caused between these three families nearly one hundred years earlier.

WHO ARRANGED IT?

- Jonathan Barker, Jr., father of bridegroom
- He had been raised by his grandfather, Benjamin Barker, from age eight,

when his father died.

- Benjamin was the youngest son of proprietor Richard Barker and lived with him until Richard's death.

I had often wondered why those fifty people of Andover and their families who had been accused of witchcraft did not sue or otherwise show their anger at those who had falsely accused them, causing them at the least to spend several weeks in a cold jail. This marriage seemed to be a partial answer, but how could it have been compelled so many years after the crime?

Helen Abbott's history of Andover's families has been posted on line. It provides much relevant information to help answer this question. Thus, there was a living link back to Benjamin, the youngest of proprietor Richard Barker's sons. It also suggests that Benjamin may have been instructed by his father to salve the wounds of 1692, since he had cared for his father during his final weeks.

DID BENJAMIN INITIATE THE IMPERATIVE FOR THE MARRIAGE?

- Benjamin had become friends with Francis Faulkner
- He witnessed Faulkner's deed to convey property to Ammi Ruhammah
- He provided the dowry for Faulkner's niece-in-law's marriage
- Faulkner arranged the marriage of Benjamin's son, Jonathan, Sr.

The healing process began during Benjamin's life. To fully understand these points, I must explain who this niece-in-law was. Abigail Dane Faulkner's husband, Francis Faulkner, had a sister, Hannah, who married a man named Pasco Chubb. This man became commander of Fort Pemaquid in what is today Portland, Maine.

During a peace parley with local Penobscot Indians in 1698, Pasco Chubb had his men attack the Indians from behind, trying to kill them. Some got away and a day or two later Indians and French surrounded the fort, so Pasco Chubb abandoned his post and sailed down the coast to Boston, where he was imprisoned for dereliction of duty. Dudley Bradstreet appealed for his release for the sake of his wife, Hannah. A few days after he returned home to Hannah, Indians came to his home in Andover, and killed both Hannah and Pasco Chubb. This couple's young daughter, also named Hannah, was spared. Francis and Abigail raised Hannah Chubb as their own child. Years later, she married John Abbott, son of Thomas Abbott, who had come to Andover from Rowley about 1660.

Bear with me now, this gets a bit complicated.

John Abbott had a brother, Joseph, who moved to Marblehead, where he married Sarah Deveraux, daughter of John Deveraux, a wealthy merchant. Deveraux bought cod from local fishermen, filleted, salted, dried it and packed it and shipped it to Boston and Philadelphia, and to England. If you are familiar with Marblehead, you might recognize the name of the man for whom Deveraux beach and Deveraux Park are named.

Marblehead was a dangerous place for young women in those days. There were several records of rapes and attempted rapes by drunken seamen. So, when Joseph's oldest daughter, Susannah reached her teens, she was sent back to live with her uncle John Abbott in Andover. Francis Faulkner arranged Susannah Abbott's marriage to Nathaniel Pettengel, and the couple settled on land in Methuen that was provided by Benjamin Barker. Abbott's history of Andover tells us that the Barkers owned "about half" of Methuen, almost all of the area west of the Spicket River.

A few years later, a second daughter of Joseph and Susannah Deveraux Abbott, Mary, was also sent to Andover to live with her uncle John. Francis Faulkner and Benjamin Barker arranged her marriage to Benjamin's son, Jonathan Barker. Before you get confused about all the Jonathan Barkers, let me explain that there were three generations of them. This was the first Jonathan, and he died in 1737 at age 28, during the great diphtheria epidemic, when his son, the second Jonathan, was just eight years old.

After the death of Francis Faulkner's wife, Abigail, he moved in with Hannah and John Abbott. When Francis Faulkner died, John Abbott was the executor of his will.

THE SINE QUA NON
THE KEY TO THE MYSTERY

Why did Pastor Francis Dane reduce his preaching in 1681?

So far, everything I have told you is fact. Now, I must use deductive reasoning to answer more of the puzzle. Let's go back to 1681, when Pastor Francis Dane reduced his preaching, forcing the selectmen to call a new pastor, Thomas Barnard.

NOT BECAUSE OF HIS AGE OR INFIRMITY

When the Selectmen tried to cut Dane's salary after hiring Thomas Barnard, the authorities agreed with his appeal, and *ordered him to increase his preaching*!

He continued to preach for 16 years and worked alone and tirelessly to end the witchcraft actions in 1693.

When Barnard was installed, the selectmen attempted to drastically reduce Dane's salary, but he appealed to the General Court, who sided with him, due to his thirty-three years of faithful service. In the Court's judgment, they strongly suggested that Dane should do more preaching. This belies the assumption (not fact) that Dane had reduced his preaching due to his age or some infirmity. He did it for some yet unexplained reason.

THE IMPERATIVE WAS INITIATED BY RICHARD BARKER

The evidence includes an historical trail that begins in December 1675, when twelve men from Andover participated in The Great Swamp Fight. Two of them were Joseph Abbott and John Faulkner.

To find the real answer, let's go back a few years to the Great Swamp Fight in December 1675 when a thousand men of the Massachusetts militia attacked a Narragansett fortified camp at South Kingstown, Rhode Island. This was the beginning of King Philip's War, intended to discourage the Narragansett Indians from joining the other tribes who had agreed to join King Philip as he attacked colonial villages later. Twelve sons of Andover proprietors were part of that militia, one of whom, Ebenezer Barker, was wounded. Two others were Joseph Abbott and John Faulkner.

KING PHILIP'S WAR

- In January 1676, Indians raided Andover. They held the Bradstreet family hostage until they learned the location of Joseph Abbot and John Faulkner.
- They killed Joseph Abbot as he worked in the field.
- They gathered the Faulkner animals in a hovel and burned them, the barn and the house.
- In the weeks following, the Indians burned the entire towns of Lancaster, Groton, Marlborough, and Sudbury, killing many residents in the

process.

All of these towns had committed atrocities against Indians in recent years.

The attack on Andover was limited, compared to the attacks on other towns. Knowing all the facts, it was clearly retribution for the actions of two men at the Great Swamp Fight. All of the Puritan leaders and all of the Andover townspeople but Pastor Dane, however, held a different view. To them, this was God's punishment for the sins of the people – He had loosed the devil to encourage the Indians to attack the settlers for their sins. There may have been one or two others who believed as Pastor Dane did – his daughters, Abigail Dane Faulkner and Elizabeth Dane Johnson.

THE CRIMES OF ABBOT & FAULKNER AGAINST INDIANS

- After the fighting ended in Rhode Island, over 200 women and children were left in the wigwams.
- The militiamen were ordered to burn the wigwams and kill all the women and children.
- Faulkner was likely one of those torching wigwams and Abbott one of those shooting women and children as they fled.

These points don't need further explanation except to point out the divergence in individuals' understanding of the Indian attack and its explanation. Once you learn the facts, you and I and Pastor Francis Dane readily understood that they were retaliation for the brutal killing of defenseless women and children. It's a simple matter of cause and effect, but not to the Puritans.

ANDOVER PEOPLE LEARN THE REASON FOR THE RAID

- It probably took a year or more. Dudley Bradstreet would have been reluctant to explain that he had given specific directions to the Indians.
- John Faulkner would have admitted his role, since he was just following orders.
- The other ten participants may have eventually revealed what happened.

PASTOR DANE WAS TROUBLED ABOUT THE KILLING OF WOMEN

- He likely read the entire Bible, searching for guidance.
- Eventually, he decided that it was wrong, and began preaching from the Gospels, about God's love for all people and forgiveness.

- By 1680 he was preaching against the actions of John Faulkner and Joseph Abbot.

RICHARD BARKER'S POSITION IN ANDOVER

- His name appears as a witness on every legal document in 17th century Andover.
- He was elected a selectman nearly every year – far more than anyone else.

Now we get back to the Barker family, and specifically, Richard Barker and his role in Andover. He seems to have been highly respected in Andover, but the reasons are not clear. My view is that he was extremely pious – he tried to be as perfect a Puritan as he could, patterning himself after John Winthrop. Winthrop kept a journal during much of his life. During his college years his journal contained daily entries of his many sins. For example, enjoying a meal more than he ought; enjoying a leisurely walk when he should have been studying or praising God.

The Puritans took the first commandment very seriously. Man was required to love and praise God during all of his waking moments. I believe that Richard Barker's comportment showed his devotion to God. I suspect that he often prayed aloud during Meeting, asking God to forgive the townspeople's sins and to strengthen the town.

- He was assumed to be one of the Elect (Sarah Vowel)
- He likely came in 1638 with Ezekiel Rogers but did not stay with him in Rowley because Rogers did not allow 'open prayer'.
- He became the chief overseer of the pastor.

In Sarah Vowel's book, "The Wordy Shipmates," she states that the Puritans were Calvinists, believing that God had chosen his elect and that there was nothing a person could do to change this. However, everyone was obliged to act as if they were one of the elect, but almost no one could. If any man did, well, he was assumed to be one of the elect. That was Richard Barker. There were other indications that Richard Barker was one of the elect; for example, that he had been blessed with six sons, and that he continued to acquire wealth, which he used to buy more land – around Great Pond and in Methuen.

My final point here cannot be found in any of the source material or in any of the books by historians. It is, however, almost a necessary conclusion to the analysis I have laid out.

CONFLICT WITH PASTOR DANE

- Richard Barker was very upset with Pastor Dane's new preaching.
- He criticized him directly and openly after the service.
- In response, Dane cut back his preaching to once each Sunday or none.

Now, I must try to explain what it was about Pastor Dane's new preaching that upset Richard Barker.

One possibility is that Pastor Dane used Jesus's parables from the Gospels to teach principles which opposed Richard's understanding of Puritan principles. For example, he may have used the parable of the Good Samaritan, where a good Israelite fell injured by the side of the road and was passed by several of his kind, but was helped by one of the despised Samaritans. The conclusion is that all are equal in the sight of God, while Puritans believed in a hierarchy that was indicated by the seating arrangement at meeting.

Another parable he might have used is that of the prodigal son, who had left his father's house and lived a shameful life, returning penniless. His father welcomed him home with a celebrity feast, forgiving him his sinful life.

Richard Barker may have openly suggested to Pastor Dane that his preaching was inspired by the devil. The people of Andover would have known of Barker's criticisms of Pastor Dane, particularly about his suggestion that Dane's preaching was inspired by the devil. At this point, the people believed Richard Barker more than Pastor Dane.

SELECTMEN CALL THOMAS BARNARD

The General Court had suggested this earlier, because of the burden of preaching twice each Sunday, plus teaching all the town's children to read and write, plus Latin & Greek to those aspiring to attend Harvard.

Andover had no Grammar School to teach Latin & Greek, since Richard Barker did not support it.

There is nothing in Andover's history to confirm that Andover had followed the General Court's requirement that every town with over fifty families have a separate school to teach reading, writing, and arithmetic, or that towns with 100 families have a grammar school to teach Latin and Greek (a requirement to enter Harvard). Mofford's new book states that Andover's grammar school was not set up until 1710. Thus, there was a heavy burden on Pastor Francis

Dane to do all of the teaching in addition to his preaching chores (two hour sermons every Sunday morning and again in the afternoon. I believe that Richard Barker would not support the teaching of Latin, because it was the language of the pope.

By the way, to contrast Andover's lack of historic documentation of its schools, Methuen's is well documented. It was founded by Stephen Barker (Enders Robinson's ancestor) in 1726 and they built the Meeting House a year later and a school six months after that. Stephen's son, Zebadiah, was the first teacher.

TWO PASTORS, TWO SALARIES

The townspeople were angry about the increased tax to support two pastors. They blamed Pastor Dane.

KING WILLIAM'S WAR

- In 1690 Indians destroyed many towns in southern Maine, killing hundreds in some.
- Mary Beth Norton: The Puritan worldview was that God was allowing Satan to move against them, for their sins.
- Joshua Scottow: Our churches must return to the good old way we have walked in.

King William's War frightened Andoverites who feared it could spread south to their town. Maine was extremely important to the leaders of Massachusetts, as it was the source of most of its wealth – furs, timber, and fish. All of Massachusetts's leaders had connections in Maine, family members who plied these trades, or investments in them. No one used common sense to see that King William's War was driven by the French from Canada, who paid Indians for each colonist's scalp they brought back. The Puritans were incensed more by the knowledge that many of the Abenakis had been converted to the hated Catholic religion. When Tad Baker conducted a twelve year archaeological dig of a wealthy mansion in Salmon Falls, Maine, one of the many artifacts he unearthed was a Jesuit ring.

Several Puritan leaders are on record for explaining the destruction in Maine to "God's providence moving against us." Governor Phipps made the same statement after his failed campaign in Quebec, perhaps to deflect criticism of his poor military strategy. The most damaging writing was by Cotton Mather, who wrote exaggerated stories of each of the attacks on Maine seacoast towns and explained all of them in terms of God's providence against the sins of the colonists.

My theory of Pastor Dane's use of the parables was in opposition to the Puritan principle of God's providence against the colonists for their sins. Richard Barker likely argued openly with Pastor Dane and may have suggested that his preaching was inspired by the devil.

WITCHCRAFT IN ANDOVER

Richard Barker had suggested the devil's influence in Pastor Dane's new preaching.

When witchcraft spread from Danvers to Andover, twenty-six relatives of Pastor Dane were charged – more than half of the total.

ABIGAIL DANE FAULKNER & HER SISTER ARE CHARGED

- Abigail seemed particularly targeted.
- Judges questioned her two successive weeks without action.
- Then, William Barker is charged and he quickly confesses and accuses the Dane sisters.

Abigail Dane Faulkner was well-known among Andoverites. They knew that her husband had a mental breakdown and that she had miraculously cured him with her knowledge of herbs. She had managed the Faulkner Tavern when her husband was incapacitated and they probably disliked her firm business-like manner. They may also have observed her different attitude towards her uncle John Faulkner, after she learned what he had done at the Great Swamp Fight.

While Abigail was extremely bright and capable, her sister Elizabeth was characterized by their father, Francis Dane, as "simple, at best, with no knowledge of witches."

ABIGAIL IS BROUGHT TO TRIAL

- With a Barker as witness against her, she is brought to trial, convicted, and sentenced to be hanged.
- Her sentence is postponed because she is pregnant.
- By the time her son was born, Gov. Phipps had stopped all prosecutions and executions.

Abigail's life was saved by her unborn son. When he arrived, she named him, Ammi Ruhammah, Hebrew for "My people have obtained mercy."

WILLIAM BARKER'S CONFESSION

- More detail than all other confessions combined.
- Surprising statement: Devil promised "all men would be equal and live bravely (not humbly). Possible suggestions from Pastor Dane's sermon.

William Barker's confession was well thought-out and crafted. It incorporated all of the other confessions the magistrates had imagined and pressured the accused to confess to. They must have loved it. This was likely the only confession which had not been composed by the magistrates themselves.

The statement, that stands out to us because of its similarity to the Declaration of Independence, stood out to the people of Andover because of its similarity to what they had heard from Pastor Dane's sermons. William Barker was implying that Pastor Dane was under the devil's influence. The statement that "all men should be equal and live bravely (proudly in modern parlance)" is opposed to Puritan principles; that there was a hierarchy among the citizens was indicated by their assigned seats in the Meeting House. The suggestion that people should live proudly was even worse. One of the bible verses well-known by the Puritans was Micah 6:8: "what does the Lord require of you but to do justice, and to love kindness, and to walk humbly with your God." Humility was a major requirement for all Puritans, especially women.

A SINGLE VOICE OF REASON VS SEVERAL VOICES OF FAITH

- Everyone believed that all fortune and misfortune was due to God's providence.
- The death and destruction by Abenaki Indians in Maine was the consequence of colonists' sins.
- God had loosed the devil to spread witchcraft in Andover.
- Puritan Faith incorporated superstition & ignorance

Everyone believed in witchcraft. There is a single verse in Exodus supporting that belief, but all pastors were familiar with 16th century history with stories of thousands burned for witchcraft in Belgium, western Germany, and eastern France, and smaller numbers in England. There were small books recounting strange postulations about the activities of witches. Cotton Mather published pamphlets reprinting some of those stories to 'educate' people of the current dangers. The most intellectual people in Massachusetts believed in witchcraft and in the preposterous witch stories they accused all of the victims of being involved in and pressing them to confess to them. Pastor Francis Dane apparently had doubts about all of it, but dared not say so. His early objections were legal ones regarding the type of evidence the judges were accepting.

The more important point is the singular worldview of the Puritans, that all events, both good and bad were the result of God's providence.

THE LETTER WHICH HELPED END ANDOVER'S NIGHTMARE

- Thomas Barnard and 30 Andoverites sign Francis Dane's "our sin of ignorance" letter.
- Richard Barker felt guilty for supporting witchcraft charges and opposing Pastor Dane.
- He died on March 18, 1693.

Pastor Dane wrote several letters to other Essex County pastors appealing for their help to stop the madness. Similar discussions were going on in Boston, with some progress regarding changes to the process. This was in response to the attitude of the people throughout the county which had turned against the trials. Finally, Pastor Dane wrote a letter which was signed by at least thirty people from Andover, including Thomas Barnard.

BENJAMIN AT RICHARD'S BEDSIDE WHEN HE DIED

Richard likely left Benjamin with the imperative to arrange marriages of reconciliation. I am convinced that this man, whom I believe helped drive the witchcraft hysteria in Andover, must have felt deep remorse when most of the authorities whom he respected decided it was a mistake. He felt most deeply about harming the Faulkner family and wanted a Barker-Faulkner marriage.

Jonathan Barker was unable to achieve the Barker-Faulkner marriage in his lifetime because of the bitterness of Ammi Ruhammah Faulkner. Ammi grew up with the witchcraft conviction hanging over his mother's and his family's heads. He was 17 years old before the General Court finally wiped the felony conviction from his mother's record. Col. Francis Faulkner had six daughters whose ages matched up well with Jonathan Barker's six sons, but he could not forget his father's admonition against the marriage.

However, I believe he laid the groundwork for the marriage in the next generation. He likely invited his cousin, John Faulkner to the marriage ceremony from his Bolton home and suggested that John's son marry the next female child born to one of Jonathan Barker's sons. That child was Dorcas Barker and, in 1808, she came down from Bethel and married Lovell Faulkner in Andover where they settled and had nine children.

If there was a villain to hold responsible for the witchcraft hysteria in Andover, it was not Thomas Barnard. He was a man of faith like all the other pastors in Essex County and all of the witchcraft judges and like Cotton Mather. If there was a villain, it may have been Richard Barker, whom the people of Andover looked up to and believed as he did. One thing is very clear, however, Pastor Francis Dane was a true hero throughout the ordeal. His story reminds me of Rudyard Kipling's poem, "If", which begins: "If you can keep your head when all about you are losing theirs and blaming it on you." Dane was alone in a sea of others who had lost their heads and blamed him, charging twenty-six of his family with witchcraft.

CHRONOLOGY

HISTORICAL EVENTS AFFECTING THE
BARKER-FAULKNER RELATIONSHIP

October 1675	Francis Faulkner married Abigail Dane
May 1689	Hannah Faulkner (sister to Francis) married Pasco Chubb
August 1692	Timothy Swan accuses William Barker of witchcraft. William Barker confesses and names Abigail Dane Faulkner his recruiter
August 1692	William Barker, Jr. testifies against Abigail Dane Faulkner
November 1692	Abigail Dane Faulkner convicted of witchcraft and sentenced to hang. Since she was pregnant, the sentence was delayed until the birth.
December 1692	Francis Faulkner and John Barker provide bail for the release of William Barker Jr. and Mary Barker.
January 1693	Gov. Phipps orders a halt to witchcraft trials and executions
March 1693	Richard Barker dies, leaves his house and land aside the road to Swan's Ferry plus land in Methuen, to his youngest son, Benjamin.
Feb. 22, 1698	Capt. Pasco Chubb, commander of Fort Pemmaquid, has his men attempt to kill Penobscot leaders during a peace

parley. They escape and return with large contingent of Indians and French soldiers and surround the fort. Chubb abandons the fort to them and escapes, sailing south to Boston, where he is imprisoned for abandoning his responsibility. He is released to return to his Andover home, on appeal by Simon Bradstreet.

Mar. 4, 1698 — Indians invade the home of Pasco Chubb, killing him and wife Hannah. Seven-year-old daughter Hannah is spared. She is then raised by Francis and Abigail Faulkner.

Nov. 28, 1708 — Abigail and Francis Faulkner arrange the marriage of their daughter, Dorothy, to Samuel Nurse, nephew of convicted and hanged witch, Rebecca Nurse of Salem Village (Danvers).

Apr. 11, 1710 — Francis Faulkner arranges the marriage of Hannah Chubb to John Abbott

January 1725 — Benjamin Barker elected Andover Representative to General Court

June 1726 — Ammi Ruhammah Faulkner, son of Francis & Abigail, married Hannah Ingalls, great niece of Abigail's mother.

April 1727 — Mary Abbott leaves her parents and siblings in Marblehead and moves to her uncle John's home in Andover.

Jan. 26, 1728 — Francis Faulkner arranges the marriage of Mary Abbott to Jonathan Barker

June 1728 — Francis Faulkner deeds to his son, Ammi Ruhammah, his house and land on the road to Swan's Ferry (across the road from Benjamin Barker's). The deed is witnessed by Benjamin Barker and his son, Joseph Barker.

Feb. 5, 1729 — Abigail Dane Faulkner died. Her husband, Francis, moved to town to the home of his adopted daughter, Hannah, and her husband, John Abbott.

Jan. 20, 1737 — Jonathan Barker, age 28, died in Methuen, leaving his wife, Mary, son Jonathan Jr. and three young daughters. Mary returns to her uncle John's house in Andover with the three girls, two of which die within two years. Jonathan moves in with his grandfather, Benjamin, who raises him until he can return to Methuen to run his father's farm.

Jonathan Barker Jr. (1728-1794) was the son of Jonathan Barker and Mary Abbott. Mary was the granddaughter of Thomas Abbott, who came to Andover around 1660 from Rowley. Her father, Joseph Abbott, was born in Andover in 1674, but he moved to Marblehead around 1694. He married Sarah Devereaux there. Mary Abbott was born in Marblehead in 1709 and she had two brothers and three sisters there. She moved to Andover to stay with her uncle about 1726 and married Jonathan Barker two years later.

Mary's uncle, John Abbott, was the husband of Hannah Chubb, who, as an infant, was orphaned when Indians killed her parents, Pasco Chubb and Hannah Faulkner Chubb, in 1698, in retribution for Chubb's betrayal at Fort Pemaquid. Hannah was raised by Abigail Dane Faulkner and Francis Faulkner. When Abigail died in 1729, Francis moved in with Hannah and John Abbott. When Francis died in 1731, John Abbott was the executor of his estate. By this time, his son Ammi Ruhammah Faulkner and baby son Francis Faulkner, were living in Acton.

WILLIAM BARKER'S FIRST CONFESSION

He admitted to have been "in the snare of the devil" for three years. Satan had promised "to pay all his debts" and allow him to live "comfortably," which he found very attractive because "he had a great family and the world went hard with him." After signing the devil's book, he had attended a witch meeting and sacrament in Salem Village with about one hundred others, "upon a green piece of ground near the minister's house." George Burroughs, a ringleader in that meeting "had summoned the witches there with a trumpet that could be heard "many miles off." Some of the witches had "Rapiers by their side." Satan chose to attack the Village first "by reason of the peoples being divided and their differing with their ministers" but the witches planned "to fall next on Salem and so go through the country."

Once they had established the devil's kingdom, "all persons should be equal and live bravely (proudly, in modern parlance – the opposite of the Puritan-required "humbly") and there would be neither punishment nor shame for sin and no day of resurrection or of judgment." Some unnamed leaders of the conspiracy had told him that there were about 307 witches in the country. "In the spring of the year the witches came from Connecticut to afflict at Salem Village but now they have left it off."

William Barker declared flatly that the sisters Elizabeth Dane Johnson and Abigail Dane Faulkner "have been my enticers to this great abomination."

THE SECOND CONFESSION[1]

A few days after his first confession, William Barker, Sr., produced a second confession from prison. "God having called me to confess my sin and apostasy in that fall in giving the Devil advantage over me, appearing to me like a black man in the evening to set my hand to his book, as I have owned to my shame. He told me that I should not want, so doing. At Salem Village, there being a little off the meetinghouse, about a hundred five blades, some with rapiers by their side, which was called, and might be more for ought I know, by Burse and Burroughs, and the trumpet sounded, and bread and wine which they called the sacrament, but I had none, being carried all over on a stick, never being at any other meeting. I being at cart a Saturday last, all the day, of hay and English corn, the Devil brought my shape to Salem, and did afflict Martha Sprague and Rose Foster by clinching my hand; and a Sabbath day my shape afflicted Abigail Martin, Jr. and, at night, afflicted Martha Sprague and Abigail Martin, Jr. Elizabeth (Dane) Johnson and Abigail (Dane) Faulkner have been my enticers to this great abomination, as one has owned and charged her to her sister with the same. And the design was to destroy Salem Village, and to begin at the ministers house, and to destroy the church of God, and to set up Satan's kingdom, and then all will be well. And now I hope God in some measure has made me something sensible of my sin and apostasy, begging pardon of God, and of the honorable magistrates and all God's people, hoping and promising by the help of God, to set to my heart and hand to do what in me lies to destroy such wicked worship, humbly begging the prayers of all God's people for me, I may walk humbly under this great affliction and that I may procure to myself the sure mercies of David, and the blessing of Abraham."

Most of the imprisoned Andover people confessed that they joined the Devil's church. Their descriptions of this hellish church—its forms, ceremonies and sacraments—are the imaginings of clerical minds. The thoughts of the ministers shine through in the words of the confessors. The confessions were extorted by persistent importunities; sometimes threats were used, and even torture. Certain fanatic clergymen were first and foremost in the efforts to extort confessions. These ministers molded the persecution into a religious shape and form. The ministers then quoted the works of their own minds (the

---

1   From *Salem Witchcraft and Hawthorne's House of Seven Gables* by Enders A. Robinson, with permission.

confessions that they zealously elicited) as proof of the Devil's plot, which they themselves claimed to dread. Cotton Mather, chief of this class, was the most forward in molding the affair of 1692 into a shape acceptable to his own illusions. The fabricated confessions revealed the whole scope of his superstitions and fanaticism. Cotton Mather used the confessions, especially references to Satan's plan to abolish all the churches and to the existence of hundreds of witches in the country, as proof of his own fantasies.

On September 16 William Barker, Sr. admitted to his confession before the Court of Oyer and Terminer at Salem. Sometime afterwards he made his escape from prison. On the back of his indictment for practicing witchcraft against Abigail Martin, Jr., it is written, "fled, persons fled." His cattle were immediately seized, but were redeemed by his brother, Lieut. John Barker, who paid £2 10s. to the deputy sheriff. About October 10, Lieut. John Barker and Francis Faulkner posted bonds for the release on bail of Mary Barker and William Barker, Jr. After six-weeks imprisonment the children were free, awaiting trial.

On January 3, 1693, the grand jury at the Superior Court of Judicature at Salem indicted both William Barker, Jr. and Mary Barker. However the two Barker children were not brought to trial at that time. A new bail bond had to be posted for the children to stay free. On January 13, 1673, Mary's father, Lieut. John Barker, together with Captain John Osgood posted "the sum of one hundred pounds to be levied on their or either of their lands & tenements, goods & chattels for the use of our said sovereign Lord & Lady, the King and Queen, on condition that William Barker, Jr. and Mary Barker having stood committed for suspicion of witchcraft shall make their personal appearance at the next Court of Assizes and General Jail Delivery to be holden for the County of Essex." At the May 10, 1693, meeting of the Superior Court of Judicature the two children made their appearance; each was tried by jury and found not guilty. Eleven years later, in 1704, Mary Barker and William Barker, Jr., first cousins, were married. Small wonder that these two, who had suffered hideous interrogation and imprisonment, should choose one another. They had eight children. He died in 1745, aged 66, and she died in 1752, aged 72. William Barker, Sr. died in 1718, aged 72; his wife, Mary, died in 1744, aged 88. The four graves may still be found in the old cemetery in North Andover.

BIBLIOGRAPHY

Abbott, Charlotte Helen. *Abbott Genealogies,* unpublished. Originals at Memorial Hall Library and digitized on line.

Bailey, Sarah Loring. *Historical Sketches of Andover, MA, comprising the Present Towns of Andover and North Andover.* Boston: Houghton Mifflin (Cambridge, MA: Riverside Press, 1880).

Dow, George Francis. *Everyday Life in the Massachusetts Bay Colony.* Boston: Society for the Preservation of New England Antiquities, 1935.

Fogle, Lauren. *Colonial Marblehead – From Rogues to Revolutionaries.* Charleston, SC, 2008.

Gagnon, Daniel W. *Historical Sketches of Methuen, Massachusetts.* Andover, MA: Merrimack Valley Preservation Press, 2003

Gagnon, Dan; Mack, Ernest, et al. *Methuen: Images of America.* Charleston, SC: Arcadia Publishing, 1999.

Lapham, William B. *History of Bethel, Maine.* Somersworth, NH: New England History Press 1981, originally printed in 1891.

Mofford, Juliet Haines. *And Firm Thine Ancient Vow, The History of North Parish Church of North Andover, 1645-1974.* Lawrence, MA: Naiman Press, 1975.

Mofford, Juliet Haines. *The Devil Made Me Do It, Crime and Punishment in Early New England.* Guilford, CT: Globe Pequot Press, 2012.

Mofford, Juliet Haines. *Andover Massachusetts: Historical Selections from Four Centuries.* Andover, MA: Merrimack Valley Preservation Press, 2004

Norton, Mary Beth. *In the Devil's Snare: The Salem Witchcraft Crisis of 1692.* New York: Alfred A. Knopf, 2002.

Robinson, J. Dennis. *Under the Isles of Shoals (Archeology & Discovery on Smuttynose Island).* Portsmouth Marine Society, 2012

Various Town Recorders, Early Vital Records of Essex and Middlesex Counties to about 1850.

Vowell, Sarah. *The Wordy Shipmates.* New York: Riverhead Books, 2008.

Wight, Carrie. *A History of Newry, Maine 1805-1955.* Self published, 1980.

Wight, Paula M. *Newry Profiles.* Self published, 1980.

PART III: THE STORY

THE
ANDOVER
CONNECTION

HYSTERIA AND FORGIVENESS
IN EARLY NEW ENGLAND

BY HOWARD KAEPPLEIN
EDITED BY MITCHELL F. BARKER

PROLOGUE

METHUEN, MASSACHUSETTS, 1768

Rivers were the highways of colonial America and Methuen was well served by two. The Spicket flowed south from New Hampshire to the Merrimack, splitting Methuen and emptying into the Merrimack.

The Merrimack was wide, a super highway. It's source was a lake in central New Hampshire, from which it flowed south turned east and passed several towns before reaching the Atlantic.

The Merrimack was so broad and deep that even square-rigged seagoing vessels would occasionally sail up to Methuen. Loggers in New Hampshire ran their best product down the river past the last falls, at Swan's Ferry, where they would load it on flat–bottom gundalows, barges and two-masted schooners to be delivered to ship-builders in Haverhill, Amesbury, Newbury and Ipswich on the coast.

South of the Merrimack was Cochichewick Brook, which drew water from Lake Cochichewick in Andover and emptied into the Merrimack. It was not a navigable waterway, but it powered Andover's first sawmill and gristmill.

The Shawsheen River flowed north through Billerica, Tewksbury and Andover. Another major river which flowed north into the Merrimack was the Concord, originating in that town and meandering west and north to just west of Tewksbury, which bordered Andover on the west.

Methuen was a relatively new town, having separated from Haverhill just 40 years earlier. In the 17th century, it was wooded and undeveloped, except for the home and property of Robert Swan. He had moved there from central Haverhill because of a dispute over taxes with town officials. He was no recluse, however; soon after constructing his cabin, he built a small boat, which he used to cross the Merrimack to attend Meeting in Andover. He was a respected member of the Puritan assembly there for many years, as were his children and grandchildren. In the late 1600s and early 1700s, several Andover residents acquired western Haverhill land and settled there.

The town grew steadily but remained largely one of small family subsistence farmers. The older towns down river were much more varied, with tradesmen and craftsmen. There were milliners, shoemakers, weavers, joiners, and small merchants who brought goods in from the established towns and also from England.

The long-established Swan family was an exception; they were Merrimack seamen, operating Swan's Ferry and a schooner. They owned the most-imposing building in town, Swan's Tavern, which lodged overnight guests, primarily loggers guiding their unshaped ship-masts on their way to the shipyards. The tavern served flip, cider, and rum. It also contained an Ordinary, which served meals to weary travelers.

Merrimack seamen were as skilled as those from the seacoast towns. While coastal sailors ventured out of land-sight and occasionally onto the high seas,

Swan's Tavern

Merrimack seamen had to navigate the turbulent estuary at Newbury. Seacoast seamen often refused to deliver cargo up the Merrimack – they brought it to Newbury where it was loaded onto Merrimack vessels which brought it upstream.

Jonathan Barker's young children often joined their neighborhood friends to walk down to the Merrimack and watch this excitement.

The children also contributed food to their family's table by fishing the Merrimack for bass, shad, alewife, pickerel, carp and eel. Thus, this broad river was important to the Barker family in many ways.

In the years to come, the Merrimack would play an important part in the lives of Jonathan's sons.

Jonathan and his family, like everyone in Methuen, attended the Congregational church in the town center. Christian teaching had changed significantly since the rigid and harsh Puritan days of the 17th century. The witchcraft hysteria of 1692 had softened what the Puritan leaders espoused. It had to, because many left the towns with strict rules to live in more liberal communities.

More important was the Great Awakening, which started in upstate New York in the 1730's and reached Methuen and other towns on the Merrimack in the 1740's. It ushered in an era of 'free thinking' which contributed to the revolutionary attitude that emerged later. Evangelists who brought this brand of Christianity awoke a new vibrancy in the people. Yet the Puritan principles of hard work and community support remained. These largely defined the Methuen people.

Until a decade earlier, Methuen men would have been proud to be called Englishmen, as many of them had fought in the colonial militia alongside English Regulars in battles against the French in Canada. But they had no direct contact with their relatives back in England, for none of them were landed gentry or of royal stock. They had no close ties in England, for their ancestors had been simple farmers there as they were now in Methuen.

The connections to England began to unravel and break in 1765. Massachusetts men had enjoyed a charter giving them independent and local government. The British government decided to change this by passing the Stamp Act, imposing taxes on the American colonies on all printed documents. They needed money to pay for the French and Indian War it had fought on this continent and felt the colonies should share that cost.

However, it made no attempt to enlist the cooperation of the Massachusetts government This set off a series of protests and led to the formation of a Committee of Correspondence by Massachusetts. The Committee sent objections to the other colonies and wrote a formal objection to England.

Eventually, the tax was withdrawn, but replaced by the Townshend Act. It taxed several imported items, including textiles, paint, paper, tea, lead and glass. By 1768, some in Massachusetts were using the term American to describe themselves.

In this soon-to-be nation Jonathan and his family had a simple life, much like many of his neighbors.

His small family farm provided food and a small income for his large family. He had eight children. His wife, Abigail, was pregnant with a ninth. Most of the children were too young to provide much help on the farm, so this would be another year of very hard work for Jonathan and Abigail.

Some of Jonathan's neighbors considered him to be a rich man. His nearly 1,000 acres of Methuen land were much more than he could farm. He sold small parts of it on rare occasions when he needed money for livestock, feed, or clothing. His other advantage was half interest in a mill, which provided cornmeal and flour for his family.

More than wealth, land or possessions, what differentiated Jonathan from his neighbors was his future: he had a rendezvous with destiny. It would not be serendipitous - he knew very well what his destiny would be, for he had much to do to realize it. It was a mission that had been given him by his grandfather and it was at the core of his very being, the driving force of his life.

Rather than add to the burden of long, hard days on the farm, his mission made those chores less tedious. Although farming was of critical physical importance, it was incidental to his life's purpose. The successful completion of his mission required years of patient pursuance, love and understanding.

In short, it made him a man above most others.

CHAPTER ONE

A FAMILY CONFERENCE

Driving April rains melted remnants of winter's snows into the raging waters of the Spicket River as it rushed past Jonathan Barker's farm on its final sprint to the Merrimack River. The rain filled trenches and furrows irrigating his fields and portending success for the 1768 growing season in Methuen, Massachusetts.

Forty-year-old Jonathan Barker was a man of average height for his day – five feet six inches tall. He was physically fit and performed most of his work on the farm with seeming ease.

He had a pleasant countenance, punctuated with eyes which displayed self-assuredness and confidence. Moreover, they conveyed an honest interest in every person with whom he conversed.

His mouth expressed not a full smile, but a friendly and caring attitude he had towards all. Jonathan's children also shared this adult relationship with him. They knew he cared about what they thought, feared or wanted.

Jonathan Barker's children all had their assigned tasks on his farm. Jon, who had recently celebrated his 14th birthday, and Benjamin, 18 months younger, both did the heavy work. In the fields they split logs for the fire and carried pails of water from the well.

Molly, 11, and Samuel, 8, handled the milking and assisted their mother to prepare meals. Hannah, 9 and Jesse, 6, kept the two youngest ones occupied.

One cool day Jon and Benjamin had refreshed the fire with more logs for cooking. As they lifted the six-quart iron pot of soup onto the trammel, Jon spoke.

"Father, tell us about grandpa Barker."

Jonathan was taken aback at this inquiry about an ancestor none of his children had known.

"There's not much to tell, actually," he said.

"He died when I was just eight. He had been taking turns with my mother, nursing my baby sister back to health. Years later I learned that they were part of the diphtheria epidemic of 1735-40. It took my baby sister and my father died just a few weeks later. Before long, it killed another of my sisters.

"Life was hard for my mother and it became worse after my father died. The day we buried your grandpa Barker, mother said something to me which shaped my life. 'Jonathan,' she said, 'you are no longer Junior. You are now the only Jonathan in this family. You are the man of the house.' It was a heavy burden to bear. I'm afraid I couldn't do it as well as I needed to."

Jonathan realized that he had opened an important teaching point for his children. He was pleased that his wife, Abigail, also realized this, and took a break from the meal preparation to take a seat beside him.

"We tried to continue working part of the farm and stay together, but we got further behind each week. Mother took the girls back to her uncle's house in Andover and I went to live with my grandfather Benjamin. Mother asked a Barker cousin to hold our farm until I could return to run it."

Samuel asked, "What did you mean about what Grandma said having shaped your life?"

Jonathan was pleased that his eight-year-old son was fully involved in the discussion.

"Good question, Samuel, I guess I mean it gave me a sense of responsibility. Maybe I couldn't replace my father when I was just eight, but four years later I could. So I moved back to the farm and began working it."

Jon looked at his father, wide-eyed. "You were just twelve-years-old, and you came back to Methuen and ran this farm all by yourself?"

"Actually, my grandfather came with me, but he was seventy-eight years old and couldn't work the fields. But he helped me a lot, in many other ways.

Grandpa Barker was a loving grandfather, an instructive and disciplining father, and a wise teacher. He was a good and wise man whose words are burned in my memory.

"Even now, I see him sitting here, guiding my words and actions. He stayed with me for several years, before returning to Andover. Grandpa Benjamin and I spent many winter days by the fire as he told me fascinating stories about the early Andover days. One day I will tell you some of them."

By now, all of his children were intently waiting on their father's every word. Jon persisted, "I still can't imagine how you handled such responsibility at that young age, father."

"To be honest, I also got help from Uncle Benjamin. He came with Grandpa Benjamin when we first came back to the farm. He got father's cow, chickens and pigs back from my Methuen cousin to get me started. He returned to Andover after a few days, but visited us several times, sometimes bringing a goat or pig for me. But I knew that I was the one responsible for the farm. I never forgot what my mother told me and I never will."

Abigail inched her chair closer to Jonathan's as she gave him an admiring smile. This got Benjamin to raise a new question. "With no father around, who arranged your marriage?"

Abigail and Jonathan grinned broadly. "Grandpa Mitchell took the first step," Jonathan said. "He sent three of his daughters to help with the farm chores, hoping I would marry one of them. I picked the prettiest and we married."

Abigail laughed. "Not really. My sisters were and still are both prettier than I am. The truth is that your father picked me because I worked the hardest. He realized that we made a good team. We worked very hard to get the farm well established before we started a family."

Jonathan became more serious as he returned the topic to one of responsibility. "I can now tell you, Jon, that the day will come when I will not be there to help you and you will be the Jonathan." It may come soon, if we go to war with England., It may not happen until you leave to start your own family. But it will come and you must be prepared for it," advised Jonathan.

"I'm not sure when I will be ready," said Jon.

"I'm ready now," said 12-year old Benjamin, as all the other children laughed. "I mean it," Benjamin protested. I want to run a farm and find my own wife and have a family soon, and I don't want to fight in any war. Why should I?" he demanded. "You can all go off to war and I will stay and work the farm."

"That's a reasonable position, Ben, I'll keep it in mind. How do the rest of you feel about war with the English?" Jonathan asked.

"I am ready to march now," Samuel, the eight year old, said, "I will be the fifer."

"If it comes to war, then we all need to join, if we are truly Americans," offered six year-old Jesse. His father beamed proudly.

"Perhaps that is when I will be the Jonathan," added Jon. "More and more, it appears that war with England may come, so we need to be prepared. But dad, tell us more about your grandfather. He must have thought you were really special to spend the last years of his life with you."

Jonathan nodded, "When my mother brought us back to Andover, Grandpa Benjamin took me into his home and raised me like his own son, teaching me the things I needed to know to run a farm. When he felt I was ready, we moved back to Methuen with Uncle Benjamin to get the farm started again. During the next eight years he spent much of his time in Methuen with me, with occasional trips back to his house in Andover. When his health began to decline, he went back to his home and I spent a lot of time there taking care of him.

Jonathan had not intended to open such a long conversation about his Grandpa Benjamin, but he couldn't ignore Jon's honest interest.

"I should tell you the most important reason why Grandpa Benjamin came to Methuen to live with me for a while. He told me that I needed to learn what happened in Andover in its early days, but especially during 1692.

"He told me my great grandfather, Richard Barker, was the first settler in Andover. He built a cabin there by 1643, at least a year before the other settlers arrived.

"One of them was Edmund Faulkner, whom he had befriended during the first meeting of the proprietors in Rowley. Three years later, Richard Barker and Edmund helped to arrange for Parson Francis Dane to come to Andover, and the three became close friends for many years.

"In 1692, fifty Andover residents were charged with witchcraft. Pastor Dane did not believe the charges, but Richard Barker and the new pastor, Thomas Barnard, did. They believed that God was punishing Andover by loosing the devil among otherwise good people. "Richard Barker felt that the biggest sin of Andover's people was the preaching of Francis Dane after an Indian attack on Andover in 1676. Pastor Dane said that the Indians were only retaliating for the brutal and inhumane way the colonists had treated them. Pastor Dane used texts from the Gospels to teach that God loved both English and Indians and that we should also love them. "Richard Barker and Thomas Barnard though, said the Indians were doing the devil's work. This was a teaching that was widely distributed in the booklets written by Rev. Cotton Mather. It was an extension of a central teaching of the Puritans, originally presented by John Winthrop in his 'City on a Hill' sermon. Winthrop compared the Puritans colony to the Old Testament stories of Israel's establishment under God's direction. The stories told how the people would, time and time again, disobey God's laws and be punished by God for doing so.

"The Puritans believed in strict adherence to the Ten Commandments. The first Commandment called for singular love of God to the exclusion of all other things. John Winthrop kept a journal beginning in his college days, in which he recorded his daily sins. Those sins included, 'enjoying my noon repast and walks on the campus, without thoughts of God and his blessings.' Thus, Rev. Mather suggested that the colonists were guilty of similar sins to a much greater degree and they were now being punished by God. The omnipotent God was loosing the devil to create witches in our midst to do mischief among us. Most Andover residents accepted this teaching and rejected Pastor Dane's.

"Late in August 1692, Grandpa Benjamin's older brother, William, was charged with witchcraft. His father Richard, convinced him to confess that, in his weakness, he had allowed the devil to control him, but now he would renounce the devil.

Cotton Mather

"The authorities asked William who had enlisted him to the devil's side. He answered it was the two married daughters of Francis Dane, since he knew they had influenced their father's sinful preaching.

"Abigail, the wife of Edmund Faulkner's son, Francis, was convicted and sentenced to be hanged. Providence saved her, but her good name and that of her husband was destroyed. Because of this, the bond of friendship between the Barkers and the Faulkner's was broken.

"It is this affair that I have been called upon to set right as you shall hear.

"In October of 1692, Pastor Barnard came to Richard Barker and told him that he had come to believe that the whole witchcraft affair was a mistake, and that he had been misled by the devil.

"He said he would sign a petition written by Pastor Dane and signed by fifty townspeople asking the authorities to end the prosecutions. Richard had a difficult time accepting this. He became depressed and conscience-stricken. He prayed almost constantly for God's forgiveness. His health declined rapidly.

"It killed Richard Barker, but before he died, he called Benjamin to his bed to hear his final wishes. He began by telling Benjamin that his older brothers were well situated with houses, which they would own when he died.

"Therefore, he was leaving his entire estate to Benjamin, his youngest son. However, he said the gift carried a price, and that Benjamin must pledge to pay it then and there.

"He held his hand tightly and said, 'You must pledge on your honor and your life that you will make it your life's work to restore the bond of friendship between the Barker and Faulkner families. If you cannot fulfill this pledge, you will pass it to your sons, and if they cannot, it will pass on to your grandsons, but no further. My soul will not find rest until this pledge is fulfilled, so your pledge is a sacred one.'

"Grandpa Benjamin told me he was only partially successful, because the pain suffered by the Faulkners was too great and they put much of the responsibility for their pain on the Barkers.

"He said Francis Faulkner held no grudge and they actually became friends. Abigail supported her husband, although she had been the one who was wronged. She became philosophical about the entire witchcraft hysteria, sympathizing with all of the accused without holding hatred for the accusers or the judges.

"She told Benjamin she understood what William Barker had done, because he was a good man who accepted the judgment of the authorities, and he was also a victim, as was she. However, Abigail held a stronger grudge against the Barkers because Richard Barker had removed her father from his role as the leading pastor in Andover, replacing him with Thomas Barnard, who cooperated with the witchcraft prosecutions.

"Their son, Ammi Ruhammah, was very bitter. He had suffered the taunts of other Andover children throughout his youth. He did not openly defy his parents, but he would not shake grandpa Benjamin's hand. He moved away from Andover, eventually to Acton.

"So grandpa Benjamin had to pass the pledge to me. He said, 'Now, you must fulfill this quest during your lifetime, because my father said it could go no further than my grandsons – but you are the one that must fulfill it.'

All of Jonathan's children sat in silence and shock. Jonathan saw that they had many questions, but realized there was not enough time to go further.

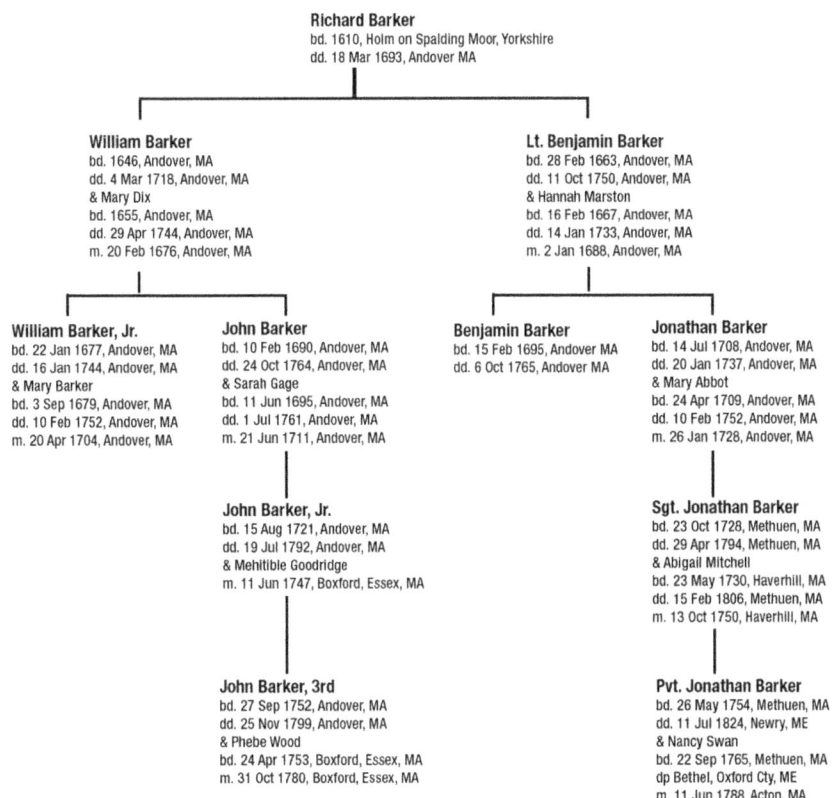

"We must return to this heavy subject when we have lots of time to discuss it. Grandpa Benjamin first told these things to me during a winter blizzard that kept us housebound for two days. Perhaps we can do the same.

"However, before we end this history discussion, I need to know if Jon and Ben have decided whether they want to learn a trade. If you do, I've got to find a local family that has that skill to take you in."

Benjamin responded quickly, "You don't have to arrange anything for me, father, I'm going to be a farmer and I can learn all about it right here."

Jonathan nodded approvingly and turned to Jon. This was the third time he had raised this issue with Jon, who was having difficulty with his decision.

"I've seen Mr. Swan's schooner at the ferry dock," said Jon, "and watched the crew at work, as they arrived and then set sail down the Merrimack. I think I would like to crew on Mr. Swan's boat."

Jonathan was happy to finally get a response from his eldest son. Training for a trade or skill always started by age fourteen, and Jon was at that point. "Fine," he said. "I will contact James Swan tomorrow."

CHAPTER TWO

A WINDOW TO THE PAST

Jon had made his decision. He would become a seaman and crew on James' Swan's schooner. Jonathan and his eldest son walked over to Swan's Tavern early one evening. James Swan greeted Jonathan warmly and was introduced to Jon by his father.

"James, I am here to request a favor of you, if I may. My eldest son has expressed an interest in learning how to sail and to crew on your schooner."

"He certainly seems fit for the task, Jonathan. He will soon be bigger than you and if he works as hard as you do, he will make a fine seaman. I believe I will eventually be able to use him on the schooner, but he would first have to apprentice on the ferry, to help him get his sea legs and learn to manipulate a craft in the difficult river currents. Would that be acceptable?"

Jonathan looked at Jon for his reaction. "I will be happy to do whatever you say to learn to be a crew member on your schooner."

"I don't have room for you to stay with my family, Jon, so you will have to agree to be at the ferry dock just after sunrise to prepare for the first crossing. You can start next Monday, if that is acceptable. My elder son, Joseph Greeley Swan, will be there to train you and work with you."

Piloting the ferry across the Merrimack was no easy task for 16-year-old Joseph Greeley Swan and 14-year-old Jon. Of the two, Jon, as he was known

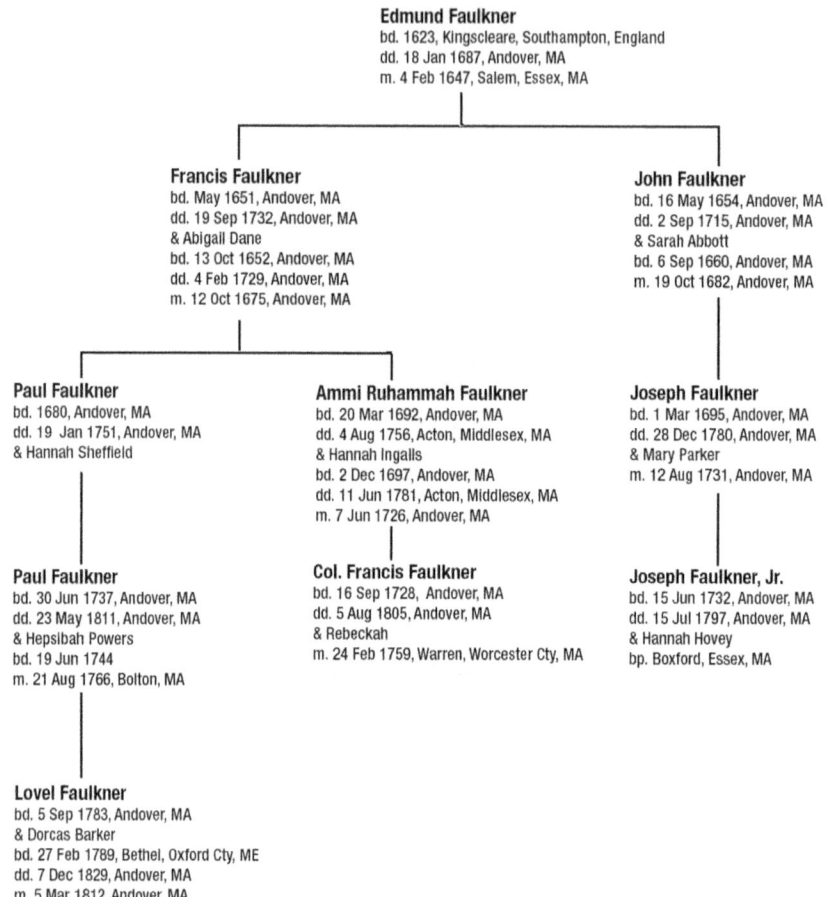

Edmund Faulkner
bd. 1623, Kingscleare, Southampton, England
dd. 18 Jan 1687, Andover, MA
m. 4 Feb 1647, Salem, Essex, MA

Francis Faulkner
bd. May 1651, Andover, MA
dd. 19 Sep 1732, Andover, MA
& Abigail Dane
bd. 13 Oct 1652, Andover, MA
dd. 4 Feb 1729, Andover, MA
m. 12 Oct 1675, Andover, MA

John Faulkner
bd. 16 May 1654, Andover, MA
dd. 2 Sep 1715, Andover, MA
& Sarah Abbott
bd. 6 Sep 1660, Andover, MA
m. 19 Oct 1682, Andover, MA

Paul Faulkner
bd. 1680, Andover, MA
dd. 19 Jan 1751, Andover, MA
& Hannah Sheffield

Ammi Ruhammah Faulkner
bd. 20 Mar 1692, Andover, MA
dd. 4 Aug 1756, Acton, Middlesex, MA
& Hannah Ingalls
bd. 2 Dec 1697, Andover, MA
dd. 11 Jun 1781, Acton, Middlesex, MA
m. 7 Jun 1726, Andover, MA

Joseph Faulkner
bd. 1 Mar 1695, Andover, MA
dd. 28 Dec 1780, Andover, MA
& Mary Parker
m. 12 Aug 1731, Andover, MA

Paul Faulkner
bd. 30 Jun 1737, Andover, MA
dd. 23 May 1811, Andover, MA
& Hepsibah Powers
bd. 19 Jun 1744
m. 21 Aug 1766, Bolton, MA

Col. Francis Faulkner
bd. 16 Sep 1728, Andover, MA
dd. 5 Aug 1805, Andover, MA
& Rebeckah
m. 24 Feb 1759, Warren, Worcester Cty, MA

Joseph Faulkner, Jr.
bd. 15 Jun 1732, Andover, MA
dd. 15 Jul 1797, Andover, MA
& Hannah Hovey
bp. Boxford, Essex, MA

Lovel Faulkner
bd. 5 Sep 1783, Andover, MA
& Dorcas Barker
bd. 27 Feb 1789, Bethel, Oxford Cty, ME
dd. 7 Dec 1829, Andover, MA
m. 5 Mar 1812, Andover, MA

in his youth to differentiate him from his father, was the taller and stronger. This was of significant advantage in this work.

The Merrimack was nearly a quarter mile wide at the crossing, and it flowed rapidly eastward towards the Atlantic during its ebb. The skiff was large enough to accommodate one horse-drawn carriage, two horses and eight passengers. It had just a single sail, which Jon set at the beginning of the crossing and usually fixed for the journey.

Jon and Joseph used the combination of the river flow and wind to effect the crossing, with occasional pole and oar thrust and constant rudder adjustment. They made three runs daily from Methuen to Andover, and then back again, an hour later. They piloted the boat and assisted passengers and their horses, loading and unloading the goods they were delivering or picking up.

During the stop in Andover, Jon would, on occasion, get some produce from the old Barker Farm and visit there with his cousin, fifteen-year-old John Barker. Joseph Swan often brought along his five-year-old sister Nancy, for her amusement and to free up her older siblings for work on the family farm. However, Nancy idolized Jon and tagged along with him, when he allowed it.

Jon was two or three inches taller than most grown men, reaching nearly five feet eight inches. He was also well developed from the heavy work he did on the family farm. Nancy enjoyed feeling his strong hands on her waist as he lifted her on board the ferry.

One day in late June, a passenger boarded on the Andover side and handed out leaflets to all aboard. The masthead read, "The Sons of Liberty" set in a fancy scroll. There was a bold headline: "ILLEGAL IMPORT DUTIES." The text explained that Parliament had passed the Townshend Act, requiring colonists to pay duties on most goods imported from England.

The Act had not been approved by the Massachusetts Assembly, which the leaflet stated was the only lawful governing body for the colony. Accordingly, the leaflet suggested that colonial merchants should refuse to pay the taxes; and if any did, colonists should not buy from them.

The leaflet also told of a Massachusetts merchant and legislator, John Hancock, who instructed the captain of his ship not to pay the duties. As a result, the English impounded the vessel. However, two days later the Sons of Liberty freed it and unloaded the goods.

After that, they hung a sign on a large tree in Boston that read "The Freedom Tree." They hung lanterns on it along with effigies of the English-appointed Governor Bernard and his tax collectors.

Upon reading most of the leaflet, Jon spoke to the man who had given it to him, "Are you one of the Sons of Liberty?"

"Well, I support them, but the active members are all in the Boston area and I live in Andover. I am just distributing the leaflets to the towns along the Merrimack. I am Joseph Faulkner, Jr."

At hearing this Jon felt his nerves tingle, remembering the story his father had told of the rift between the Faulkner and Barker families. "I hesitate to give you my name because of the enmity between our families. I'm Jon Barker."

"I have no quarrel with the Barkers. Your father visited mine fifteen years ago, seeking to mend the schism. My father explained that it was Frances

Faulkner's wife, Abigail, and especially her son, Ammi Ruhammah, who would not speak to the Barkers.

"Abigail was a strong, principled woman. She broke off cordial relations with my grandfather, John Faulkner, because of what he did during the Great Swamp Fight. Your father can explain all of this to you. My father told him that he should visit Ammi Ruhammah Faulkner in Acton to try to mend the rift. I don't know whether he was able to see him before he died – two years ago."

John Hancock

Jon was full of questions, but he decided that Joseph Faulkner was right – he should ask his father to answer them. However, he was somewhat pleased to know that some of the Faulkners could still be friendly with the Barkers.

He returned to the leaflet. "My father told me that the king and parliament were treating colonists in a way that ignores our English citizenship yet independent government, and that this may eventually lead to war."

"Your father is a wise and patriotic man. I hope that most people will feel the same, but I am concerned that some merchants want to pay the duties and sell goods at higher prices. They want to keep their business going. They don't realize that patriotism requires sacrifice from all of us."

By then the skiff had reached the Methuen dock and Joseph was preparing to disembark with his horse. "Good day to you, Jon. Perhaps I will see you again on my return."

Jon and Joseph Swan tied the skiff to the dock and helped passengers with their horses and luggage. Joseph Faulkner rode out of sight towards Haverhill. Jon did not see him on either of the last two southern trips that day.

That evening, as the Barker family was preparing for supper, Jon spoke to his father.

"I had an interesting passenger on the ferry today. It was Joseph Faulkner of Andover." He told his father he had no issue with the Barkers – that it was only Ammi Ruhammah Faulkner of Acton who did.

"That's right, Jon. Joseph's father told me that his branch of the family was also shunned by Abigail Dane Faulkner, long before the witchcraft business. It seems that John Faulkner was one of twelve militiamen from Andover who attacked the Narragansett Indians in 1675 there.

"Because of what John Faulkner did then, the Indians came to Andover, burned the Faulkner farm and killed all their animals. "Abigail Dane Faulkner was furious when she learned why the Indians attacked the Faulkner farm and never again spoke to John Faulkner, his wife or children."

Benjamin, listening intently to their father's explanation, now joined Jon. "What terrible thing did John Faulkner do?" asked Benjamin.

"Before I answer that I should tell you a little more about the battle with the Narragansett Indians, which became known as The Great Swamp Fight. It was a vicious encounter, which lasted nearly two hours. Several of the militiamen were killed and many more were wounded, including Ebenezer Barker. But at the end several hundred Indian warriors were dead and the rest had fled.

"Two days before the battle, the Andover militiamen marched ten hours to assemble with the rest of their forces at Dedham. The next day they trooped another eight hours to the swamp near the Indian camp. There they slept a few hours until dawn. Through a foot of snow they proceeded through the bogs to a fortified Indian village and attacked it.

"The story of the victory in the Great Swamp Fight was told throughout Massachusetts and the militiamen were called heroes. The Andover group included sons of several of the founders: Joseph Abbot, James Frye, John Ballard, John Lovejoy, John Parker, John Faulkner, and Ebenezer Barker. These families were proud of their sons' bravery and success in this historic battle."

Jon could not wait any longer for the answer to Benjamin's question. "Then why did the Indians attack only the Faulkner farm and not those of the others? Why was he different from the other militiamen?"

Jonathan replied, "After the battle was over and the remaining warriors had fled, there were still hundreds of women and children in the village wigwams.

After discussion the officers gave orders to burn the wigwams and kill all the survivors.

"John Faulkner was one of three militiamen who ran around torching all the wigwams. Many women and children stayed in the tents and burned to death, but many others tried to flee and were shot dead by militiamen at their officers' orders. One of those who followed that order was Joseph Abbot. When the Indians came to Andover, they burned the Faulkner farm and killed Joseph Abbot as he worked in the field. They also captured his seven-year-old brother, but he was returned six months later."

"How did the raiding Indians know the location of the Faulkner and Abbot farms?" asked Jon.

"To get that they went first to the finest house in town, the Dudley Bradstreet house. The Indians threatened to take Dudley and his family captive, unless told the location of those two farms. Dudley had no choice but to tell them what they wanted to know. Actually, finding the location of the two men they sought was rather complex. The town was originally laid out with each family having just two or three acres clustered around the meetinghouse so that all would be within walking distance to Sabbath Meeting. Later, they were allotted much larger meadow acreage where they could do their farming. Residents kept their livestock on their in-town property but did little in the way of crop cultivation there. We know that the Indians attacked the Faulkner in-town property, because they destroyed all of his livestock and also his house where he kept all the early town records. However, Joseph Abbot was working in the fields, so that was likely in the family farm in the meadow outside of town.

"Only after this attack did the militiamen tell what happened at the end of the Great Swamp Fight. It made no difference to most people, who were still proud of the militiamen. But Abigail Dane Faulkner refused to speak to John Faulkner or his family after that.

Benjamin was still confused. "There are three different Abbott families in Andover. How did they know the right one where they would find Joseph?"

"You are quite right, Ben. Dudley must have told them exactly where to find Joseph. Eventually, many in town realized this and held a grudge against Dudley. It would figure into what they did during the witch hysteria.

"Abigail's fury was not exhausted by shunning her brother-in-law, John Faulkner. She also asked her father, Pastor Francis Dane, to speak out against

Great Swamp Fight

the murder of innocent women and children.

"Parson Dane hesitated. He knew that would go against all the teachings of the Puritan leaders and the feelings of most of the Andover people. But a year later he learned that the Narragansett Indians had burned Providence and 77-year-old Roger Williams had confronted them, asking why they turned against people who had been friends to them. They answered that the local settlers had turned against the Indians by assisting invaders from the north and west. Further, their leader said God was on their side, for they killed only fighting men while the colonists killed women and children.

"This convinced Parson Dane that it was time to speak out against un-Christian behavior against the Indians. When he did, the Andover selectmen began looking for a new pastor. Sixteen years later they would charge Abigail Dane Faulkner, Elizabeth Dane Johnson and several others of the Dane family with witchcraft."

Jon was deeply troubled by this whole story. "Why did the militiamen attack the Narragansett village in the first place?"

Jonathan replied, "The militia leaders had learned that Chief Metacomet, also known as King Philip, was contacting all the tribal leaders in southern Massachusetts and Rhode Island to get them to attack many towns in the colony. But they knew that the Narragansetts had not yet agreed to join the rebellious tribes. They struck in hopes that it would deter them from joining

King Philip. It had just the opposite effect. Two months later, they joined the Nipmucks and Pokanokets, and torched Massachusetts towns including Lancaster, Groton, Medfield, Marlborough, and Sudbury.

"Andover was fortunate to suffer only a minor attack in comparison. But the fury of the Indian attacks was a response to injustices they had suffered. For example, Lancaster and Groton had raised a bounty of a thousand pounds, which they offered to its men for killing Indians. A bounty was offered for each male Indian scalp and smaller amounts for scalps of women and children. A party of twenty or more Lancaster and Groton men went out searching for Indians and returned several days later with more than one hundred scalps, enough to collect the entire bounty. Probably, most of the scalps were of women and children.

"Lancaster was the first town burned after the Great Swamp Fight. All of the houses on the west side of the Nashua River were burned to the ground. The next day the entire town of Groton was burned."

Benjamin had been listening closely to all that his father was telling them. He was clearly shocked as his expression changed from pain to disgust and to sorrow.

"All of this does not give me a very good feeling about the early settlers. We had been told that the Puritans were primarily driven by their strong Christian faith, but their behavior does not seem very Christian to me."

"That is an excellent reaction, Ben. It shows how much we have learned during the past hundred years. But you need to hear the other side of the story to understand why the colonists acted the way they did. The Puritan leaders were convinced that the Indians were agents of the devil. They said that God was angered at the colonists for their sinful ways and He had loosed the devil to send the Indians to attack the colonists.

"Cotton Mather wrote several small books with this theme and he gave examples of Indian attacks throughout New England, especially in Maine. However, we now know that the Abenaki Indians in Maine were being paid by the French to help them resist the attacks by the English colonists against French forts in Maine, New Hampshire, and Canada.

"That was not the case in Massachusetts where the various Indian tribes were relatively peaceful until Metacomet convinced them to retaliate against the colonists. This was for injustices they had received at the hands of the colonists, including broken agreements, exile enslavement and excessive punishment.

"The Andover selectmen called a second pastor a few years after the Great Swamp Fight. Rev. Thomas Francis Barnard, had attended Harvard College with Cotton Mather. Barnard became Mather's voice at Andover's First Parish meetinghouse. He was a very forceful and convincing speaker and soon became the primary pastor in Andover. "So, you see, the Andover people were thinking and doing as they were advised by the Puritan leaders. If you consider the hard life the Andover settlers had had during the first fifty years after their arrival, this is quite understandable.

"They had come to a dense wood, which they had to clear for their houses and farms. There had been outbreaks of smallpox and other diseases, and there had been many severe winters.

"Richard Barker was elected one of the three or four selectman almost every year. They guided the town affairs. Much of their concern was with how the colonists behaved, paid for building of the meetinghouse and parsonage and supported the pastor. The people had great respect for the pastor and the Puritan leaders in Boston and accepted their direction without hesitation."

Jon sensed that his father was about to end the discussion so the family could have supper. "Father, there is another question from Joseph Faulkner that you have not answered. Did you ever go to Acton to speak to Ammi Ruhammah Faulkner before he died?"

"I did, Jon. In fact, I rode down there just a week after I met with Joseph Faulkner. I found the Faulkner mill in South Acton quite easily. There I met Francis, the son of Ammi Ruhammah Faulkner. I told him about the sacred assignment I had received from my grandfather.

Francis listened politely, and then he said, "Did your grandfather tell you about the misery William caused my father and my grandparents? Do you know that my grandmother lived for another ten years with the witchcraft conviction still standing over her head? Did you know that many people in town still believed that she was a witch for many years? They could dismiss the testimony of young people and others with poor reputations, but the testimony of a Barker could not be questioned. My father is in our house across the street, I will take you there, but I am sure that he will not see you."

"He was right. When Ammi Ruhammah learned that I was a Barker from

Andover, he slammed the door as he shouted, "Go away and don't come back!"

"I went again a few years ago, and had a nice discussion with Francis Faulkner. He told me that he had tried several times to convince his father to meet me and give me a chance to apologize. His father said he would take his hatred for the Barkers to the grave and he never wanted to see one again. He said that my quest would have to wait until his father died and then it would be up to him and me to work out a solution."

Jon smiled as he breathed a sigh of relief. "That sounds promising, father. When will you go to Acton again?"

"It will have to wait until you are a little older. I believe that the solution he has in mind may involve you, as you mature to full adulthood. But we will have to discuss that at another time."

CHAPTER THREE

AN UNPLANNED VOYAGE

As the summer of 1768 rolled on, there were ever increasing signs of trouble between the colonists and the English Regular soldiers.

The many campaigns against the French in Acadia, Quebec, and northern New England had been a heavy burden on England. To recover some of the loss it levied taxes but this did not sit well with the colonists, who felt they were being treated like subservient Africans, rather than as English citizens. As unrest grew, governor Francis Bernard requested that England send more Regular soldiers and seamen to Boston.

Despite the increasing danger, James Swan continued business as usual, making river trips to Newburyport loading goods. Weekly he followed the coast to Boston for other merchandise. The co-owner of James's schooner docked it at Amesbury, and generally had men available to serve as crew for a single trip. By July, James Swan felt it was time for Jon to start working on his trips to Boston. It was hard work, but Jon was built for the task, and enjoyed the challenge.

Occasionally winds were calm and the vessel moved slowly. Young Jon Barker was able to sit at the helm for instruction from Mr. Swan. At one of these times, James decided to reveal to Jon more about the Swan family and what might lie ahead for him.

"My brother Caleb was a brilliant student, so dad sent him to Harvard College, where he graduated with distinction in 1738. He became an officer in the Colonial militia assigned to lead a regiment in the campaign against Louisburg, the large fortress on the coast in New France.

There he was joined by another officer, Joseph Frye from Andover, who quickly was assigned control of the militia. It was a hard-fought campaign, but they captured Louisburg from the French. Joseph Frye became a hero and was promoted to Colonel. Caleb and Joseph became good friends, and Caleb married Joseph's niece, Dorothy Frye.

"Joseph Frye was a leading citizen of Andover and was elected the town's representative to the General Court several times. Although he was a career military officer, he always returned to Andover between campaigns in the French & Indian War. Besides his role in the capture of Louisburg, Col. Frye was in the major assault against the French and Acadians in Nova Scotia in 1755. He took part in several other operations of the War, most on the Maine coast or on one of its major rivers.

"In 1762 the General Court and House of Representatives granted a six square mile parcel of land in Maine to Joseph Frye on either side of the Saco River at the New Hampshire line. Joseph had to coordinate the settlement of 50 families there within a short time, and they all had to build substantial houses.

He contacted friends, including my brother. In 1763, some of his friends arrived at what was called Pequaket at the time, after a nearby Indian village. He contracted with some of his friends to build a large house to be ready when he arrived. The house would have a stone foundation, forty by sixty feet.

"Joseph had other duties, both in Andover and in the military, so he was not ready to move his family to Maine until 1766, when he learned that my brother was ready to go. Caleb asked if I would take both families there and I agreed.

"Two of my nephews, Joshua and Timothy Swan, were available as crew in addition to my son Joseph. Joseph Frye could aid in navigation, based his many trips up the coast of Maine. It was quite an assemblage on the ship: Joseph Frye, his wife, Mehitible, their six children, Caleb Swan, his wife Dorothy and their five children, me, my son, and two nephews.

"One of the most challenging parts of the journey was passing through the turbulent estuary at the mouth of the Merrimack. The eastern flow of the river met the tidal waves of the sea to cause a massive churn which whipped small

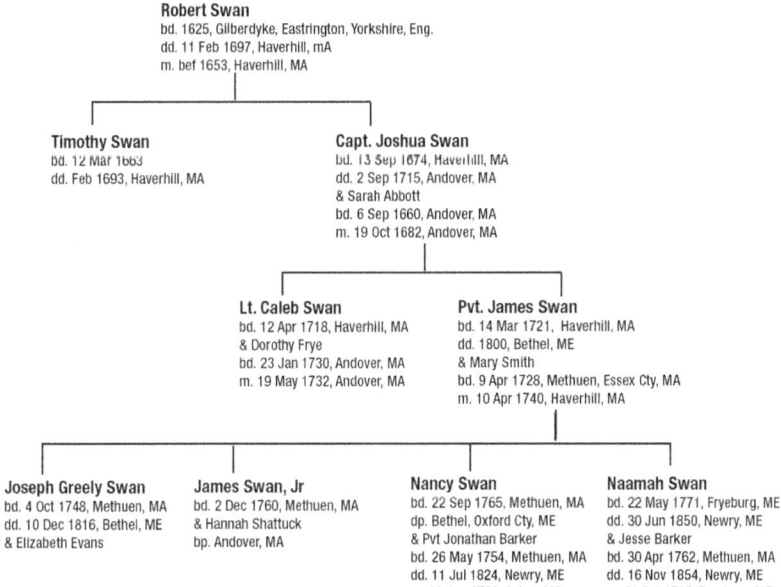

Robert Swan
bd. 1625, Gilberdyke, Eastrington, Yorkshire, Eng.
dd. 11 Feb 1697, Haverhill, mA
m. bef 1653, Haverhill, MA

Timothy Swan
bd. 12 Mar 1663
dd. Feb 1693, Haverhill, MA

Capt. Joshua Swan
bd. 13 Sep 1674, Haverhill, MA
dd. 2 Sep 1715, Andover, MA
& Sarah Abbott
bd. 6 Sep 1660, Andover, MA
m. 19 Oct 1682, Andover, MA

Lt. Caleb Swan
bd. 12 Apr 1718, Haverhill, MA
& Dorothy Frye
bd. 23 Jan 1730, Andover, MA
m. 19 May 1732, Andover, MA

Pvt. James Swan
bd. 14 Mar 1721, Haverhill, MA
dd. 1800, Bethel, ME
& Mary Smith
bd. 9 Apr 1728, Methuen, Essex Cty, MA
m. 10 Apr 1740, Haverhill, MA

Joseph Greely Swan
bd. 4 Oct 1748, Methuen, MA
dd. 10 Dec 1816, Bethel, ME
& Elizabeth Evans

James Swan, Jr
bd. 2 Dec 1760, Methuen, MA
& Hannah Shattuck
bp. Andover, MA

Nancy Swan
bd. 22 Sep 1765, Methuen, MA
dp. Bethel, Oxford Cty, ME
& Pvt Jonathan Barker
bd. 26 May 1754, Methuen, MA
dd. 11 Jul 1824, Newry, ME
m. 18 Jun 1788, Acton, MA

Naamah Swan
bd. 22 May 1771, Fryeburg, ME
dd. 30 Jun 1850, Newry, ME
& Jesse Barker
bd. 30 Apr 1762, Methuen, MA
dd. 16 Nov 1854, Newry, ME
m. 21 Oct 1788, Fryeburg, ME

vessels mercilessly.

"After that it was almost glassy sailing up the coast to the mouth of the Saco River. There smaller boats were for hire upriver. Since it was late in the day, we all stayed on board to sleep until early morning, when we could begin the Saco River journey to Pequaket.

"At dawn, I returned to Methuen with my crew. The Frye and Caleb Swan families boarded riverboats and continued their journey.

"Six months later, I received a letter from Caleb, telling me that the river trip to Pequaket took three days. He said that there was plenty of good land and everyone was working to clear it and build houses. His enthusiastic letter told me that I should seriously consider taking my wife and family there to join him.

By the end of 1767, the town was renamed Fryeburg, and Joseph was elected as its representative to the General Court."

Jon discussed all of this with his father and brothers each evening during supper. His father was aware of much of it, being a friend of James for several years. Jonathan was pleased to see that Jon was developing a good relationship with his friend as well.

Trips to Boston had to coincide with ebb tide on easterly travel through the estuary at Newburyport and a rising tide on the return. Such was the case on the day of Jon's fourth trip to Boston on the schooner in August. The trip to Boston went smoothly and James dropped anchor in the harbor. James, Jon and Joseph boarded the launch and as they lowered it, another boat approached containing an English officer and a Regular. James turned to Jonathan and said, "This looks like trouble."

The officer asked James to identify himself. When James did, he said, "You are now in the service of His Majesty's Royal Navy. We will take you to your assigned ship." Jon was terrified. A hundred thoughts ran through his head. Where were they going? How long would they be away? How would his parents learn of his predicament?

They rowed a short distance to a barque staffed by a crew of colonial seamen. They all boarded, immediately pulled anchor and set sail eastward towards Castle Island in the harbor. James was ordered to take the helm, but he was able to whisper to Joseph and Jon to capture and disarm the officer and Regular on his signal.

About a quarter of an hour into the trip, something far at sea seemed to catch James' attention. He squinted, then pointed to something in the distance, "Ahoy!", he said, startling the officer and Regular as they turned to see what he was pointing at.

Jon and Joseph were able to quickly overcome their adversaries. They brought the English seamen down to the brig and locked them there, as the colonial crew cheered.

James, Jon and Joseph then piloted the barque around Castle Island and back into the harbor. A merchant friend of James spotted him as the barque entered the harbor. He shouted to some others to stand by, as he boarded a launch to meet James at his schooner.

Then he shouted to James, "Let us help you pick up your goods quickly, so that you can be on your way."

As James lowered the launch from the barque, he shouted to one of the colonial crewmen, "Give us half an hour before you release the captain." The crewman gave him a thumbs up. He then boarded his friend's launch and made his way to the helping hands of the merchant's friends. Within the half hour, the merchandise was loaded on James' schooner, the anchor lifted, and sail and rudder set for the return trip to Methuen.

Jon's heart continually pounded in fear other English seamen or Regulars would capture them. He kept looking about as he tried to help with the chores. However, once they were moving swiftly out of the harbor and north, he began to breath normally.

James instructed Jon what must be done. "I need to take my family to Fryeburg, to avoid arrest by the Regulars. They will surely come looking for me within a day or two. I will stop at Amesbury to tell my partner of my predicament.

"He will assist us in our journey upstream to Methuen and send ahead to warn my wife Mary, and my children that they must pack all they can easily carry, so we can sail for Fryeburg within a few hours.

"I will need your help loading the schooner. When we arrive in Methuen, I want you to run to your father and ask him to help as well. He and I have been friends for many years, and this may be the last time I see him. I would also like you come with us up to the mouth of the Saco River. After my family and I have begun our trip upriver, you will need to help crew the schooner and take it back to Amesbury and my partner's dock."

"Will you do all of that, Jon?" he asked. "It will be my pleasure, Mr. Swan," replied Jonathan.

When Jon arrived home, he roused his father and told him all that had happened. His father agreed to do all that James Swan had asked, but said, "Jon, you have had a trying day and have many hours of work ahead. You must sleep while the Swan family prepares for Fryeburg. I will help James and his family and return to wake you for the final loading."

Although physically exhausted, Jon could not sleep for some time, as he kept re-living the engagement with the English officer. By the time he eventually rejoined the others at the dock, there were just a few items left to be loaded on the schooner.

His father met him. "Jon, I have decided to make this trip with you. Abigail agrees that it will help us as we consider such a move for you and your brothers when you are ready to venture out on your own."

Jon was happy with this plan. He quickly completed loading and helped each of the family members board. As the schooner set sail, Jon and his father waved to his mother, brothers and sister.

They soon reached Newburyport and were able to leave the estuary without losing any belongings. James, Joseph, and Jon had secured all boxes and luggage so the violent tossing of the ship caused no harm or alarm to the women and children. James' wife, Mary, had a vomiting spell, but the others were fine. Mary was pregnant and it was beginning to show. They began the sail up the coast with a favorable but moderate wind.

In time, James had an opportunity to talk seriously to Jon and his father. "I have told you about my brother, Caleb and his friend, Joseph Frye, and how they encouraged me to move to Fryeburg to start a new life. I thought that I might do it one day, but the English have advanced my schedule. Caleb will be there to greet me and help to build a house for my family. There is fertile land for many more settlers and cooperation which fuels the pioneer spirit of the settlers."

Jon's father had heard all of this from James Swan some time ago. "When you told me about Fryeburg you said you hoped I might move there with you. I believe I should raise my family in Methuen and leave it to them to start their lives in Maine with you. I have tried to give my sons the spirit of their ancestors, so they would be eager to face such a challenge."

Jon became excited at the prospect. "I would like to go as soon as I can." Young Nancy Swan smiled happily when she heard Jon say that he would come to Fryeburg.

Jon's father then surprised his son with more news. "Jon, your mother agreed that you and I should spend at least two days on the Saco River trip, so we will be better prepared for your own trip. We will lease boats for all of us, and will help James and his family carry their belongings around the falls upriver."

James then turned more somber. "Your own move may be delayed by war, Jon. I fear there will be much more trouble with England. They keep sending Regulars to Boston and imposing more taxes. The colonists will not stand for it. "The Sons of Liberty" will not miss an opportunity to disrupt England's high-handed treatment of the colonists.

"The Sons of Liberty is an informal group, but is supported by Samuel Adams and John Hancock, which gives it respectability and strength. These are historic times and you must be alert to what is going on in Essex County and in Boston, Jon."

Jon, of course, knew all about the Sons of Liberty, but he was pleased to hear James' words about the situation. "Father has prepared all of us for what lies ahead. We will join the militia as soon as we are of age, and we will serve when we are called."

When the schooner arrived at the mouth of the Saco they dropped anchor and had supper together. As darkness settled in, they set blankets on the lower deck so they could sleep until dawn. When the sun rose, Jon was the first awake and begin to untie the boxes and luggage and move them to the deck for disembarking. As Mary came up, she became sick again. James came to her aid and comforted her.

Mary spoke quietly, almost apologetically, "James, this is not a good time for me to be pregnant, for there will be much work for me to set up house in Fryeburg."

"I am confident that my brother's wife, Dorothy, will help you during your last hours of pregnancy and with the birth of our child. I expect that this will strengthen our relationship with Caleb and Dorothy and that they will be the godparents to our daughter or son." These prospects comforted Mary, who smiled softly.

James disembarked, helped Mary off the schooner, and contracted for passage upriver. Jonathan helped unload their belongings. The other children scrambled down and Jon helped Nancy. After the riverboats were loaded, they all found a seat and began the long hard row up the Saco River.

The river voyage was slow and difficult, requiring boats being carried around two falls. They also stopped twice to camp for the night.

On the last of these stops, a lone Pequaket Indian greeted them. James soon learned that he was called Sabattis, and that he was friendly to the settlers in Fryeburg. Sabattis helped James and his family set up camp for the night and ate with them. James opened a flask of rum and shared a cup with Sabattis, who thanked James profusely for it.

After a time, when the family members were settling down to sleep, Sabattis left the camp briefly, to relieve himself. When he returned, he snuck up behind James and tried to wring his neck, but James reached back and grabbed Sabattis' elbows and threw him over his head. Sabattis landed on the fire, but quickly jumped up, laughing. After wiping the coals from his backside, he smiled and offered his hand to James, saying, "You are my friend for life; I will do what you wish, any time."

The next morning, Jon and his father prepared to leave the Swan family and row down to the sea and the schooner which awaited.

It was time for Jon to say goodbye to his father's friend and his employer. James reminded him, "Jon, don't forget your promise – I expect to see you and your brothers in Fryeburg before many years." Jon shook James' hand and replied he would come as soon as he could. He then began to help load the riverboats. After the belongings were safely aboard, James helped his wife and baby aboard, as his older children climbed on alone.

James reached to help board Nancy but she pulled away, saying, "I want Jon". Jon picked her up by the waist and as he turned she wrapped her arms around his neck and whispered clearly, "When you come to Fryeburg, I'm going to marry you." Jonathan blushed as he set her in the boat. He could not help but respond to her adoring smile with a smile of his own. Jon and his father shouted a last goodbye to Joseph, James, Mary, and the rest of the family, as they began to move upriver.

Sabattis did, indeed, help James and his family as they settled at Fryeburg. But the greatest help came from James's brother, Caleb, and his wife, Dorothy. The men built a log cabin that provided shelter for their first winter. This was a simple building that would protect James and his family from Maine's cold winter months. Caleb had helped to build several such structures for his own family and friends in Fryeburg, so it went up quickly. On several occasions during the next weeks, Caleb and James drew plans for a more permanent house they could build the following summer. First priority, however, would be to remove brush and a few trees so James and his sons could cultivate two or three acres for corn, wheat, beans, potatoes, and beets.

In spring, Mary gave birth to her eighth child, Nathaniel. In May 1771, Mary's ninth child was born, with Dorothy's help. This time it was a girl and she asked her devoted friend, Dorothy, to name her. Dorothy chose to give her the name of her own mother, Naamah – a biblical appellation meaning 'the beautiful'. The name followed the Puritan principle of naming children after people in the bible, although many people were no longer following it.

CHAPTER FOUR

SNOWBOUND

Jon and the other crew members were able to sail the schooner down the coast to Amesbury and dock. Jonathan and his son, Jon, then walked six miles to the Barker farm in Methuen, where they were greeted by Abigail, who embraced her husband and son warmly. The other Barker children gathered around them in celebration.

Jonathan spoke to all of them. "I am proud of Jon for what he has done this summer. He has come a long way towards becoming 'the Jonathan'. We can now all work together to bring in the harvest and prepare for winter."

Within days, Jon learned that James Swan's older brother, Timothy, was selling the Swan's share of the schooner, and that he would take ownership of Swan's Ferry. Timothy had no need for Jon's services on the ferry, since his own sons: Joshua, Timothy, Jr., and Caleb would handle it. However, he agreed to keep Jon on until first snow. After the adventures of August, September passed rather quietly.

During the ferry stops in Andover, Jon was able to spend more time with his cousin, John Barker. On one of those occasions he asked his cousin what he knew about his great grandfather, William Barker, the confessed witch. "Did your grandfather tell you much about the witchcraft business?"

"He was just a baby when it all happened. When he was older his father refused to discuss it. He said that it was painful and he would prefer to forget it. What he did learn came from his older brother, William Barker, Jr., who was fifteen when he and his father were charged as witches.

Grandpa John learned that Will Jr. was convinced by his grandfather, Richard Barker, to confess. Richard persuaded him that all people are sinners and some are more easily led by the devil into more sins than others. Since so many good people had testified that Will and his father were witches, it must be true. He argued that the officials would go easy on him if he confessed.

After meeting with Pastor Barnard, he confessed. Then Richard Barker influenced his son, William Sr., to confess, telling him that William Junior might be hanged unless he did so.

Next, one of the magistrates told Will Jr. that his life would be spared if he repented and named other witches that he knew. He was horrified to think that he would be hanged because he didn't know any other witches. But that problem disappeared when he was taken to Salem and examined by Judges Hathorne and Corwin in the presence of Martha Sprague – who named many witches.

She said she saw his apparition --or spirit -- and that of the widow Mary Parker riding on a pole to be baptized by the devil at Five Mile Pond.

Eventually, he agreed that he had done so. One of the judges asked if Abigail Dane Faulkner, Elizabeth Dane Johnson, Mary Parker, Samuel Wardwell and his wife and two daughters were also there with him. He said they were.

This testimony was later read at the trial of Mary Parker. She was convicted and hanged, even though she never confessed."

Jon could hardly believe his ears. "What a horrible lack of justice! Didn't anyone speak up in her defense?"

"People were afraid that if they did, they would also be charged as witches. Eventually, Parson Dane wrote a letter protesting the trials. That was in October when many more people were upset that their children were in Salem prison.

Many people signed Parson Dane's letter. Even Parson Barnard signed, as he no longer believed that all of those charged were really witches."

"In the end, what happened to Will Jr.?"

"Francis Faulkner posted a bond for his release after six weeks. The following year, the charges were dropped by order of Governor Phipps. But Will Jr. was tormented to think he had a hand in the death of an innocent woman.

During the six weeks he was in prison he became good friends with his first cousin, 13-year-old Mary Barker. She was arrested a few days before Will Jr. and was treated much the same.

Richard Barker convinced her that she must be guilty, and then Judges Hathorne and Corwin got her to name her uncle, William Barker Sr., Abigail Dane Faulkner and Elizabeth Dane Johnson as witches. Fortunately, none of them were hanged, but Mary was still very troubled about her confession being used against them. Eleven years later, Will Jr. married his first cousin, Mary Barker."

"What a terrible state of affairs! Did the people of Andover eventually apologize to the families of the innocent people they had put in prison and hanged?

"Not immediately. Pastor Barnard realized that something needed to be done to heal the rift between those charged and those who brought the charges of witchcraft. He preached about peace and forgiveness and offered his apology for having been taken in by the devil. As for those who had been hanged, there was a lingering belief that they were witches and had been lawfully convicted by respected judges and juries. Many years later one of the judges, the only one, Samuel Sewall, apologized for his role in the witchcraft affair. Only then did some begin to doubt the guilt of even those who had been hanged.

"As I said, my great grandfather, Will Sr., was too embarrassed to show his face. He stopped attending Sunday meeting. Several families moved to the South Parish, and others moved to Methuen, or to Wilton, Milford, or Amherst, New Hampshire.

Of those convicted in the hysteria, three from Andover were hanged and one died in prison; they were buried in a mass unmarked grave near Gallows Hill in Salem."

Jon thanked his cousin, John, for telling him about this embarrassing family history which he had learned to accept without judgment. When he got home for supper, he told his brothers and sisters and father all that he had learned.

"Well, that's a good start, Jon. Unfortunately, there is much more to the story, but it will have to wait for a snowy winter day, when we all have more time to talk."

As the fall approached, Jon heard many passengers discussing a boycott against British textile goods. He heard men talking about building looms for their wives and daughters and others who had already done so, or had one made. Many women in Haverhill were weaving material for their own clothes. Some in Methuen and Andover were doing it as well. 'Homespun' became the watchword of the day.

The Essex Gazette, began publishing in August.   It reported that the Massachusetts General Court had sent a "Circular Letter" to the other colonies asserting the Townshend Act was illegal and only the colonies could tax themselves. Governor Bernard was outraged and ordered the General Court to rescind the letter. The vote against rescission was 92-17.

Five of the seventeen delegates voting to rescind the letter were from Essex County. They were immediately removed from office by their towns.

The Essex Gazette continued to publish news supporting the spirit of revolution right up to the Battle of Bunker Hill in 1775.

In October, ships arrived in Boston Harbor with two brigades of troops, which Governor Bernard had requested to enforce the import duties. Jon read about this in the newspaper and in Sons of Liberty flyers, which Joseph Faulkner continued to distribute.

One flyer contained a lithograph showing the arrival of the troops in Boston Harbor. It was by Paul Revere, whose engraving emphasized Boston's churches, lending credence to the argument that the troops were a war-like gesture in peaceful Boston.

November passed quietly, then first snow fell early in December, ending Jon's work on Swan's Ferry. He had grown taller and stronger during his fourteenth year and looked more mature than his years. Despite his size and age advantage over his siblings, he still lacked self-confidence. When possible, he would defer to Benjamin during any family discussion.

Jon spent the next few weeks chopping enough cords of wood to last through the winter.

Snow fell heavily every week in January 1769. By mid-February, it was more than three feet deep and the shoveled pile at the side of the path to the barn reached Jon's full height - five feet nine inches. Jon and Benjamin had shared the snow shoveling with their father, but now only Jon could throw it above the pile.

They had a narrow path cleared to the barn, where they needed to make regular trips to milk the cows, gather eggs, retrieve wood, and feed the livestock. On several of the snowy days, there was little to do, as blizzards roared outside. On one of those days, Jonathan spoke to his children about the winters he had spent with his grandfather, Benjamin Barker.

"This is a good day for me to begin to tell some of Barker family history I learned from Grandpa Benjamin. He told me some of these stories over and over, because he said he wanted to be sure I would remember and tell them accurately to my children."

Molly's face lit up. She was always pleased to be part of a family discussion where she was on equal footing with her brothers. She was, perhaps, more interested in the family history than her siblings. She had a happy disposition, issuing a glow that permeated the family as they gathered around the fire. "I had been hoping you would tell this story soon," she enthused.

"I will start at the beginning then, with the story about Richard Barker, the first settler in Andover. He grew up in Holme-on-Spalding Moor in the East Riding section of Yorkshire County, England. The moors of Yorkshire County are characterized by wide expanses of heather on gently rolling hills. It was rather sparsely populated but had a fine 16th century cathedral, which sits on the highest hill. Richard's attendance there became less regular as he became disenchanted with the high Protestant church mass and hierarchy of the Church of England.

Many local farmers learned to clear the heather and replace it with the plants

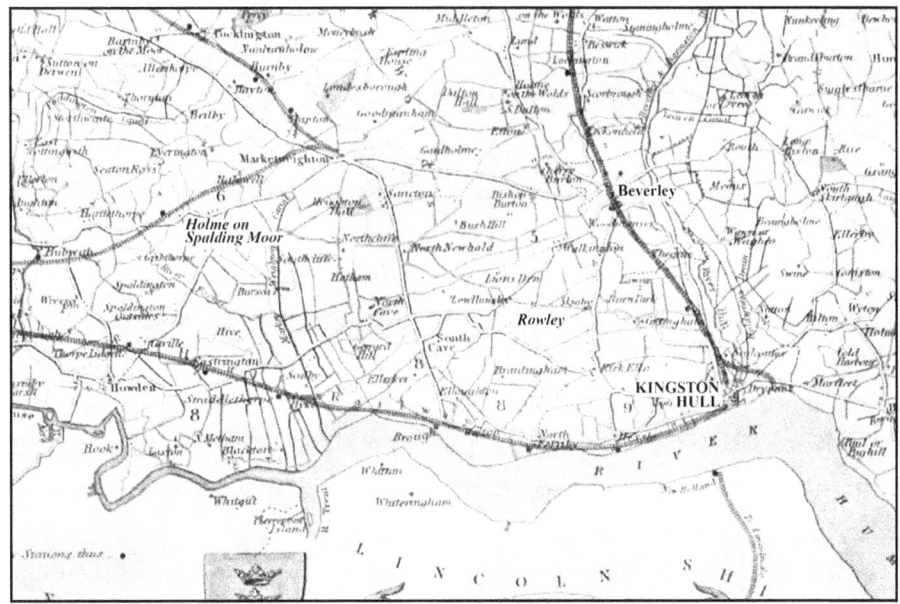

used to make hemp. Richard became a successful farmer and processor of the hemp fiber, used for making rope. Every week he led an oxcart with hemp to the harbor at Hull, for shipment to London. During one of his trips, he passed through Rowley, where he learned that Rev. Ezekiel Rogers was a Puritan preacher there. After that, he began to travel to Rowley to attend meeting.

"He came to Massachusetts in 1638 on the "John of London" with Rev. Ezekiel Rogers and cousins James and Thomas Barker. James and Thomas settled in the new settlement of Rowley with Rev. Rogers, but Richard was not happy there. Although Rev. Rogers appeared to be a virulent Puritan preacher, he prohibited lengthy "free prayer" by others in the congregation.

"Rogers wanted complete control and considered such prayers to be competition against his rule. Richard attended Meeting at Rowley, and occasionally in Newbury and later, Haverhill. He built his first house in Rowley Village, which later became Boxford. But he was looking for a better situation.

"During his early years in England, Richard had become a pious Puritan. His cousin, James, had grown up in Stragewell, Suffolk, not far from John Winthrop's home in Boxford.

"He moved to Yorkshire to follow Rev. Rogers, who had inspired James with his fiery sermons. James also gave Richard a copy of John Winthrop's sermon, "A Model of Christian Charity". James gave it to him just before Richard departed for America. In it Winthrop described the new Puritan settlement in Massachusetts as "a city upon a hill."

"Richard Barker drew great inspiration from that sermon – more than anything he heard from Rev. Rogers. It guided his life in America.

"As years passed, many Massachusetts pastors drew parallels between the Old Testament texts, which told of the land God gave to the Israelites, and the Puritan settlers in Massachusetts. They read passages from those texts, which told of the unfaithfulness of the Israelites and God's punishment.

"For many years, this was a dominant theme of many Puritan sermons in Massachusetts. People were encouraged to develop "the fear of God" in order to live more purely. The good people of Andover accepted this teaching and it contributed greatly to an orderly community, with little crime. It also resulted in the people having great respect for the pastor and leaders of the community, whose guidance they accepted without question.

"Richard learned that Pastor Ward of Ipswich was assembling people from

Ipswich and Newbury and seeking permission to start a new settlement at Cochichewick, on the Merrimack River. One Sunday, Rev. Rogers announced that he had agreed to coordinate their efforts at a meeting in Rowley. This was exciting news to Richard, and he attended it. After some discussion, Rev. John Woodbridge presented the Oath of Allegiance, which all of the proprietors would sign.

"John Woodbridge signed, then Edmund Faulkner. Several of the others began discussing a problem — that they had already signed the oath at Ipswich or Newbury. While they argued, Richard signed the oath and he spoke forthrightly, urging the others to sign so that they could get on with the settlement. He earned the respect of the others for his demeanor and Christian sentiments, but the meeting ended without agreement. Several refused to sign, saying they took their oath very seriously and could not repeat it to a different town. Richard was convinced that they would soon agree, so he moved from Rowley Village and built a house in Cochichewick (which later became Andover) by 1643. He was instrumental in getting the proprietors together a few months later, when all signed and the process went forward.

"John Woodbridge, the first pastor, and Edmund Faulkner purchased the Cochichewick lands from the Indian sagamore, or chief, Cutsamache. Those plus Simon Bradstreet, whose wife, Anne, was a daughter of Thomas Dudley, would be the town leaders.

"Bradstreet had been one of the founders of Ipswich, along with John Winthrop Jr. Richard Barker and John Osgood were recognized as the next most important proprietors for their role in bringing the others together and for Richard's deep devotion to Puritan principles.

"Only two years later, John Woodbridge had to return to England to settle his estate. Richard Barker and Edmund Faulkner were assigned to travel to Ipswich to find a new pastor. They returned with Francis Dane, who served as Andover's pastor for forty-five years. For many years he preached the traditional sermons, which provided firm guidance to Andover residents and punishment for those who strayed from the accepted norms.

"Each year, the proprietors – the original settlers – elected "tithing men" with authority to enter any resident's home unannounced to look for any violations. These included a failure to strictly observe the Sabbath, which started at sundown Saturday and ended Sunday night. If they entered Saturday after dusk and smelled cooking, the violator would be named at Sunday meeting and required to stand, confess and repent. Other violations included failure to pay taxes or attend Sunday meeting.

"After the Indian raid in 1676, Parson Dane's sermons changed. It seems his daughter, Abigail Dane Faulkner may have urged him to preach much more from the New Testament gospels. He began with a sermon about the sanctity of the life of all of people, and the militia's sin in killing Indian women and children at the Great Swamp Fight.

"Richard Barker, who was primarily responsible for relations with the pastor, was very upset about this sermon. He began to search for an assistant pastor, a position which the ruling council in Boston had suggested for the settlement some time previous to that.

Other things were changing in town, as well. Paul Faulkner moved his family to the South Parish, as did George Abbott, the tailor, and Thomas Chandler, who opened a tavern there. It was difficult for these families to travel to meeting every Sunday, so their attendance became irregular. Parson Dane excused these once-forbidden absences, but this also angered Richard Barker.

"Richard Barker convinced the selectmen to select Rev. Thomas Barnard as the assistant pastor. Thomas Barnard had attended Harvard with Cotton Mather, and his sermons were more traditional. The selectmen were happy with one of his sermons, in which he referred to Cotton Mather's book on the devil's use of the Indians against the colonists. Mather said that God had allowed the devil to punish the colonists for their sins. The townspeople took this to mean it was right and just for the militia to have killed all of the Indians, including women and children.

"After 1685, Thomas Barnard did most of the preaching, while Francis Dane preached less than once each month. They tried to greatly reduce Parson Dane's salary to pay the new pastor's salary but Francis Dane protested to the General Court in Boston and they agreed with him.

When Dane did preach, his sermons were more about the teachings of Jesus, and the love that God has for all people."One Sunday he went further. He told the parable of the prodigal son who had left his father and lived a sinful life until he needed help to survive. When he returned home, his father slew a calf and had a feast to celebrate. There was no punishment. This, he told the meeting, showed that God loved each of them and they should not fear God for

He would not punish them for minor sins.

"He said it was wrong that people were required to stand before the meeting and confess sins which should only be confessed to God in prayer.

"Richard Barker was upset about this sermon. He believed it would undermine the selectmen's authority and could lead to anarchy.

"A major premise of the Puritan settlements was a hierarchy of the families in each town. This was reflected in the seating order in the church pews. Each time the church was rebuilt (which occurred every 30 or 40 years), a committee of three members would determine the seating order. Back in 1681, when the church was re-built, this process became a central point of disagreement among the townspeople. Some leading citizens tried to avoid being part of that committee, but were forced to serve.

"A few weeks after the Prodigal Son sermon, Pastor Dane told the parable of the good Samaritan. This parable told of how an injured Israelite lay by the roadside. Several of his countrymen saw him, but passed, without helping. Eventually, a Samaritan (a tribe generally despised by the Israelites) helped him. Pastor Dane said this taught that all men are equal in God's eyes, and they should also be equal in ours. Richard Barker was furious. As he left the meetinghouse with his sons and their families, Benjamin and William Barker heard their father speak sternly to Parson Dane.

" 'No punishment for sin? All men should be equal? This is not the kind of Puritan teaching I have known!'

"Parson Dane put his arm around Richard's shoulder and smiled. 'It is from God, Richard.'

"Richard turned quickly so that Parson Dane's arm fell from his shoulder. 'I fear it may be more from the devil,' he said as he walked briskly away.

"Others heard what Richard had said and soon everyone would know, including Thomas Barnard. Those words would come back to haunt Richard and lead to his troubled death a few years later.

"I have been talking for quite a while now and wonder how much of this you have heard and understood."

Jon responded quickly, "I believe I understand most of it, father."

Ben, Molly and Hannah nodded in unison, "Me too."

The younger Samuel said, "I don't know what it all means, father."

Jonathan was pleased at the rapt attention of his children and the understanding the older ones apparently had of this important family history. "Let us take a break from this history lesson for some other activity. We can continue after supper, by candle light."

That evening, Jonathan asked Molly to repeat what she could remember of his talk that afternoon. "Remind me about how it starts," Molly urged.

Jonathan replied with the hint of Richard Barker's youth in Yorkshire, England. "Oh, yes," she said and continued rapidly through much of the story, pausing occasionally to recall the year of certain events. Hannah, Jon and Ben interrupted her two or three times to provide minor corrections and additions.

Jonathan was happy about his older children's recall of his presentation, knowing that their recitation would help store this history in their minds.

"Let me continue, then. I think I should now turn to Abigail Dane Faulkner.

"Edmund Faulkner, one of the most respected proprietors, arranged the marriage of his son, Francis, to Abigail, the younger daughter of Rev. Francis Dane in 1675. She had been well educated by her father and was probably the most intelligent woman in Andover. When townspeople learned that Abigail had stopped speaking to her brother-in-law, John Faulkner, after the Indian raids of 1676, they did not take kindly to her.

"The couple raised seven children and Francis operated his father's tavern until he suffered from a mental breakdown or mania. This stopped him from managing the tavern, so Abigail took over those responsibilities as well as her child-rearing chores. She was better at running the tavern business than her husband. Eventually, Francis Faulkner's mental deficiencies improved, due to herb treatments by Abigail. Later, when witchcraft charges were brought against her, this was seen as a sign of a witch.

"The tavern clients did not mind her serving them food and drink but they were not happy with her strong business-like dealings with them. They also suspected that she had urged Parson Dane to speak out against the militia's killing of women and children at Swansea in 1675. This was not acceptable behavior for a Puritan woman. All were expected to be humble, especially women, and particularly a pastor's daughter's obedience to her father. Not being meek was another attribute of a witch.

"This gives you some background for what followed. I will try to give you an easy way to understand the 1692 witch hysteria in Salem and Andover.

"It was like a firestorm because it spread quickly. The makings of a firestorm are a spark, fuel, and something like the wind, to make it spread.

"In Salem and Andover, the equivalent to the fuel was the fear and superstition of the people. The wind was Rev. Cotton Mather, who spread fear among the people. Most of the Puritans believed that witchcraft existed and that witches were controlled by the devil. They also believed that God was all-powerful and that witches could only operate with God's permission, which He gave when the people had sinned against God. Everyone knew the Bible verse from Exodus 22 which states, "Thou shalt not suffer a witch to live." Cotton Mather preached about this when stories of witches in Danvers started. He wrote about previous instances of witchcraft in Connecticut, but he also wrote about the many attacks by the Indians in York, Falmouth, Wells, and Salmon Falls, Maine, emphasizing the fury of the devil's work. He exaggerated and distorted the stories with regard to the cruelty of the Indians. He failed to mention that some of the Indian attacks were in retaliation for crimes of the colonists against the Indians or that the French, who had paid the Indians for their assistance, directed some of the attacks.

"The spark occurred in Danvers, which was Salem Village in those days. Rev. Paris had a young Indian slave woman from the West Indies named Tituba working in his house. She taught his young daughter and some friends about mysterious rites and lore. During one of these lessons, the girls lost control of themselves; screaming, yelling, tearing their hair and throwing themselves to the floor in anguish. Rev. Parish was unable to calm them. Their condition worsened and they appeared to be in fits of pain. Dr. Griggs was called to examine some of them, but could find no clear reason for their behavior, and suggested that witchcraft might be at work.

Rev. Parish gathered pastors from neighboring villages to meet with him, observe some of the girls, and discuss the situation. They soon agreed that witches had taken hold of the girls. Pressure was put on the children to tell who afflicted them and they named Tituba and two local wives, Sarah Good and Sarah Osburn. Those were arrested on February 28, 1692. A trial was arranged to be held in Salem, conducted by Magistrates John Hathorne and Jonathan Corwin. By this time everyone in Danvers and Salem were talking about witches being at work in their midst. A huge crowd assembled at the trial.

The two women denied their guilt but Tituba readily confessed and proceeded to tell a wild tale of the witches who were at work in Salem.

The afflicted girls now felt empowered and began to name other witches. Other people in town who were suspicious or held grudges against some townspeople named them as witches.

Soon there were formal charges against several innocent people, who were put in jail and eventually on trial. During the trials, the judges pressured all of those charged to confess, but none did. The girls' affliction failed to subside and their answers to doubting questions of several magistrates were consistent. Soon, there was a growing belief that the village faced an outbreak of witchcraft. Rev. Cotton Mather of Boston began to visit Salem regularly to accelerate the process. Within three months, over thirty people from Danvers and Salem town were charged and soon, people from other towns were charged."

Jon interrupted this long discourse. "How did this firestorm spread to Andover?"

Abigail interrupted, "Jonathan, before you answer that, let me put the younger children to bed. I am not sure if any of them can follow such a complex story at this late hour."

Jonathan looked around and saw that Samuel was only half awake and Jesse and Symonds Epes were already asleep on the floor. "Let's put the story aside for another day. Let me help you with the boys."

Jonathan woke Jesse and Symonds Epes and led them to their cot as he carried three-year-old Amos. When the children were all tucked in, Jonathan and Abigail embraced warmly for a long time. Abigail spoke softly into Jonathan's ear, "Our children are so fortunate to have such a loving father. On a day when the elements whirled furiously outside, they were so engrossed with your story that they scarcely noticed and passed the day in perfect calm and pleasure."

Jonathan kissed Abigail passionately. "It is I who am fortunate to have a woman who gave me these lovely children and who nurtures them with such tenderness."

CHAPTER FIVE

MASSACHUSETTS DRIFTS FURTHER FROM BRITAIN

The Barker family awoke to a blazing sunrise that invaded their bedchambers like a trumpeter calling them to duty. There was much work to be done to clear the snow so that they could return to milking the cows, feeding the other animals and bringing wood for the fire. Yet there was time for play in the snow by the younger ones, while the older boys built forts and dug tunnels for snow fights. For several days they worked and played hard until they fell exhausted into their cots after dark.

Winter's harshness mellowed, yielding an occasional day or two when the snow would melt. After the noon meal one day, Jon asked his father to return to the story of how the witch hysteria spread from Danvers to Andover. Benjamin, Molly, Hannah, and Samuel added their pleas, "Yes, father, please tell us."

Jonathan drew the older children around him on the floor by the fire while Abigail sat between Jesse and Symonds Epes, not yet seven and five years old. She held three-year-old Amos on her lap.

"Jon has asked an important question, 'How did the firestorm of the witch hysteria spread to Andover?' Well, three sparks set it off. The first were the two Allen sisters, Mary and Martha. They were daughters of Andrew Allen, one of the proprietors of Andover. Mary, the older, married Dr. Roger Toothaker of Billerica, and moved there. Dr. Toothaker often entertained his patients with strange but interesting stories. When the witch hysteria began in Danvers, people talked about it throughout Essex County.

"Dr. Toothaker told about a séance he held at his house during which his daughter killed a witch. A few days after telling this, Dr. Toothaker was arrested and brought to Salem for questioning. He was charged and jailed in May 1692. Ten days later, his wife, Mary, and her sister, Martha were arrested.

"People had been looking for a way to get back at Martha since she and her husband, Thomas Carrier, had moved back to Andover from Billerica two years earlier. There was a smallpox epidemic in Andover soon after. Four of the Allen family in Andover were infected and died, swiftly followed by nine others in town. Everyone believed that Martha had brought smallpox to Andover, despite showing no signs of the disease herself.

Eventually, the selectmen ordered her quarantined at home. She defiantly went about town while all the infected were dying. When she was arrested and charged with witchcraft, the Salem judges moved swiftly against her. She loudly protested her innocence throughout the questioning and trial and even on gallows hill, just before she was hanged.

"The other sparks were two dying Andover residents who probably suffered from an unknown disease. The first was the wife of Joseph Ballard, another early settler of Andover. He did all he could to comfort her and have her treated by physicians, to no avail. During a visit to their home, Rev. Thomas Barnard suggested that his wife might be the victim of witches at work in Andover. He encouraged Joseph to ride his horse to Danvers and fetch Ann Putnam and another of the afflicted accusers there, which he did. When they arrived, Rev. Barnard assembled the afflicted girls and Andover residents who had had disputes with the Ballards and others in town. After a prayer to begin the meeting, the afflicted girls pointed to one after another in the room, accusing them of witchcraft. Within a few days, people began accusing others of witchcraft and the girls were used to confirm the accusations. This continued for several weeks until fifty Andover people had been accused of witchcraft.

"The final spark was the one which affected the Barkers and Faulkners. Nineteen-year-old Timothy Swan was also suffering from an unknown malady. He experienced several painful bouts, which suggested to Rev. Barnard that he was being attacked by witches sticking pins in a poppet, a kind of doll. This was a practice of certain groups in the West Indies. The ritual had been taught to some of the afflicted Danvers girls by a servant. Rev. Barnard brought Ann Putnam and the other Danvers girl to his bedside, along with others who had visited him to comfort him. One of those was William Barker, son of Richard Barker. He was quickly pointed out as one of Timothy Swan's tormentors, and thus, a witch. Soon, his son, Will Jr. was charged as well.

"William Barker was a simple man, who did as he was raised to do: respect authority and carry out what he was told by those in authority. His father convinced him to confess that, in his weakness, he had allowed the devil to take control of him, but now he would renounce the devil.

"When other authorities questioned him, he was asked why he became a witch. He said that the devil had promised that all of his debts would be paid and that life would go easy for him if he signed the devil's book. He said when the devil ruled, all men would be equal, live bravely and there would be no punishment for sin. Everyone recognized these statements as having been preached by Rev. Francis Dane.

"They asked what the devil looked like and he answered, 'a black man.' When they asked if he had ridden on a witches' broom to a meeting with other witches, he agreed that he had and named Abigail Dane Faulkner and Elizabeth Dane Johnson as also being witches. Asked if the meeting was attended by a pastor he said, 'Yes." He said it was Rev. George Burroughs, who he knew had been arrested in Wells, Maine and brought to Salem where he was charged with witchcraft."

The children were incredulous. Molly asked, "How could they charge a pastor with witchcraft? Didn't the Puritans believe that pastors were chosen by God and above reproach?"

"You are quite right, Molly. But George Burroughs was not your regular pastor. He had served as a pastor in Danvers for a short time, during which he and his wife lived in the home of a local family. When he moved to Maine, those he had lived with told of how Rev. Burroughs had mistreated his wife. A year after he settled in Maine, his wife died and Rev. Burroughs returned her to Danvers to be buried. He soon remarried but his second wife died two years later and he married a third time. One young woman in Danvers had lived in Maine at the time and after her return, she charged that George Burroughs had murdered his two wives.

"The most serious charge against Rev. Burroughs was related to the books that Cotton Mather had written, claiming that all of the Indian raids on settlers in Maine were directed by the devil. George Burroughs had lived in three towns in Maine. Each time he moved away from a village, it was attacked by Indians within a few weeks, with many people killed and houses burned. Thus, it was reasoned that the attacks were the work of a witch, and that witch was Rev. George Burroughs.

"After his trial, at which he denied all of the charges, he was quickly sentenced to be hanged. On gallows hill, he said an impressive prayer, asking God to forgive those who had wrongfully accused and convicted him. Standing nearby was Cotton Mather, who called him "the king of hell." A few minutes later, Martha Carrier was hanged, and Cotton Mather named her "the queen of hell."

"The important point in all of this is that William Barker was an unwitting accomplice to the conspiracy targeting the Dane family. The Barker name was held in high esteem, so a Barker witness against the Danes was critically important. Many in town were upset with Pastor Dane, because they were taxed to support two pastors. They blamed it on Pastor Dane, who had reduced his preaching because Richard Barker no longer approved of him.

"It was Richard Barker himself who assisted the Dane and Faulkner enemies by his angry reply to Rev. Francis Dane, suggesting that his Bible lesson was from the devil and not God. William heard this statement and took it to heart, and Richard realized this.

"Now you can understand why this eventually led to Richard's death and why he made my grandpa Benjamin promise to restore the bonds between the Barkers and Faulkners. He felt responsible for this miscarriage of justice.

"When Abigail Dane Faulkner was tried for witchcraft, the leading witness was William Barker. He repeated all that he had said. Abigail was found guilty and sentenced to be hanged. However, she was pregnant and the Puritans would not destroy an unborn life, so sentence was delayed until after the birth of her child. Fortunately, Governor Phipps ordered an end to all witchcraft trials and executions a month before Abigail's child was delivered. It was a boy she named Ammi Ruhammah, which, in Hebrew, means "my people have obtained mercy." This unusual name partially met the requirements of the

Puritan naming tradition – that all names should come from the Bible. Abigail chose a more meaningful name, but one which did not appear in the Bible as such. It was an amalgam of two Hebrew words, which appeared separately in another context.

"Judge Hathorne, who had sentenced Abigail to be hanged was furious at being over-ruled by the governor. He wanted the sentence to be reviewed in another trial, but Gov. Phipps would have none of it.

"Hathorne's objection kept a cloud over Abigail's head for another ten years, while her conviction was still in effect. Ammi Ruhammah grew up under this cloud and was the target of many taunts from other children, who called him "son of a witch." Finally, she appealed to the governing council in Boston, which set aside her conviction.

"There are other lessons from the Andover witchcraft affair which I will teach you at another time. This is too much for Samuel and Jesse to understand just now. Next winter we can review this story so that we can all know why we need to share the challenge which Richard Barker gave to his son, Benjamin."

As the spring of 1769 approached, the Essex Journal and Ipswich Sentinel carried increasing reports on the Massachusetts boycott of English goods, as a protest against the Townshend Act.

The boycott succeeded, with very few merchants importing English goods, and those who did lost most of their patrons. English merchants complained of their lost business. Soon, Parliament repealed the Townshend Act and replaced it with a single tax – on tea. This was intended just to show the colonists that England had the right to tax them.

The year passed quietly for the Barker family, in contrast to the exciting events of 1768. In September, Abigail gave birth to her ninth child and third daughter. Having named her first daughter for her grandmother and second for her mother, she consented to naming this daughter Abigail. Molly and Hannah helped their mother care for the new baby, as well as for three-year-old Amos. The other five boys shared camaraderie with their father, working together on farm chores and house maintenance.

This made the Barkers more productive farmers, producing ample fruits and vegetables with excess quantities to store for the winter and sell to some neighbors. These sales, in addition to an occasional sale of a pig or goat, provided cash to buy material for clothing the growing family. Like most residents of Methuen, Andover, and Haverhill, they bought homespun fabric from the women of Haverhill. Although English fabric was finer, they happily used homespun, so as not to pay English taxes.

The newspapers also carried stories about Boston boys and their run-ins with the English Regulars. Clad in their bright red coats, the boys named them "lobsters." The Sons of Liberty reported these run-ins were caused by the Regulars but there were clearly attempts by the young men to provoke confrontation. The political climate in Boston was a tinderbox, awaiting a spark of revolution.

As winter approached, the Barker family began to spend more time together by the fire after dusk. One evening Molly recalled her father's witchcraft stories and asked, "Father, last spring you told us you had more to say about the Andover witchcraft episode which you would tell later. Besides, I still have questions about it that I would like you to answer."

Jonathan invited her to ask her questions and she responded, "How many people were charged with witchcraft in Andover, and how many were executed?"

Jonathan responded that he believed there were more than fifty Andover people charged with witchcraft, more than all who were charged in Salem and Danvers combined. Of those, only eight were convicted and four executed. Many others spent several weeks in Salem prison, several in the basement, sleeping on lice-infested straw. They were given only water by the prison guards. They had to rely on family visitors for food. However, some families were unable to make the four-hour walk to Salem to bring food.

Jonathan went on to explain that the judges convicted those eight because they honestly believed they were guilty of witchcraft – they exhibited many of the traits of witches. For example, Martha Carrier had not attended Sunday meeting regularly; her demeanor was never humble and she showed no respect for those in authority. Moreover, they were convinced she purposely spread smallpox to Andover, killing thirteen people, including five from her own extended family.

Samuel Wardwell was also executed. He also exhibited the traits of witches, performing magic, telling fortunes and stories of mysterious creatures and happenings. Four others were convicted because evidence suggested they probably caused the deaths of Timothy Swan and Goody Ballard. More likely, those two died of some unknown disease.

Abigail Dane Faulkner was the more difficult case, Jonathan explained. As the daughter of Parson Dane, she was a model Puritan in most respects. She was respectful towards the elders, but not so much to ordinary men she served at the Faulkner tavern, so many men in town disliked her. She was as knowledgeable about herbal remedies as any physician, and some suspected this art as witchcraft. She had almost miraculously nursed her husband back to health after he suffered from mental illness, which also raised suspicions of witchcraft. When she was named as a witch by Ann Putnam, the authorities told her she should confess. She responded in a way that could not be called disrespectful, but the authorities felt insulted by it nonetheless. She said, "God would not want me to confess that of which I was not guilty."

She was questioned at length at least twice over two weeks, with no clear evidence to bring her to trial. Finally, however, William Barker was arrested and named Abigail and her sister as two who had recruited him to the devil's side. They then had a witness from a family of unquestioned credibility and so they brought her to trial and convicted her.

The case of Mary Parker is a puzzle, perhaps even a mistake. When they told her she should confess to being a witch, she responded that she knew nothing of it and insisted that they must have the wrong Mary Parker, for there were two others of that name in Andover. Her protests were ignored and eventually they got 15-year-old Will Barker Jr. to name her as a witch. Based solely on this, she was convicted and hanged. This shows how highly esteemed the Barker name was, that the word of a 15-year-old grandson of Richard Barker was sufficient to send a wrongly-charged woman to the gallows.

Jonathan said that it was now necessary for him to explain in more detail why the Barker name was held in such esteem.

At this point Jonathan paused for what seemed a long time. He had never cried but now came as close as he ever had, as his eyes misted over. The many days he had spent cross-legged on the floor at the foot of grandpa Benjamin's chair came back to him. The fire set his grandfather's visage aglow, highlighting every distinguishing cleft and wrinkle that his strength of character and the years had carved into it. The picture was burned into his memory and never failed to move him.

Jonathan had always felt blessed that this great man had devoted so much

Samuel Adams

of his later years to a father-less grandson. Now, he sensed an impossible burden upon him. He believed he was much less a man than his grandfather, yet his task was much greater. He had many children of different ages. How could he pass on all the complex and important lessons that he had received to each of them.

As these thoughts raced through his mind he said, "Grandpa Benjamin told me all of these things several times over many years as I grew up in his Andover house. It was all very confusing until I was in my later teens. I think the next part is the most important and the most difficult to understand, so I believe we should let the matter rest for another year. We will pick it up again next winter.

Before the winter of 1769-70 passed, several incidents greatly ignited the sparks which would eventually erupt in revolution. There were regular encounters between young colonists and the English Regulars. The Sons of Liberty and their supporters named merchants who were not observing the boycott of imported taxed goods. They went further, ransacking their shops and hanging the owners in effigy on the Liberty Tree, and organizing crowds to block the entrance to those shops.

On February 22nd, they had posted a large "Importer" sign in front of the North End shop of Theophilis Lillie. A large crowd gathered and prevented customers from entering. A Royalist neighbor, Ebenezer Richardson tried to drive the crowd off, but they pelted him and his house with stones, breaking his windows and doors and hitting his wife and children. Richardson came to his window with a musket, threatening the crowd if they did not disperse. It remained and Richardson fired, the pellets wounding one man and killing twelve-year-old Christopher Seider as he bent over to pick up a stone.

At his funeral on February 25th, two thousand people followed as the body was taken from Faneuil Hall around the Liberty Tree back to the Provincial House (which later became known as the Old State House) and then to the Granary Burial Ground. The Essex Journal reported that John Adams said, "Mine eyes never beheld such a funeral."

After that, there were daily confrontations between the locals and the Regulars. The soldiers, who were sent to maintain order, had all they could do to defend themselves from the crowds of ruffians.

On Monday evening, March 5th, a hoard of men and boys marched through Dock Square in Boston, determined to confront the Regulars. They eventually isolated a sentry and abused him until seven Regulars arrived to free him. As the confrontation continued, the crowd grew in size and rowdiness until nearly a thousand were shouting and throwing snowballs and ice at the Regulars. They taunted the soldiers with cries of "Fire if you dare" and "Are your weapons loaded?"

In the confusion, first one and then several Regulars began firing, killing five and wounding six in the crowd.

Boston Massacre

Paul Revere and others soon proclaimed the killings "The Bloody Massacre". Samuel Adams organized meetings to urge speedy trials and convictions of the Regulars and the captain of the troop that fired on the crowd. Public funerals were held for the victims, attended by hundreds of people.

A measure of calm was restored when the captain's trial was held and he was found not guilty. John Adams, his lawyer, showed that the Regulars fired after they heard what they thought was an order to fire, but that the voice that shouted that had come from the crowd and not from where the captain stood.

Still, Samuel Adams and John Hancock made sure that "The Boston Massacre" remained in the minds of the colonists by establishing a day of remembrance each March 5th for several years thereafter.

This event became the topic of discussion at the Barker homestead throughout the winter and spring of 1770. There were lively discussions, with Molly taking the side of the Regulars, pointing out that they were victims of severe harassment by an unruly mob of antagonists. Jon and Benjamin took the opposite view in support of the colonists, saying they were rightfully opposed to having the Regulars stationed in Boston acting as policemen when they were not needed or wanted. Moreover, they said that Massachusetts had their own authorities and that England had no right to impose these outside police on their peaceful lives. Jonathan encouraged more thoughtful discussion of the situation by his children, stating that this would not be the end of the matter. Clearly, he said, Sam Adams, Paul Revere and John Hancock were intent on stoking the fiery and resentful attitude of many colonists, until the Crown withdrew the troops. Otherwise, they were prepared for revolution.

The English governor tried to bring calm to Boston by removing the Regulars to Castle Island in Boston Harbor. He also had the Townshend Act repealed, eliminating all duties on imported goods from England with the exception of a small tax on tea. This was kept to show the colonists that the king had the right to impose taxes. Moreover, they felt that the tax was so small that the colonists would overlook this token of their authority. They were wrong.

CHAPTER SIX

A MATURING BARKER FAMILY

The early 1770's were productive at the Barker farm. The Barker boys grew bigger and stronger and worked harder. Benjamin became more productive than his older and taller brother, Jon, and clearly enjoyed working hard. Young Jesse idolized Benjamin and worked alongside him on many chores. Samuel worked with Jon, but at a less aggressive pace. Jesse made a competitive game of the two teams, as they undertook similar chores. He exulted as he and Benjamin often won against their older brothers.

Molly helped young Symonds Epes with his chores, while her younger sister, Hannah, cared for the youngest boy, Amos. These growing family bonds would strengthen even into their adult years and provide encouragement and support for one another throughout their lives.

Jonathan Barker had inherited considerable Methuen land from his grandfather – more than he could use in his younger years. As he and Abigail were getting their farm and family started, he sold off parcels to raise the money he needed. Now, however, his maturing family was clearing and cultivating more of his land each year, growing more staple crops of corn, potatoes, tomatoes, carrots, beets, beans, and squash. They also added new crops each year, primarily berry patches, apple and peach trees. The family joyfully celebrated crops harvested for the first time.

Barker livestock also expanded markedly. Jonathan acquired additional cows and chickens to provide milk, eggs, and cheese for his voracious sons and daughters. The goat herd provided entertainment to young Amos and baby Abigail and the Barker diet was much more varied and interesting with the addition of goat's milk and cheese. They also added several more pigs. Jonathan purchased a second horse and a small carriage so he and Abigail could ride to meeting in comfort.

Each winter, Jonathan would encourage Jon, Benjamin, and Molly to re-tell the stories he had taught them about the witchcraft era and the Barker family's role in it. Hannah, Samuel, and Jesse were now old enough to understand and be interested as their siblings recalled the stories. The children discussed and corrected one another or responded to questions from the younger ones. Jonathan sat back, observing the excited interest of his children, pleased that they were able to recall these important details and embed them into the minds of his youngest children.

In early December 1773, Jonathan felt it was time for him to impart the final and most important chapter of his story. His youngest son, Amos, was seven years old and even he was engaged when his older siblings told the oft-repeated stories.

Before the opportunity for this arose, another major event took place in Boston. A ship arrived from England, laden with tea. It stood in Boston harbor awaiting payment of import duties for the tea, before it could be released to the merchants. The colonists insisted that the ship should return to England, because they had no intention of paying the taxes. The governor announced that this would not be done.

On December 15th, a committee was organized in Boston, led by Paul Revere and Joseph Warren, to plan the destruction of the tea. The next night several men, disguised as Indians, boarded the ship and threw the cases of tea into the harbor. This was patterned after the successful Gaspeé Affair of

The Boston Tea Party

June 9, 1772.

The merchants of Providence and Newport had been conducting a very profitable but forbidden import-export trade with countries other than England. Britain sent a two-masted schooner, the HMS Gaspeé, to intercept and destroy the merchandise. A small boat from Newport, heading for Providence, approached the Gaspeé and ordered to allow boarding by the Gaspeé. Instead, they maneuvered the Gaspeé onto a sand bank and escaped.

The next night, in moonless darkness, 60 of Rhode Island's leading men with painted faces and Indian headdress rowed out on longboats and surrounded the Gaspeé at close range before they were discovered. They boarded, overcame the captain and crew, and rowed to shore in their long boats. They burned the ship, destroying it. Despite several months of investigations and trial, the British were unable to identify any of the perpetrators.

The day after the Boston raid, Paul Revere and others from the committee began traveling to the major towns of Massachusetts, defending the tea's destruction. Jonathan traveled to Ipswich to attend one of those meetings.

When Jonathan returned to his children, he explained what had happened. He related that the governor demanded payment for the destruction and that the committee had agreement from the leaders in Boston that they would not pay. Vowing not to repeat the unhappy result of the Gaspeé Affair, Parliament passed a law called "Coercive Acts" to punish Massachusetts. These laws cancelled Massachusetts' charter and forbade town meetings, importation of gunpowder, muskets and other munitions. Jonathan also told his children that Paul Revere planned to visit New York and Philadelphia to enlist support.

In September 1774, the First Continental Congress met in Philadelphia, with representatives from every colony but Georgia. They voted to prevent Britain from enforcing the Coercive Acts and to take retribution against Britain for this action. They also suggested every town organize a militia and equip each private with a musket, powder, lead balls, and a bayonet.

The mood throughout Massachusetts was quite aggressive towards Britain and its Regulars stationed there. Before winter passed, Methuen organized a militia and more than 150 were designated 'minutemen', ready to march on short notice. Jonathan and Jon were among them. Samuel asked to be accepted as a fifer. During the winter, they met weekly at the school for training and instruction. When the weather permitted, they met twice a week and marched on the roads.

The event of December 16, 1773 became known as "The Boston Tea Party" and was a rallying point much like "The Boston Massacre." Soon, the word "revolution" was used in public conversation, and was raised in conversation at the Barker homestead regularly.

At least one day each week, Jonathan and his older children took turns reading aloud various reports from the Essex Gazette and Essex Journal. While Continental Congress delegates assembled in Philadelphia, British troops took control of the largest store of munitions in Massachusetts, at the Powder House in a section of Cambridge later called Somerville. When news of this reached the towns, people panicked in Salem and Marblehead, fearing an attack from the Regulars. Many moved to inland towns or Nantucket island.

One snowy afternoon in January 1775, the Barker family gathered to celebrate Hannah's sixteenth birthday. She had developed into an appealing maiden with long blond hair and her father's flashing blue eyes. She was uncomfortable being the center of attention – less secure than her older sister, Molly. She preferred to be busy caring for the youngest children: Abigail, and Elcy, while Molly cared for eight-year-old Amos. She drew some strength from thirteen-year-old Jesse, who admired her beauty and helped her with some of her chores. Jonathan and Abigail smiled with pride, as they presented Hannah with small gifts they had made or acquired.

After the celebration, Jonathan asked his children if they were ready to hear the final most important chapter in his story about the Andover witchcraft hysteria. All were eager to hear; Jon, Benjamin, and Molly had been ready for a few years, but Jonathan had urged them to wait until more of them were old enough to understand it all.

This maturing Barker family had gathered many times to discuss the 1692 witchcraft hysteria in Andover, and how it affected their ancestors. Jon was now a fully grown twenty-one-year-old, five feet ten inches in stature, Benjamin a handsome and fit twenty-year-old. Molly had blossomed into an attractive young woman, nearly eighteen. Samuel, fourteen, and eleven-year-old Symonds Epes had heard the stories enough that they, also, had some understanding of them.

Jonathan began, "You must all be patient because this story starts more than 150 years ago, before the Puritans came to Massachusetts. I have already told you that the most important Puritan leader, John Winthrop, had been the major influence on Richard Barker's Puritan beliefs. But, there was another important Puritan leader in the large group that came to Boston in 1630. That was Thomas Dudley.

"In England, he had been steward for the Earl of Lincolnshire when the elder Earl died, leaving his estate in deep debt. Within three years, Thomas Dudley restored the estate to profitability, by carefully managing the large staff and expenses and increasing rents. The Earl's estate was called Sempringham, which was a small village, all of whose inhabitants either worked for the Earl, or were tenant farmers on the his estate.

"During that time, a friend of Thomas Dudley died, leaving a 14-year-old son, Simon Bradstreet, who had just started college. Dudley agreed to take the son on as an apprentice, after he completed his studies. Thomas Dudley taught him all that he was doing as steward on the estate and soon he handed off most of his responsibilities. Simon Bradstreet lived in Thomas Dudley's home as a member of his family.

"As the years passed, Thomas Dudley's daughter, Anne, became enamored of Simon. She saw him as a young version of her father, whom she adored. In 1630, when Thomas Dudley became part of the Puritan contingent that sailed to Boston, Simon Bradstreet was 28 years old, and Anne Dudley was 16. They married and sailed with the elder Dudley.

"Simon Bradstreet was given major responsibilities as the towns of Boston,

Charlestown, Cambridge and Watertown were established. In 1633, it was decided that a new seaport town with an inland river should be established. That town was Ipswich and John Winthrop Jr. and Thomas Dudley took five others to establish it. Simon and Anne Bradstreet joined them.

"These settlers all had wealth enough to bring carpenters and joiners who built substantial houses for them. Anne Bradstreet was maturing and writing poetry, with the encouragement of her father, husband, pastor, and other intellectuals in Ipswich. She built one of the largest libraries in the colony and enjoyed her life in Ipswich.

"In 1638, confrontation between Puritans, Catholics and the formal protestant Church of England led many Puritans to leave England, fearing a bad outcome. Among these late immigrants was Ezekiel Rogers, an energetic and ambitious Puritan pastor, who brought more than fifty families from Yorkshire. He was given permission to establish the town of Rowley in northeastern Massachusetts.

Richard Barker came with them and spent time in Rowley, but was waiting for approval for another town. By 1640, permission was granted to establish the inland town at Cochichewick Plantation, on the Merrimac River, but it was necessary to find a pastor and two capable leaders before final approval.

"John Woodbridge, who had taken part in the petition to establish a settlement at Cochichewick Plantation with his brother, Nathaniel Woodbridge, agreed to be pastor. He had been a teacher at Boston Latin School as he was principally a scholar. However, since his father had been a pastor, he also aspired to that position and was pleased to accept the role which had been urged on him by Thomas Dudley, his father-in-law.

"Among those wishing to settle at Cochichewick Plantation was Edmund Faulkner, the only man who was given the gentleman's title of "Mr." All of the other prospective settlers were simple farmers. The settlement could not proceed without a qualified leader.

"The prospective settlers were becoming impatient with each passing month. Finally, Thomas Dudley told his son-in-law, Simon Bradstreet, that it was his duty to accept this leadership role.

"Simon was extremely reluctant, because his wife, Anne, was very happily settled in Ipswich. She had many supportive relatives and intellectual friends there. She also had a fine house and more than one thousand books, which would be difficult to move. However, Bradstreet could not refuse, so he promised to move to Andover within a year after the first settlement there.

"After a year's delay the settlement was begun. This occurred after Edmund Faulkner and John Woodbridge bought the land from the Indian sagamore, Cutsamache.

"As promised, Bradstreet joined the settlement in 1646, after the proprietors had cleared land for their houses and began to cultivate small farms. By this time, Cochichewick Plantation was incorporated as the town of Andover. Bradstreet established various town offices and arranged for annual elections.

"A small temporary meetinghouse was built, since Sunday meeting was central to Puritan life. Pastor Woodbridge provided religious instruction to the new settlers in his Bible-based sermons, as well as practical instruction. All of the Puritans looked forward to the Sabbath each week, and to the meeting and the long sermons, often two hours or more in the morning and again in the afternoon. They took very seriously the Bible's story of God's creation in six days followed by a day of rest, and its example for all people. They worked very hard during the week and needed a day of rest. They also enjoyed meeting all of their friends in the Meetinghouse. As for the long sermons, those were the main source of education and serious thinking about life's important issues.

"Besides the pastor's preaching, the meeting included singing of the Psalms. Every settler had his own book of psalms and one or two probably had a Psalm book with music. The other important aspect of a Puritan service was 'open prayer.' Any member could stand and pray aloud at any quiet time in the meeting.

"Richard Barker often prayed in this manner. The content of his prayers demonstrated the depth of his Puritan beliefs. He prayed as John Winthrop had done when he was away at school. He prayed for God's forgiveness for his many sins, such as resting more than he needed when there was much work to be done; enjoying a tasty meal and other things which we now think are not sins.

"He also made intercessory prayers, asking God to bless his fellow Andover citizens and help them to better please their God. Richard Barker's devotion and strong faith endeared him to the people of Andover. He was trusted by everyone to be honest, and was asked to witness nearly every legal document created in Andover during his lifetime, including wills, inventories, and property deeds.

"There was another, more important, reason why the people of Andover looked up to Richard Barker. All of them were devoted Puritans and accepted the teachings of John Calvin. Calvin, who lived in Switzerland from 1509 to 1564 had been one of the first Protestant reformers after Martin Luther. He taught that God had chosen, or elected, those who would live with Him in heaven. The choice was made before birth and there was nothing anyone could do to become one of the elect. All were charged with acting as though they had been chosen, knowing that few actually were. Almost none of them could act in this way, but Richard Barker did and so he was believed by other Andoverites to be one of the elect. The people also assumed that the leaders and pastors were among the elect, and they accepted their own roles of being in a lower status.

"During Andover's first few years, Simon Bradstreet saw that John Osgood stood out as a bright and political leader. With Bradstreet's support, Osgood became Andover's first representative to the General Court in Boston. Bradstreet also supported Richard Barker as one of three selectmen, who would manage the town's affairs.

"Those affairs largely related to the meetinghouse, its construction, the support of the pastor, and to the Puritan behavior of the people. After being re-elected to a selectman's position for many years, Barker was recognized as a partner with the pastor, and later, as the overseer of the pastor.

"When John Woodbridge resigned as pastor after less than three years to return to England on family business, it fell to Richard Barker and Edmond Faulkner to find a replacement.

"They traveled to Ipswich and returned with Rev. Francis Dane. Pastor Dane served faithfully and acceptably for many years. However, as I've related before, at some point he began to change. He became more lenient and understanding of people who occasionally missed Sunday meeting. His preaching became less about the fear of God and of the sin of man and more about the need of all people to love one another and accept their shortcomings.

"Richard Barker was not pleased with these changes. In 1681, he convinced the other selectmen that Francis Dane had to go, and that the town needed a new pastor. Some of you will remember that I told you some of this a few years back, but I feel it should be repeated for you who were too young to understand at that time.

"The changes in Pastor Dane began after the Great Swamp Fight in 1675, when twelve sons of original Andover settlers returned heroically to the town. However, when Indians struck only certain homes in Andover a few months later, it became clear that the attacks were in retribution for the slaughter of over two hundred Indian women and children at Swansea. The Indians attacked only the homes of those who had taken part in that slaughter.

"A year later, Pastor Dane preached about the good Samaritan, saying that the parable taught us that all of God's creatures were equal and deserved the same respect. This was contrary to Puritan belief, which was that God had chosen some to be wealthy, some to be wise, but most to be humble workers who must show respect to those placed above them.

"Later, Pastor Dane preached on the parable of the prodigal son. He noted the repentant, sinning son was forgiven by his father. The father, who represented God did not punish the son. The message was that minor sins by Andover people should not be publically pointed out by the elected tithing men and the people should not be required to stand in disgrace at meeting.

"These two sermons greatly enraged Richard Barker and he firmly rebuked Pastor Dane for espousing positions contrary to Puritan teachings. He demanded that Dane apologize at the next meeting and admit he was wrong. The pastor said that he was sorry that his sermon had so upset Richard, but that he must remain true to his faith and his calling. He said he stood by the teaching of his sermon. "In that case," replied Richard, "you are no longer my pastor." As a result, Pastor Dane would come to meeting on some Sundays and have no sermon to give.

"When Richard Barker and the other selectmen chose a second pastor, they picked a strict traditional Puritan pastor named Thomas Barnard.

"As I told you earlier, he had been a classmate with Cotton Mather at Harvard. When the witchcraft hysteria began in Danvers in 1692, Mather's booklets drove the hysteria as they blamed the devil that God had allowed to infect the people because of their sins. Thomas Barnard accepted Mather's teaching and fanned the witchcraft hysteria when it arrived in Andover a few months later.

"About fifty people were charged with witchcraft in Andover, more than the total charged in Danvers and Salem combined. In each family there was at least one person who was either charged with witchcraft or accused someone of witchcraft. When the long tragic affair ended, we might expect that the town had been torn apart with hatred, but that did not occur. The petty issues, which had gotten some to accuse others of witchcraft, were accepted as Cotton Mather told them, 'We were misled by the devil.'

"Even Rev. Francis Dane, who opposed the witchcraft business from the start, held no malice for Pastor Barnard or anyone else. In his long letter which helped to end the affair, Dane wrote of 'our sin of ignorance' when it was not his sin, but that of Rev. Barnard and other townsmen. He described in detail how 'we so easily gave up our spouses and our children to baseless charges.'

"Even at this point Pastor Dane exhibited the same Puritan trait that had been espoused by John Winthrop in his famous sermon about establishing 'a city on the hill.' The premise was that all Puritans were to act in unison for the good of all and the glory of God.

"Unfortunately, the unjust witchcraft charges brought painful consequences to many. Women and children spent several weeks in the cold basement of Salem jail with very little to eat. For Abigail Faulkner and others it took ten years after the affair ended to get convictions put aside by the state legislature. Abigail's son, Ammi Ruhamma, grew up in a cloud of taunting suspicion by other children. He held a deep hatred for the Barker family, whom he held responsible for what happened to his mother and to him. As a young adult, he left Andover and moved sixteen miles southwest to Littleton and then to nearby Acton, where he built a successful textile business.

"Others moved from Andover as well, some to Andover's South Parish, which had hired a more liberal pastor. One of Richard Barker's sons moved across the Merrimack River to the western part of Haverhill to settle land they had received from their father.

"Stephen and his son, Ebenezer Barker were among the founders of what became Methuen. Before their first year there had ended, they established a grammar school, which Andover never had. Andover children received basic education from the pastor; Richard Barker had not considered it important to establish a school to prepare students for a Harvard education. Primarily, he opposed the teaching of Latin, which he considered the language of the Catholic Mass and the Pope. However, knowledge of Latin and Greek were prerequisites for admission to Harvard College. Clearly, Stephen and Ebenezer believed differently, they likely held the Andover witchcraft affair a result of ignorance and superstition and they should ensure things would be different in Methuen.

"Another who left was my grandfather, Joseph Abbot, grandson of Thomas Abbot, who had come to Andover from Rowley around 1660. Joseph moved to Marblehead on the coast, where the Puritan pastor was more tolerant. In fact, many in Marblehead did not attend meeting at all, since most were fishermen and seamen.

"As Barkers, we must accept a major part of the responsibility for Andover's witchcraft affair, since Richard Barker was most responsible for it. At the end of his life, he understood that, and that led to his charge to his son, Benjamin, to help repair the Barker name.

"Benjamin set out to do that, forming a close friendship with Francis Faulkner, husband of convicted witch, Abigail. Together, they spoke at meeting often about the need for accusers and accused to forgive. They proposed that the best means of reconciliation was to arrange marriages between their children. Several did so.

"The efforts of Benjamin Barker and Francis Faulkner helped bring peace and reconciliation to Andover after the horrible and upsetting witchcraft affair. Benjamin's efforts went a long way towards restoring the Barker name among his fellow citizens.

"To show their respect and thanks, Andover elected Benjamin Barker to the highest office the town could grant. He was Andover's representative to the Massachusetts General Court in 1725, elected when he was 62 years old. No other Barker had ever held that office.

"Now, you may understand that some of you have a role to play in the reconciliation between opposing families from the witchcraft hysteria. The involved families are Barkers, Swans, and Faulkners. I need to arrange a marriage between one of you and a Swan family member. This should not be difficult, as James Swan has told me he would be pleased if one or more of my sons married one or more of his daughters. The Faulkner marriage will be more difficult, so I will have to work on that more with Francis Faulkner of Acton."

Samuel was concerned that the Barker-Faulkner marriage could not be arranged because of Francis Faulkner's objections. He spoke up, "Would it be acceptable if one of my daughters married a Faulkner? Is it necessary for the marriage to be with one of your children?"

Jonathan was pleased at Samuel's apparent willingness to help. "I suppose it might be acceptable, but only if Francis Faulkner helped arrange the marriage. His father was the last person harmed by the actions of Richard and William Barker. Francis knew very well the pain suffered by his father and grandmother. A Barker-Faulkner marriage which did not involve him would not serve the purpose of reconciliation."

Such a long monologue would have strained the attention span of children in any other family. But Jonathan's children sat at the foot of a man who was more than their esteemed father. They considered him as great as Benjamin Barker, the grandfather Jonathan loved and admired so deeply.

The older children had waited patiently to hear this last chapter in the story and sat mesmerized as the startling facts were finally revealed to them. The six older children barely moved a muscle throughout Jonathan's presentation. Only eight-year-old Amos fidgeted and ten-year-old Symonds Epes held Amos' hand and helped him to be quiet.

Finally, Jonathan fell into silence and gazed at the faces of his children with a loving expression that told them he would help them to understand his lesson better, if they had questions. Instead, they rose, one by one, embracing him to show their love and thanks. After a few minutes, they all retired for the evening.

CHAPTER SEVEN

REVOLUTION

In 1774 and 1775, popular commemorations marked the anniversary of the Boston Massacre throughout Massachusetts. The atmosphere for confrontation with the Regulars became more heated each week.

Jonathan, Jon, Benjamin, and Samuel continued to drill with the Methuen militia. At a militia assembly on Feb. 14, 1775, there was a call for enlistment, a commitment to march on short notice should they be called. Jonathan, Jon, and Samuel all signed up. Benjamin was reluctant. Jonathan agreed he would remain at home to run the farm while the others were away.

There was also musket practice with live rounds for all but Samuel. Other Barker cousins were a part of the Methuen militia, including 21-year-old Nehemiah, son of Moses Barker's brother, Ebenezer. In addition there were nineteen-year-old Peter Barker, great grandson of the founder of Methuen, Stephen Barker, and grandson of Methuen's first teacher, Zebediah Barker. Three other Barker relatives were also in the Methuen militia.

Militiamen elected their own officers. Colonel James Frye was voted regiment commander to lead two companies from Methuen and one from Andover's North Parish. Captain John Davis was to lead one of the Methuen companies, which included Sgt. Jonathan Barker and his son, fifer Samuel Barker and cousin, Private Peter Barker. Major Samuel Bodwell led the other

Methuen Company and it included Private Jon Barker, four Barker cousins and three Pettingal cousins.

With increasing tensions between the colonists and the British, many left their homes in Boston, remaining were only the loyalists, English Regulars and a few patriots, including Paul Revere. Revere and a few others established a network able to signal plans of the Regulars. It was clear there was a plan to disarm the colonists of all gunpowder and cannon and prohibit importation of guns or powder.

On April 17th, Revere learned the Regulars would leave Boston and march to Lexington to arrest John Hancock and Samuel Adams for treason and send them to England for trial. Then they would march to Concord to capture cannon and powder they knew the colonists stored there. Word went to the militia in every town to march on a minute's notice to prevent these steps. By April 18th, Methuen's militia began preparations.

Jonathan Barker assembled his family in a working group, to prepare muskets, lead, powder, water and other provisions that he, Jon and Samuel would need for the long march to Lexington and Concord. They then lay on their beds at night, trying as best they could to sleep despite their nervous excitement, concern, and, yes, fear – at least on the part of Jonathan and Abigail for the safety of their children.

Jonathan and Abigail lay in a long embrace, trying to quench the trembling. No one could know what was in store for Jonathan and his children on April 19, 1775, but both sensed it would be a day they would not soon forget.

At 3 am on April 19th, a rider from Woburn warned the militia in Tewksbury then reached the Merrimack River where he shot his musket three times to warn the Dracut militia. They assembled and by five had crossed the river and joined with the Tewksbury militia in their march towards Concord.

A young Barker cousin in Dracut then rode east to warn the Methuen militia, which repeated the alarm at six. In Jonathan Barker's house, Jon and Samuel heard the musket alarm first, and roused their father. Soon, all of the family were up, dressed and actively about their assigned chores. Benjamin brought in wood and stoked the fire going. Molly and Hannah milked. Symonds Eppes collected eggs. Abigail, Molly, and Hannah prepared boiled and scrambled eggs, bread and milk for the entire family, as they sat down together. The fire and cooking smell provided a warm atmosphere that comforted them in the face of potential peril.

The Barkers stood and joined hands as Jonathan offered a short prayer of thanks and plea for safety during their time ahead. The family ate in silence. There was an eerie sense that history was unfolding in their midst, and that they would be part of it. Jonathan, Jon and Samuel ate quickly, then assembled their backpacks and muskets. Abigail, Hannah and Molly embraced them while Benjamin and Jesse

Paul Revere

patted their backs. The three militiamen stepped outside as the glow of the sun appeared on the eastern horizon. They walked swiftly towards Swan's Ferry and joined others along the way. Because it had been a mild winter and spring had arrived early, albeit with little rain, their heels stirred up road dust, engulfing them like a fog.

By 7 am the two companies of Methuen militia crossed the Merrimack and assembled at North Parish Church in Andover, where they joined the third company in their regiment, led by Capt. Thomas Poor (which included Jon's cousin-friend, John Barker). Colonel Frye addressed the regiment, explained their mission and marching route – through Tewksbury, Billerica, and Bedford to Concord.

He then instructed his company commanders to give the order to march. As more than three hundred men headed southwest, Samuel played "The White Cockade" on his fife, accompanied by the company drummer. The music and drumming provided a spirited atmosphere as the men moved briskly with a sense of purpose. As they passed through Tewksbury, women and children cheered them on.

An hour before noon, they arrived at Billerica Common, where they rested. Pollard's Tavern served them cider, biscuits and cheese. By noon they were on their way towards Bedford. Now, fifer Samuel Barker played "The Brick Master March" and "The Rogues March," which seemed to re-energize the

Methuen men, who had covered over ten miles on dusty roads.

Approaching Bedford, a messenger arrived on horseback from Concord with news of the confrontations with the British Regulars at Lexington. At Concord Bridge, the Regulars had ordered the militia to disperse, but they stood their ground, knowing their force was equal to that of the regulars, since it included militia from Acton, Concord, and Sudbury. In the chaotic confrontation, weapons were fired and both sides had dead and wounded before the British officers ordered a retreat. The militia pursued as they headed back towards Lexington. The messenger said they must turn east towards Lexington in order to join the chase.

An hour later, they entered Lexington and paused briefly at the meetinghouse, which had a large puncture from a cannon ball. Locals described a confrontation with the Regulars on Lexington Green. The militiamen simply stood their ground when ordered to disperse. The Regulars opened fire and the militiamen attempted to flee, but eight were killed, most shot in the back. The British suffered only one wounded. The Methuen militiamen were angered by this news.

Samuel Barker played "The White Cockade" as they marched out of Lexington. Soon, they saw bodies of dead Regulars and some militiamen. They passed houses with broken windows and doors; some still smoldered. There were also dead horses and hogs. Regulars obviously entered every house looking for plunder.

As they neared Menotomy, the houses were closer together and nearer the road. The dead and wounded from both sides were more numerous. Samuel was shocked by this sight and no longer able to play his fife. Jonathan moved up to walk beside his not-quite-fifteen-year-old son to calm him. No one was prepared to witness such bloodshed at what they had expected to be a simple confrontation and standoff. Now, it was clear that they were involved in a war that was not all the doing of the colonists.

The militiamen were emotionally and physically exhausted as darkness arrived. Upon entering Cambridge they met an aide to General Heath (whom they learned was commanding all of the militia regiments). They were instructed to join other companies setting up camp near Winter Hill by the Mystic River in Cambridge. They were told the British had escaped to Charlestown and the fighting had ended, at least for this day. They were asked to stay a few days until new orders could be determined.

For the first time since the brief lunch stop in Billerica, Jonathan was able to talk to both of his boys – Jon and Samuel. Although they had not participated in any of the shooting battles of the day, they had seen first-hand the gruesome results. They were all still shaken but relieved calm was now upon them, at least for a few hours.

They joined in setting up some of the tents that had been provided by the local militias and were thankful as food was distributed, albeit the same simple cheese, nuts and bread they had eaten for lunch. Later, blankets were distributed by women from nearby Cambridge homes.

As they prepared to retire, an unusual spring thundershower seemed to celebrate the American victory. Jonathan thought of how the rain would be welcomed on the first newly seeded fields back home.

A few hours later, Jonathan and his two boys were awakened by local militiamen and their wives, who were offering ham and eggs to be cooked for breakfast. They gratefully accepted and moved to a group that had set up a fire for cooking. They ate with fellow Methuen militiaman Peter Barker and John Barker from Andover's North Parish. All expressed their shock at what they had seen the day before. There was strong enmity towards the barbarous behavior of the Regulars, who killed women and old men in the houses along the way. The dead were only trying to prevent their property from being looted.

In time, the men turned their thoughts and discussion to the families they had left in Methuen and Andover. They wondered how long they would have to stay in Cambridge before returning home.

At this point, Samuel drew his fife from his backpack and began to play a non-marching tune he enjoyed, "The Darling Swain." The music attracted others to join their group and listen. One of them, a drummer, lightly tapped a rhythmic accompaniment.

When they had finished the tune, the visiting drummer said, "You play quite well; I wish Luther Blanchard could be here to play with us, but he was wounded at North Bridge."

"I was told I was safe from hostile fire – how did your fifer come to be shot?" asked Samuel.

"The Regular who shot him was a Hanoveran, and they apparently deeply despise the march, "The White Cockade," that Luther was playing. He was among the first to be hit, right after they killed Captain Isaac Davis. By the way, my name is Francis Barker, and this is one of our Acton officers, Major Francis Faulkner."

"My name is Samuel Barker – perhaps we are cousins. Did your ancestors come from Andover or Methuen?"

"No, they came from Pembroke, by way of Concord." Replied Francis.

Jonathan Barker now stepped forward and spoke to Major Faulkner, "I thought I recognized you, but it has been a few years since I visited you in Acton."

Francis Faulkner was forty-seven years old – the same as Jonathan Barker. He was a bit taller than Jonathan and stood erect with a serious demeanor. The change in his appearance since Jonathan last saw him was primarily his hair; he had lost most of it. It provided him an air of respectability befitting his office.

As Jonathan shook his hand he asked, "Did you take part in the fight at Concord Bridge?"

"My company stood behind Captain Davis' company, but we got involved in the fighting as we chased the Regulars out of Lexington towards Menotomy. General Heath ordered me to move against their left flank, so we were able to kill or wound several of them as my men kept running ahead in the woods, then coming back towards the road and firing, and repeating this many times.

"It got more difficult when we got to Menotomy because the houses were more tightly spaced and closer to the road. When a militiaman entered the homes from the rear and fired through the front windows, a Regular would race inside and kill him before he could re-load." I finally ordered them not to enter any house."

Major Faulkner and Jonathan Barker continued to relate their experiences during the long march through Concord, Lexington, and Monotomy, before arriving in Cambridge. Then Jonathan said, "Providence has brought us together on this historic day so we may resume our discussions on how to achieve reconciliation between the Barkers and Faulkners. I feel our lives are truly linked."

Francis Faulkner frowned. "I don't share your understanding or feeling about this linkage or reconciliation you speak about. What I learned from my father still rings in my ears. He often told me the Barker legacy is that Olde

Andover is frozen in time – in Puritan superstition and ignorance of the 1650's, while a new, enlightened, energetic, and intellectual Andover is emerging in the Shawsheen River Valley to the south.

"He said Francis Dane was leading Andover into the 18th century with sermons about God's love and forgiveness of sins. Richard Barker rudely pushed him aside and brought in traditional Puritan Thomas Barnard, to preach fear of God and punishment for minor sins. This created the climate for the witch hysteria, when fifty innocent Andover people were charged with witchcraft, including many from the Dane family.

"My grandmother suffered for many years, as did my father, Ammi Ruhammah. With all this, how can I be convinced my life is linked to yours in a positive way?"

"Your grandfather and mine became good friends after the witchcraft business," answered Jonathan, "When your grandfather transferred his Andover property to your father, the deed was witnessed by my grandfather and his oldest son."

"It doesn't prove anything. I understand they lived near one another, so it was just convenient to use Benjamin Barker as a witness. Do you have any stronger proof?"

"Your grandfather arranged my parents' marriage."

"How can you possibly know that? What was your mother's name?"

"Mary Abbot. She was a daughter of Joseph Abbot, a brother of your uncle, John Abbot, who was married to Francis Faulkner's adopted daughter, Hannah Faulkner Chubb."

"I know about John and Hannah Abbot, but I still don't see any proof that Frances arranged your parents' marriage."

"After the witchcraft affair, Joseph Abbot rejected the strict Puritanism of Andover. He moved to Marblehead, where religion was much more relaxed. He married the daughter of John Devereaux, a wealthy merchant who ran a fish salt-packing and shipping business.

"On the surface, life in Marblehead seemed good to Joseph, until he and his wife had daughters who began to mature. Most men in Marblehead were fishermen or merchant seamen. They were often weeks at sea. When on land they drank to excess. Nearly every man in Marblehead was arrested for public drunkenness at least once. Worse, it was not safe for a young woman to be out alone, even during the day. There were many rapes, most not reported or prosecuted.

"When Joseph's oldest daughter, Susannah, was sixteen, he sent her to live with his brother, your uncle John Abbott, in Andover. In 1720, Frances Faulkner arranged her marriage to Nathaniel Pettengel. The dowry was twenty acres of land in Methuen, which my grandfather gave to Mr. Pettengel for the nominal sum of ten shillings, to ensure a legal transfer. It was a gesture of friendship on Benjamin Barker's part to your grandfather. The couple settled on that land. The Pettengel children and grandchildren still live in Methuen – they are my cousins."A few years later, another of Joseph's daughters, Mary, was sent to live with John and Hannah Abbot in Andover. In January 1728, Francis Faulkner and Benjamin Barker arranged her marriage to my father, Jonathan Barker. I was born nine months later."

Francis Faulkner listened carefully. He reacted with surprise at first, then warmed noticeably toward Jonathan. "Your story is quite compelling. I am moved to give your proposal more serious consideration. However, it would be a dishonor to my father's memory if one of my daughters married one of your sons. We will have to find another way to this reconciliation. By the way, I assume that Samuel is your son – is he your oldest?

"No. This is my oldest. His name is also Jonathan, but we call him Jon. I have another son, Benjamin, who is older than Samuel but younger than Jon. We agreed that he would run the farm, while the three of us are away."

Francis shook Jon's hand and spoke to Jonathan, "You must be proud of these fine boys. I will remember them as I consider our future plans. But now, I must check with the militia staff to see if I have orders."

In the afternoon, wagonloads of provisions arrived from western towns. The Committees of Safety had ordered generous amounts of bread, meats, beer and milk for the militiamen. Jonathan and his two boys ate heartily for the first time in three days.

As the day wore on, word spread about the final engagement in Cambridge, before the Regulars escaped to Charlestown and Boston. Militiamen continued to pour into the towns surrounding Boston, cutting off all supplies to the redcoats. A standoff would ensue for several days while the generals on both sides plotted their next moves.

Three days after their arrival in Cambridge, Major Bodwell ordered his company to gather their belongings and be prepared to march back to Methuen in the morning. Captain Davis told his men to wait for their orders, which came two days later. When Jon arrived home alone, his mother trembled with fear as he approached her in front of the house. She had heard of many casualties and was terrified that her beloved husband and young son might be among them. Jon quickly put her mind to rest as he embraced his mother and greeted his brothers and sisters. Two days later, Jonathan and Samuel arrived to the cheers of their brothers and sisters.

The next day was spent in quiet celebration and reflection. The three veterans told the family about their experiences, and their encounter with Francis Faulkner. They then retired shortly after nightfall so that they could get back to work on the farm at daybreak. Benjamin, Jesse, Symonds Epes, Molly and Hannah had gotten sufficient crops started to nearly match what the whole family had done in 1774.

Their return to normalcy would not last long, however. Jonathan, Jon, and Samuel returned to their regular militia meeting the following week, and received orders to be prepared to return to Cambridge on May 17th. They said their goodbyes again, and marched with their companies to Cambridge.

They joined others already camped, this time in larger tents, which had been prepared in their absence. They also heard stories about what might lie ahead for them. Without approval from the Continental Congress, Connecticut sent Major Ethan Allen and his Green Mountain Boys to Fort Ticonderoga. Massachusetts sent Colonel Benedict Arnold with a company of men there. They were surprised to meet one another outside the fort, yet they joined forces to burst through the gates. They found it guarded by just forty-five over-aged Regulars. The combined forces easily overcame them and took them prisoner. Allen then took the British Fort at Crown Point further north in the Champlain valley. Arnold went further north to capture the small British fleet on the Richelieu River. Allen had left a small number of local militia to guard the fort. The combined yield of these small victories was a treasure trove to the arms-starved Americans: seventy-eight serviceable cannon, six mortars, three howitzers, thousands of cannonballs, eighteen thousand pounds of musket balls, and thirty thousand flints.

In Cambridge, the militia leaders watched the redcoats day and night, so they might be prepared for their next move. Eventually, it became clear they were preparing for an attack, probably on Charlestown. The militiamen waited impatiently. To keep them busy, their commanders put them through marching maneuvers for an hour or more.

Jonathan and his sons met Major Francis Faulkner again during this period. He drew Jonathan aside and said, "It seems to me your first marriage of reconciliation should be with someone from the family that accused William Barker of witchcraft – a Swan. Have you thought about that?"

"I have been planning that marriage for several years. James Swan expects Jon to marry his daughter, Nancy, when Jon settles in Maine after the war. I have suggested this plan to Jon and he is open to it."

"If you invite me to that marriage, I will have a plan for a Faulkner-Barker marriage to present to you then."

Jonathan smiled broadly and shook Francis' hand. "That will be something to look forward to."

CHAPTER EIGHT

RETURN TO BATTLE

As a sergeant, Jonathan was considered a junior officer and regularly updated on plans for his company and regiment. Major Francis Faulkner also met informally with him almost every day, to tell him the news he had heard.

They realized the many militia companies that had marched from towns throughout eastern Massachusetts, Rhode Island, Connecticut and southern New Hampshire were camped in a big semi-circle, to keep the Regulars confined in Boston.

This became known as the Siege of Boston. The English had scarce supplies of fresh milk, cheese and meats. They controlled the seas, but that did not help with fresh food needs. The militia leaders knew that the Regulars would have to take some military action to alleviate this.

Colonial spies passed the word that the English commanders were considering a ground attack to the south on Dorchester neck and Dorchester to capture cows and other livestock. They were also planning an attack to the north on Charlestown. The colonial leaders were considering their options.

On May 26th, Jonathan had breakfast with Jon and Samuel. "Jon, today is your 21st birthday and you are now an adult in every respect. You now have the authority and the responsibility for your future well-being. Have you given thought to this?"

"I have felt for a long time that my future would be in Maine, near James Swan's farm. I expect I will marry his daughter, Nancy, and raise a family in Maine. In the meantime, it seems that we may be busy fighting a war with England and I assume our family will support that."

"Spoken like an adult, Jon. It does appear we are in the beginning of a war with England. We don't know how long we may be needed but it will certainly disrupt our lives and the output of our farm.

"Last year was our best year ever, with you, Benjamin, Samuel, and Jesse working hard in the fields, and Molly and Hannah doing a great job with the cows, pigs, sheep and goats, besides helping your mother to take care of young Abigail and Elcy. Benjamin and Jesse have already begun to plant the same amount of crops as last year, but they will not be able to tend them if the three of us miss the entire growing season."

Samuel joined in, "Symonds Epes has grown bigger and stronger since then – he will probably do almost as much work this year as I did last year."

"I would just as soon stay on the farm, if you agree," added Jon. "I was most upset at all the dead I saw in Lexington and Monotomy last month. If this war continues to be like that, I may not be a good soldier at all, so I would be better off on the farm."

"Let's see how things go during the next few weeks. If the fighting becomes intense and casualties high, I would much rather you were back in Methuen, working the fields. We can continue these discussions as things change."

As time wore on, activities in the camp degraded to a level Jonathan would have preferred his sons not experience. The doings of camp followers with the men was seen by his boys. There was other lewd behavior, much drinking and rowdy language. It required a constant guard. Drunken men frequently approached the Barker camp and offered liquor to the boys, but Jonathan turned them away.

Finally, on June 16th, Jonathan, Jon and Samuel were ordered to march to Cambridge Green. They arrived at six o'clock, and shovels were distributed to every man. At dark they marched past Prospect Hill and along Charlestown Neck to Bunker Hill. A small, but densely populated town sat just to the south, containing about twenty-five buildings. Bunker Hill bordered the mouth of the Medford River to the north, later renamed Mystic River. The militia was ordered to dig a dirt fortress 140 feet square and six feet tall at the top of the hill. Soon, this was changed and they moved further south to Breed's Hill, although some companies remained on Bunker Hill, awaiting clearer instruction.

Jonathan, Jon and Samuel moved with most to Breed's Hill, where they worked feverishly through the night. The work continued through

Battle of Bunker Hill

the morning of June 17th, as they built a breastwork that ran easterly from the fort to the marsh. In the early afternoon they constructed a rail fence shield to protect the west flank. Throughout the morning, the British fired canons to disrupt their work, but the balls fell harmlessly on the south side of the hill. However, the fire had its effect on Jon and Samuel, as they shuddered with each blast.

All the militia were tired and hungry by then, so Jonathan's company, along with several others were ordered back to Bunker Hill, where they might be called upon later. Benjamin Farnum's Andover Company, which had been resting on Bunker Hill, moved into position in the Breed's Hill fort, along with several others. By early afternoon, fresh militia troops were in place behind the fortress walls. Col. John Stark's five hundred New Hampshire militiamen were in position along the log barricade which ran from the Mystic River to Breed's Hill.

Soon, the British arrived from Boston on long boats. Jonathan, Jon and Samuel watched nervously as the Regulars assembled on the Charlestown shore and formed into ranks. Seeing hundreds of uniformed and well-trained soldiers about to move against comparatively untrained and undisciplined militiamen who had been simple farmers just a few months earlier, struck fear into the Barkers.

From the top of Bunker Hill they had a good view of the militia on Breed's Hill, as well as the Regulars, as the attack began . They were struck with the terror of the last seconds, almost as if they were in the line of fire. As the British advanced, the Barkers heard the orders of the militia leaders to "hold your fire", lest some of the younger men shoot impetuously before the enemy was in range.

The same call issued from Col. Stark to his men, although they were well-trained and reputedly the best marksmen in the colonial militia. Col. Stark and his New Hampshire militia stood in contrast to a regiment from nearby Salem that had returned home on April 20th following the engagement at Lexington and Concord, assuming that confrontation had ended all hostilities.

Behind the breastworks that Jonathan, Jon and Samuel helped build, were 1,200 militiamen and eight artillery pieces. The Regulars had three canon on the shore and bombarded the militia positions as they stormed the barricade and the hill to the fortress. They were answered by fire from the militia artillery and soon, by a cacophony of muskets from both the Regulars and militiamen, and orders shouted by officers on both sides. The noise was deafening, even back on Bunker Hill where the Barkers observed the action. The combatants later described it as a continual sheet of lightning, accompanied by a deafening roar like an uninterrupted peal of thunder. Jon and Samuel shivered with fear, dropping their heads with each canon blast – although they were a safe distance from any danger. Jonathan held them close and spoke some words of comfort, which could not be heard, even by Jonathan.

The attacks were repelled, with heavy casualties for the Regulars. Two hundred dead and wounded lay on the south and west side of Breed's Hill. The noise of canon blasts and musket fire were now replaced with the eerie moaning of the many wounded. The Regulars carried most back to the long boats for evacuation to Boston. Still others remained, groaning continuously. It was a sound which would resonate in the ears of Jon and Samuel each time they slept – for several weeks.

The Redcoat officers ordered a second attack, but the results were no different. The only militia casualties were among Colonel Stark's regiment, which faced the Regulars nearly eye-to-eye, albeit with breastwork partially protecting them. They, in turn, inflicted the greatest casualties on the Regulars, each musket ball dropping a Regular.

The militia was running low on ammunition and called for back-up troops and ammunition, but none arrived. Jonathan wondered why his company was not summoned, since they had some ammunition. Apparently, the officers decided it would take too long to bring up replacements and decided to hold on for one more assault, before ordering a retreat.

On the third assault, the militia's ammunition was quickly depleted. The Regulars scaled the walls and began hand-to-hand combat with bayonets. Now, Jonathan and his boys sprang up, partly in fear, but more in expectation of orders to retreat and to help guard the retreat of those from Breed's Hill. That order soon came and they raced down the hill to join the retreating heroes.

Very few of the militia were equipped with bayonets, so they fought with the butt ends of their muskets, allowing the others to retreat down-slope towards Bunker Hill.

Possibly with his last musket ball, freedman Salem Poor (a former slave of the Poor family of Andover) killed a high-ranking enemy officer. Later, the General Court commended him for bravery.

As cousin John Barker started down the north side of Breed's Hill, he encountered Lt. Isaac Abbott, sitting and holding his wounded leg. John knelt facing him and thrust his right hand under his buttocks and his left arm around his back. He lifted him onto his shoulder, shouting, "Hang on, Isaac, the Regulars shan't get you." He continued rapidly down the hill and joined the orderly retreat along the Mystic River. For many years, Andover schoolchildren would read a poem about John Barker's bravery at Bunker Hill.

While the militia suffered just a few casualties during the first two assaults on the hill by the Regulars, they took heavy casualties retreating after the third assault. The battle was a victory for the British, for they controlled all of Charlestown. However, they suffered nearly twice as many dead and wounded as the militia. From their positions on Bunker Hill, Jonathan, Jon, and Samuel Barker had witnessed many men from both sides killed or wounded.

As they joined the militia retreating to Cambridge, Jon spoke to his father, "No one can question now whether we are at war with England. And a fierce and deadly war it is. I have no appetite for another battle like this. Yet I marvel at the bravery of cousin John. I am sure I could not have done what he did. With the Regulars shooting at me at close range, I would have been running as fast as I could, ignoring the wounded along the way."

"Don't sell yourself short, Jon. People often rise to the occasion, and I believe you might have, as well. You did it on the British barque when they tried to impress you into their navy along with James Swan."

"I was younger and more foolhardy then. Besides, no one was shooting at me."

Young Samuel walked quietly as his older brother and father spoke. He was clearly shaken with the experience. The British suffered greater losses during this than they would in any other single battle. The New England militias had gained the respect of all the colonies, and were now supported in their efforts.

The Barkers slept on Cambridge Green that night. Jon and Samuel spent a fitful night reliving the horrors they had seen that day. Jonathan lay awake for a long time, concerned with how Abigail was coping with their absence. He often reached out for her in his sleep – touching instead one of his sons. When he awoke Jonathan quickly began a letter.

June 18, 1775

Dearest Abigail,

By the time you receive this, you will have heard about the battle they are calling "Bunker Hill" that was fought in Charlestown yesterday. Jon, Samuel and I were close enough to observe the fighting, but we were not involved. We are all safe and unharmed. Our cousin, John Barker of Andover, did fight – heroically – and I will tell you more about that when we return.

We have heard that the Continental Congress met in Philadelphia three days before the battle. They appointed George Washington to lead all the Continental forces and promoted him to general. He is expected to arrive in Cambridge in two weeks and we are to await his arrival for further orders. You will be pleased to hear that Jon has decided not to return to serve in the new army for some time. He will be able to help tending this year's crops and with the harvest.

I miss you terribly. Your love sustains me, even from afar. I also miss our children. Please embrace each one for me in turn, knowing that I can picture each as you do so: Molly, Hannah, Benjamin, Jesse, Symonds Epes, Amos, Abigail and Elcy.

With everlasting love,

Jonathan

Elaborate preparations were made for the arrival of General Washington. The fifers and drummers – 250 in all – were to assemble as a company and parade before the General and his party. Samuel was excited to be one of this group. Behind them, more than ten thousand militiamen would stand at attention in their individual companies.

When Washington arrived on July 3rd, an audible stir passed through the assemblage. The General was much taller than any other man there – six feet two inches. He wore a bright blue coat, three-cornered hat and white britches and sat on a large white stallion. He was, indeed, an imposing figure who inspired awe, pride and allegiance among his men.

Washington surveyed the situation and discussed strategy with his staff. Despite their victory in Charlestown, the British still suffered from the Siege of Boston. They had not remained in Charlestown but returned to Boston after sacking and burning the town. Washington believed the British would attack again, either by sea to Cambridge, or, more likely, Dorchester Neck.

During May and June, many of the regiments built barracks for themselves as wood and nails arrived from their towns. In mid-July Andover and Methuen sent materials for Major Frye's regiment. This was welcomed work for Jonathan, Jon and Samuel, despite the summer heat. With the help of so many men, some of them experienced house-wrights, joiners, and carpenters, the buildings went up quickly.

They would be sheltered from the thundershowers which inevitably occurred during July and August. General Washington's purpose went beyond that reason, however. He needed most troops to remain well into the winter, to repel any British attack.

Washington asked all the men to re-enlist for one year in the new Continental army. On July 14th Jonathan and Samuel enlisted for just three months, but asked for a start date of October 5th, so they could return home to help with the harvest. Jon followed through on his agreement with his father and did not enlist. Early on July 15th Jonathan and his two sons set out on foot for Methuen. It was a time of bonding for them. They now had a common history as soldiers in the war of revolution.

As they headed north out of Cambridge into Woburn, Jonathan spoke to his younger son. "Samuel, you are still a month away from your fifteenth birthday, yet you are a soldier who has seen a lot of war. After this, your friends back in Methuen will seem like little boys."

"I am looking forward to seeing them, again, father. Although I am proud of my service, I do not feel superior to them, just blessed to have had an opportunity they didn't. It was all because of my ability to play the fife."

"Your example has been partly responsible for General Washington's new directive asking every able-bodied man between the ages of fifteen and sixty to enlist for one year. I would not want 15-year-old boys to be killed in a battle like Bunker Hill. Probably he has in mind that most of the younger men might be fifers or drummers, and those that are not would serve in the rear."

"I should think it might depend on how good they are with a musket. If a 15-year-old can shoot accurately, he could be as good a soldier as a 25-year-old."

"You have become too smart for your age, Samuel. I can't argue with your logic. I would rather think about getting home with your mother and the rest of our family, and back to work with them in the fields."

Jon and Samuel answered in unison, "Aye, aye to that, father."

When they finally reached Andover, the moon was rising and it was too late for the last ferry to Methuen. As they prepared to sleep on the green in front of North Parish Church, they admired the church clock. Jon and Samuel remembered their father telling them that the clock had been a gift from his Uncle Benjamin.

Jon asked, "What about your uncle Benjamin – didn't he have any children?"

"My uncle Benjamin had always told his father that he was not 'the marrying kind' and that he would not have children. He was a wonderful person – the best friend to all of his seven sisters – but he was steadfast about not marrying. Grandpa Benjamin and Rev. John Barnard had many long talks with him to try to convince him that it was his Christian duty to marry and have children. He always listened politely but replied he felt that God had created him the way he was, and he was at peace with that.

"When Parson Barnard died, Reverend William Symmes replaced him and he was more understanding in his relationship with Uncle Benjamin. Grandpa Benjamin left most of his estate to Uncle Benjamin. When Uncle Benjamin felt he had only a few years left, he donated a fine silver chalice to the church. When Andover built a new church, Uncle Benjamin bought a fine clock for it. A few months later, he died. Rev. Symmes was seen many times admiring the clock Benjamin had given to the parish, but I believe he was really thinking about what a fine person Uncle Benjamin was, and that, perhaps, God did make some people differently, and we all need to learn to accept that.

"I remember your Uncle Benjamin," Jon added. "I always liked him, and I think everyone did."

At sun-up, they walked to the dock and took the ferry home. It was a grand reunion celebration. Jonathan agreed they could all take a day off from work in the fields so they could sit together and talk about all of their experiences during the past two

General George Washington

months. The Barkers had grown as a stronger and more loving family, partly due to their separation and the experience of the war.

When Jonathan and Abigail retired to their chamber, they could not delay their passion. They enjoyed each other's body and ultimately fell asleep still clinging to one another.

For several days the Barker family worked hard, harvesting corn, weeding and thinning the other crops, tending to the animals and renewing neighborhood friendships. Word spread there was a food shortage, particularly grains for bread, so the Barkers planned to market much of their output. The income would be needed, as there had been no pay for military service thus far, only paper promises.

Samuel was right about 11-year-old Symonds Eps. He and 13-year-old Jesse had been working as a team. Together they often exceeded 20-year-old Benjamin's output. Even 9-year-old Amos was a considerable help to Molly, milking cows; feeding pigs, cleaning their pens, and tending goats. One evening, as Jonathan was congratulating his children on their accomplishments, Samuel asked about his younger brother's unusual name.

"How did Symonds Epes come to have that name?"

"It's a story I skipped when I told you about early Andover. Do you remember my telling you that my grandfather Benjamin was elected Andover's representative to the General Court in 1725?" Most of the children nodded or replied, "Yes."

"Well, while serving in that position in Boston, a man named Symonds Epes befriended him. Symonds helped him understand the Court's procedures. He was a member of the senior legislative body, which had more prestige and authority.

"He was the grandson of William Symonds and Daniel Epes. Both came from England to Ipswich around the same time Richard Barker arrived in Rowley.

"William Symonds and Daniel Epes were wealthy and Oxford- educated. In fact, less than a year after his arrival, William Symonds bought most of north Ipswich from John Winthrop, Jr., including all of Plum Island and Castle Hill Neck. About that time, he was named Justice of the Peace and performed the marriage rites for Andover's Pastor Francis Dane.

"One evening while Symonds Epes sat next to Benjamin Barker as all the representatives supped together, he inquired about Benjamin's family in Andover.

"After Benjamin told about his father and the witchcraft hysteria, Epes told Benjamin what his grandfathers had related to him about Simon and Anne Bradstreet's life in Ipswich before their move to Andover. He also told him about Anne Bradstreet's father, Thomas Dudley and how Simon had been apprenticed to Dudley back in England. He further explained that his grandfather had written to the governor in 1690, asking a delay in the execution of Dorcas Hoar of Beverly.

Grandpa Benjamin always appreciated the kindness shown him by Symonds Epes, a man of such high station. I heard about this fine gentleman so much that I named my fifth son after him."

Symonds Epes beamed. "It would be nice if I could become wealthy and powerful one day, like my namesake." The other children laughed. Jonathan interjected, "It will be enough if you just have the fine character of that gentleman, Essey (as he was often called in the family)."

Abigail concurred, "Being the sons and daughters of Jonathan Barker, I believe you will all have that character."

Summer faded quickly into fall, and the harvesting work proceeded apace. Soon it was time for Jonathan and Samuel to march back to Cambridge for their three-month tour of duty.

The Siege of Boston was still in place. It was a cat and mouse game, as British ships patrolled the coastline, threatening to bombard the coastal cities, or worse still, set them afire as they had done in Falmouth, Maine. Many families moved inland from the coastal cities, while the men guarded against any landing. The sailors of Beverly, Salem, Marblehead, and Ipswich also became privateers, intercepting

General Henry Knox

merchant ships headed for Boston with supplies and gunpowder for the British. Meanwhile, General Washington needed all the troops he could get to guard against attack by the British on Cambridge from the sea, or on Dorchester via Dorchester Neck. Major Francis Faulkner's company was assigned to protect Dorchester Heights.

The short fall and early winter tour of duty passed quickly and without major involvement for the Barkers. Most of the activity had been along the north shore where British ships threatened to come close enough to burn towns. They were driven off by defending seamen from those towns. Other seamen added cannon to their small boats so they could intercept merchant ships bringing supplies to Boston.

As Jonathan and Samuel were departing in late December, they heard about Henry Knox who had taken a small company up to Fort Ticonderoga to bring back dozens of cannon and tons of cannonballs to attack the Regulars in Boston. On December 9th with a party of three hundred soldiers and teamsters, Knox shoved onto Lake George with over-loaded gondolas. At the lower end of the lake, he acquired 160 oxen, several span of horses, and more than forty heavy-duty sleds. They transferred all of their cargo to the sleds and continued their journey over land. Near Albany, they carefully crossed the ice-covered Hudson. During the second week in January, they crossed the snow-covered Berkshire mountains, finally reaching Springfield on January 20th. Knox then left to ride on to advise Washington of his success, while his men continued to move east with their cargo.

The cannon were hidden around Cambridge until one night Major Francis Faulkner led a company to help build a redoubt for the cannon on Dorchester Heights. Under General Artemis Ward, his men then helped others install them on the redoubt, aimed at British ships in the harbor, and at British positions in Boston. England's General Howe awoke and realized his position was indefensible, so he negotiated the freedom to evacuate Boston, giving a promise not to burn any buildings. Since then March 17th has been celebrated as Evacuation Day in Massachusetts.

In August of 1775, King George III proclaimed the colonies to be in open rebellion, and ordered a forceful response. During the winter, Britain hired large numbers of German troops to assist them. In the spring of 1776 they sent dozens of armored ships to New York loaded with the reinforcements. They would participate in an offensive aimed to cut off New England from the other colonies.

George Washington anticipated this and moved his army to Long Island and Manhattan. He sent some of his officers up the Hudson to West Point and Albany. Future service by the Barkers was likely to be in those areas.

Back in Methuen the Barker family spent much of the winter and early spring in long family discussions about the war and its consequences. They celebrated Hannah's 17th birthday on January 16th, Molly's 19th birthday on March 1st and little Amos' 10th birthday on March 21st. The reduced workload of the winter months combined with the maturing family's capability left more leisure time.

One day in March, the older children returned from a walk down to the ferry dock with a copy of a pamphlet they purchased from a man exiting the ferry from Andover. He was Samuel Philips, Jr., who had re-published the pamphlet he said was being discussed by everyone in Cambridge and Philadelphia. It was written anonymously by a friend of Benjamin Franklin's, who published the first edition in January. The title of the pamphlet was "Common Sense." The family sat down and began reading it together, each of them taking turns reading a page or two. The first few pages were philosophical and difficult for most of the children to follow. However, when they got to the major part of the book, entitled, "Thoughts on the Present State of American Affairs," they quickly became engrossed.

When it was Samuel's turn, he read, "The Sun never shined on a cause of greater worth. 'Tis not the affair of a City, a County, a Province, or a Kingdom, but of a Continent - at least one eighth part of the habitable Globe. 'Tis not the concern of a day, a year, or an age; posterity are virtually involved in the contest, and will be more or less affected even to the end of time, by the proceedings now. Now is the seed-time of Continental union, faith and honour."

A while later, Jesse read this passage, "The present winter is worth an age, if rightly employed; but, if lost or neglected, the whole continent will partake of the evil; and there is no punishment that man does not deserve, he who, or what, or where he will, that may be the means of sacrificing a season so precious and useful." They paused to reflect on what they read. "He writes very well," noted Molly.

"He makes me proud that I have been involved in the fighting until now, said Jon.

Samuel interjected, "But he inspires me to get involved in what is yet to come."

Jonathan explained, "There is much more than the war in what he has written. He is telling us it is time for all the colonies to declare themselves united against England and that we are no longer a part of England. Molly is right about what this man has written. It is not only clearly written, it is powerfully inspirational. I can understand why everyone is talking about it in Philadelphia and Boston."

Soon, each Massachusetts town was taking action, spurred on by what they read in "Common Sense." The legislature in Boston asked each town's representative to voice approval or disapproval of a motion by Massachusetts on the independence of the thirteen colonies from England. Every Massachusetts town voted to support the proposal. Soon, the Continental Congress in Philadelphia began debate on the measure. On July 4, 1776, representatives of each of the colonies signed The Declaration of Independence. That day became the most important holiday in America for centuries.

Later that year, after the disastrous loss of the Battle of Long Island caused widespread desertions, everyone learned that the name of the author of "Common Sense" was Thomas Paine, when he published a new pamphlet, entitled, "The Crisis." This work aroused more passion than his first. It began with the sentence, "These are the times that try men's souls." It was an appeal to every American to participate in the war against England and to persevere in good times and bad. George Washington ordered his officers to read this pamphlet to their regiments. The Barker family read it as they had the first and were equally inspired by it.

Samuel pronounced, "I will enlist for the duration of the war. I want to be part of this great historic event."

Thomas Paine

Mother Abigail shuddered. "Don't be so hasty, Samuel. Give it more thought. You are very young to be putting your fife aside for a gun."

"I can do both, mother. I will begin target practice with my musket soon. Mr. Philips told me he had built a mill on the Shawsheen to grind saltpeter and sulfur so he could make gunpowder for the Continental army. He said he still didn't have the right mixture but he expected to solve that problem soon."

Jesse added, "I can hardly wait for my fifteenth birthday, so I can enlist, but it's still a year away."

"It seems the younger Barker boys will do the fighting, while Benjamin and I run the farm," added Jon. I suspect the food shortage will continue for some time, so our large farm can contribute a lot, if we both stay here"

CHAPTER NINE

TURNING POINT AT SARATOGA

By the last Sunday in July 1776 the Declaration of Independence had been read at every meetinghouse in Massachusetts. It had been published in every newspaper, copies printed and distributed widely. One of these came to the Barkers. They sat together to take turns reading it, sentence by sentence.

Jon, the eldest, read first, "When in the course of human events it becomes necessary for one people to dissolve the political bands which have connected them with another . . . ."

Benjamin continued, "We hold these truths to be self-evident, that all men are created equal, that they – why does this sound so familiar to me?"

"Who can answer that?," asked Jonathan.

Molly quickly replied, "It was what William Barker said in 1692, as part of his confession. He said the devil promised all men would be equal and live bravely."

Jon chimed in, "That's right! Our heroic cousin John Barker can now be proud of his great grandfather and not be ashamed for being charged with witchcraft. He was ahead of his time. He knew the class system the Puritans brought from England was wrong. Now our new country is declaring it for all to see and hear.

" Perhaps this will encourage Francis Faulkner help us reconcile the Barker,

Battle of Valcour Island

Swan, and Faulkner families," added Jonathan.

Jonathan and his children worked hard, preparing and seeding larger fields than before. Methuen's militia acquired gunpowder from Samuel Phillips. Samuel and his father took target practice in the heat of August and September.

As September wore on news came of a major defeat of Washington's army at the Battle of Long Island. Washington was outmanned, two to one and the British had over 400 armored ships on Long Island Sound and in the East River. Total disaster was averted by General Glover's industrious seamen from Marblehead and Salem, who worked through the night evacuating nearly 10,000 trapped troops from Long Island to lower Manhattan. When the British awoke, the Americans were fleeing up the west side of Manhattan to safety.

This was hardly the end of the Battle of New York, however. Several battles ensued on Manhattan, with disastrous results for Washington's army. When the last of these was ending, Washington had crossed the Hudson with a remnant of his army, and watched the final engagement through his telescope. His eyes teared up as he watched his men drop their rifles and raise their hands in surrender, only to be run through by the swords of the English Regulars. On top of these losses, nearly 3,000 Americans had been captured and placed on decrepit prisoner ships, without sufficient water or food. More than 1,000 died of dysentery and scurvy.

Before these events, a call came for new enlistments from Essex County. Samuel Barker enlisted for three months in Captain Eliphalet Bodwell's Company. They marched to Albany on October 1st.

Upon arrival, they were ordered to march to Fort Ticonderoga, where some were put on newly constructed armored schooners and four row-galleys. They ferried further north. Bodwell's Company marched up the shore to

Valcour Island, where they joined Col. Edward Wigglesworth on the row-galley Trumbull.

On October 11th, 1776, Samuel Barker was in a decisive naval battle at Valcour Island near the west shore of Lake Champlain, under General Benedict Arnold. Arnold engaged the superior British fleet with the row-galleys Congress and Washington. The Congress was captured and there were heavy casualties on the Washington. They all fought valiantly for several hours, until fog set in at dusk. Then, Arnold ordered

Benedict Arnold

his damaged fleet to sneak past some of the British ships, heading south to Buttonmold Bay, where the larger British ships would have run aground in the shallow waters. Then they stripped their ships of armor, carried their wounded ashore and torched the abandoned ships at Buttonmold Bay.

Arnold was left with just 150 men and the British pursued them as they headed south to Crown Point. They reached their goal just ahead of the British, so Arnold ordered the fort burned and his weary men headed towards safety at Ticonderoga. The Americans suffered 80 dead, many wounded and 120 taken captive in the Valcour engagement. Although defeated, they so delayed the British advance towards New York, that British General Carleton decided (with winter coming on) to return to Canada. Samuel Barker was among 60 who were wounded and released, after treatment at Fort Ticonderoga. Before leaving, Carleton released 200 captured Americans under a flag of truce. They were so effusive in their praise of Carleton that General Arnold decided to send them home to prevent desertion.

Samuel returned home in early January, his minor wounds fully healed. His enthusiasm and confidence were depressed by his most recent experiences. He joined his brothers and sisters in their winter chores on the farm, taking comfort from the close-knit Barker family. During family discussions, it was Jesse who questioned Samuel the most about the Battle of Valcour Island.

Despite the danger and depression from these defeats, Jesse still longed to be part of the action. Abigail was happy that he was yet too young for that. She was also happy Jon and Benjamin had no appetite for war.

The war was going badly and many believed that it was only a matter of time until it was lost. After the defeats in battles on Long Island and Manhattan, the British forces had grown while Washington's army was steadily depleted by the end of short enlistments, and desertions. They were poorly equipped for winter marches and encampment; most were without boots or shoes. The English were led by General Cornwallis and General Howe. They were accompanied by an two squadrons of Hessians led by Colonel von Donop and Colonel Rall, plus an elite squadron of Hessian Jaegers, commanded by Captain Johann Ewald. The Hessians were not mercenaries, but a professional army that had been brought to America via a treaty between the King of England and the Prince of Hesse. The Hessians were renowned for their professionalism and discipline. Several English officers had spent time in Hesse to receive training.

Rather than engage Washington's army in a battle in New Jersey, Cornwallis pursued a tactic of chasing the Americans from New Bridge, Hackensack, Newark, Brunswick, and Princeton His plan was to wear down the smaller American army in hopes of an end to the war without massive bloodshed. Washington, however, was of a different mind. At Princeton, his men finally found comfortable quarters at the college. By the time the British arrived there, Washington had moved south to the Delaware River near Trenton. He organized a defensive line along twenty-five miles on the Pennsylvania side of the river. He was receiving reinforcements from the Pennsylvania militia, equipped with river galleys, and artillery. When the British arrived at Trenton, they moved towards the river but were met with heavy artillery fire from the other side. General Howe sent some of his troops down the river looking for boats, but found none.

Howe had decided to retire to winter quarters, as his troops were exhausted. But he was encouraged to believe that his army was in control and proceeded to disburse it across the state of New Jersey to encourage the Loyalists and to be in position to take control of the country. Meanwhile, Washington had received 2,500 additional forces, formerly led by General Lee. Lee had resisted orders from Washington to join him earlier in New Jersey. He was eventually captured by the British when he was in a tavern, away from his troops. Washington was also receiving new recruits weekly and was being joined by local militias.

On the English/Hessian side, their forces were getting weaker. New Jersey militia General Philemon Dickinson organized a series of attacks north of Trenton, taking control of the countryside that Cornwallis expected to control. They succeeded by striking the Hessians again and again, causing casualties, but then fleeing to avoid a face to face battle. At the same time Pennsylvania militia General James Ewing repeatedly made raids across the river to destroy Hessian outposts under artillery support on the west shore. They did their damage quickly and left before Colonel Rall realized what had happened. When he tried to strengthen his defenses, Ewing struck again with a larger force. On December 21st Ewing sent several men with blackened faces across the river, who set several house afire and returned to the other side. The Hessians incurred only minor losses of men, but they lost much sleep and were physically weak and tired.

Colonel von Donop then took the offensive and attacked the Jersey militia near Mount Holly. There were a series of skirmishes with casualties on both sides. On December 23rd Donop had arrived with a larger force and attacked the American militia. Outnumbered, they retreated and Donop decided to stay the night in the fine abandoned homes of wealthy residents of Mount Holly. Von Donop took up with a wealthy widow in one house and was so enthralled that he stayed there through Christmas.

On Christmas night, a winter storm hit Trenton and the exhausted Hessians were relieved, expecting to get their first good night's sleep in eight days. The storm was severe, with near hurricane force winds driving a cold rain that turned to sleet and snow. Washington had meticulously planned crossings at three points. His main army would cross with him at Johnson's Ferry and McConkey's Ferry, ten miles north of Trenton. Ewing's force was to cross at Trenton and another force was to cross ten miles south of Trenton. These two failed, because of the ice on the river.

Washington's crossing was successful largely due to the seamanship of the Marblehead sailors, part of General Glover's New England militia. General Washington had given command of the crossing to Henry Knox, a big heavy man who shouted orders with a thundering voice. Many believed the operation would have failed but for the stentorian lungs of Colonel Knox. Knox was able to bring eighteen artillery pieces across the river. This added two hours delay to the crossing, to add to the two hour delay in starting. Washington

General John Stark

feared he would be too late to surprise the enemy, arriving after sunrise in Trenton. However, the storm grew more fierce, driving the heavy rain and snow so that visibility was very poor. While waiting on the Jersey side, he gave detailed orders to his officers about his plan of attack on Trenton. At the village of Birmingham, he split his army into two divisions: one moving further inland before heading south to Trenton from the northeast, and the other heading directly south.

The two American divisions converged on the town just after 8 am and began attacking Hessian outposts with artillery and muskets. On the river road, General Sullivan's division included New Hampshire's John Stark. Within an hour Colonel Rall had been alerted and was rallying his troops to battle. He came to the false conclusion that his army was surrounded on every side, not knowing there was a path of escape to the southeast. Rall fought fiercely but was overcome by Washington's superior tactics and strength. When he became mortally wounded, his junior officers eventually surrendered. Twenty-two Hessians were killed and 83 seriously wounded. On the American side, two officers were wounded; one being Lieutenant James Monroe, who later became the fifth president of his country. Several soldiers died from the elements during the crossing.

In mid January, news came of George Washington's glorious victory in the Battle of Trenton. This victory lifted the spirits of the Barkers and all Methuen and Andover residents. Jonathan Barker answered the call for new enlistees in April and was assigned to Col. Jacob Gerrish's regiment of guards in Bristol, Rhode Island.

They were expecting the 900 Hessian prisoners taken at Trenton to be transported by sea to Bristol. However, the prisoners were kept in Pennsylvania. Gerrish's regiment remained in Bristol to protect the citizens from raiding British ships roaming the coastline looking for provisions. After two months Jonathan was released from duty.

When he returned home, Abigail greeted him with tears in her eyes.

"Jonathan, Samuel re-enlisted a month after you left. I could not convince him to wait for your return. He kept quoting Thomas Paine's booklet about the present crisis and about 'summer patriots and sunshine soldiers.'

"He left with several others from Methuen and Andover to join Captain Samuel Carr's company and they marched June 1st back to Albany, to join Colonel James Wesson's Ninth Regiment. He has become very headstrong and resolute after all of his military service. Despite Washington's victory at Trenton, there is no prospect of an early end to this war. He has already been hurt once, I fear he may face greater danger in this new service."

Jonathan embraced Abigail for a long time, trying to calm her fears. "Samuel has become a grown man long before his time. He may be headstrong, but he is also wise. He is well trained and knows how to control himself during danger and stress. He may be engaged in more combat, but he is prepared for it."

Abigail's fears for her son's safety and well-being were justified. Nothing could prepare Samuel Barker for the almost continuous action he saw from August 6th thru October 20th after arriving in Albany.

It began when his company was ordered to assist the New York 3rd Regiment to search for weapons and supplies among the dead and wounded at the Battle of Oriskany. Samuel was horrified to find his cousin, Samuel Pettengel, among the many dead. He had left Methuen with his wife six years earlier, to settle in a more fertile farming area in the upper Hudson River Valley. However, on July 17, 1777, Nicholas Herkimer, head of Tryon County Committee of Safety issued a proclamation, warning of an impending attack by a regiment of Loyalists and Seneca Indians. He issued an urgent call to arms and Samuel Pettengel was one of 800 untrained farmers to answer the call. Lt. Col. Barry St. Leger led the British regiment but the main attack came from two Seneca chiefs and their men. Most of Herkimer's men were killed before a remnant retreated.

There were more dead in one small area than Samuel had seen before – even at Bunker Hill. He helped gather up muskets, powder horns, and two artillery pieces and returned to the regiment. Soon they were under attack by elements of Burgoyne's army and this siege continued for 21 days until a large relief force led by General Arnold arrived.

On September 19th, Col. James Wesson's 9th regiment was entrenched on Bemis Heights on Freeman's Farm when Burgoyne's army began several offensive attacks. Samuel's regiment was held in reserve for most of the day, but when the enemy threatened the American left flank, General Arnold called for more forces and Colonel. Ebenezer Learned's brigade, including Wesson's 9th regiment repelled this attack. Soon they were forced to retreat, losing their loftier position. However, the Continental army inflicted heavy casualties on the enemy. Samuel Barker was part of the last action and hasty retreat.

As time wore on, the American army gained reinforcements almost daily, while Burgoyne lost men. Before the first Freeman Farm engagement, he sent 800 men east to Bennington where he expected only light resistance. His goal was to steal food, horses and draft animals for his army.

He encountered General Stark's New Hampshire militia of 2,000. Samuel had seen General Stark in action at Bunker Hill. Very few of Burgoyne's forces returned from Bennington, as a large Indian contingent fled back to Quebec and 700 British and Germans were captured.

When Stark led his men into combat, he rallied them saying: "There are your enemies, the Red Coats and the Tories. They are ours, or this night Molly Stark sleeps a widow."

Some of Stark's men, who chased the fleeing English, related Stark's words to General Learned, who used them and the news of the victory to inspire his troops. Morale was very high as Burgoyne's forces advanced on them once more.

On October 7th, the Americans outnumbered Burgoyne's army by several thousand. Burgoyne was planning to attack the Americans, who strategized their defense. Samuel was, again, a part of Learned's Brigade, which defended the center.

Burgoyne attacked on the right flank, but was repelled. Benedict Arnold then led a charge of Learned's men through the gap between redoubts toward the rear, where the American left flank circled behind the British. Furious fighting continued until dark. Arnold was hit twice and was out of action for six months. At the end of the day, the Americans had re-taken Bemis Heights and suffered less than half the casualties of Burgoyne's army.

On the morning of October 8th, Burgoyne retreated to the fortified position he had held on September 16th. By October 13th, a vastly superior force of Americans surrounded his army at Saratoga, and he was forced to surrender his force of 6,000.

News of this victory spread rapidly throughout the colonies and to Europe. Because of it, the French joined the battle as an ally to America. Previously, they had provided important supplies and equipment, but the Saratoga victory caused them to send a fleet to rival the British, as well as troops and some talented officers.

During the two days following victory, terms of surrender were negotiated and plans made to move the prisoners to Cambridge. Five hundred militia, under Lt. Col. James Brickett, were assigned to accompany the prisoners. They were separated into groups: the English prisoners were to take a northerly route through Northampton Massachusetts while the Germans took a southern route through Great Barrington and Worcester. Major Francis Faulkner took half of the militia to guard the Germans.

While preparations were being made, British fifers played a tune they preferred, "The World Turned Upside Down." Samuel Barker had not heard this before, so he befriended a British fifer to teach it to him. While they played, Major Faulkner spotted Samuel and shouted, "Private Barker!"

Samuel feared he was in trouble for consorting with the enemy, but that was not the case. Faulkner approached him, "I thought I recognized the young Barker fifer I met in Cambridge. Did you take part in the hostilities here in Saratoga?"

"Yes, sir, it was my good fortune to do so. I have been attached to General Learned's Brigade since June."

"Then you have seen a lot of action for such a young man. Your father must be very proud of you."

"I wrote him only once and don't know if he received my letter. I didn't get one from him, but hardly anyone has received mail here. You may see him when you arrive in Cambridge. He has been assigned to Col. Jacob Gerrish's Regiment. Guarding prisoners is their primary responsibility."

"I will surely look for him when I get to Winter Hill. He and I still have to discuss plans for your older brother's marriage. But you and I must talk some more. Your father will want me to tell him all about the battles you have seen. You must tell me everything"

The two talked for a long time, as Samuel excitedly described the action of the armies he watched and was part of, during the past few months. Finally,

General Glover signaled to Major Faulkner that it was time to go, and he quickly excused himself and shook Samuel's hand.

"Godspeed to you, sir." Samuel had developed an avuncular attitude towards Major Faulkner. He was pleased his father had also developed a relationship with him that would eventually lead to the Faulkner-Barker marriage his ancestor had wanted.

By the time the English and German soldiers arrived in Cambridge on November 7th, they had met up and marched together, with General Burgoyne and General Glover leading the way. A large crowd had gathered, church bells were rung and canons fired.

The Germans were separated again and marched under Major Faulkner to Winter Hill alongside the Mystic River in Cambridge (which later became Somerville). The English were marched to Prospect Hill near Charlestown Neck, next to Bunker Hill.

Francis Faulkner was required to stay at Winter Hill until Colonel Gerrish's guards arrived, five weeks later.

When that day happened, he was very happy to be relieved, and see his friend, Sergeant Jonathan Barker again. After greeting Colonel Gerrish, he approached Jonathan, who was standing beside a tent, back turned slightly away, and engaged in animated conversation with two sturdy-looking young men.

"What took you so long, friend? I thought you would never come."

"I came as soon as they called me, Francis. I guess nothing happens quickly in the military. I would like you to meet two more sons of mine. This is Benjamin, who has been running the farm in my absence and Jesse, who has been anxious to serve, now that he is fifteen."

"You told me Benjamin chose to remain on the farm while the rest of you served. What changed?"

"Benjamin and Jesse have always been very close. When Jesse reached his fifteenth birthday he was eager to serve, at least for a few months."

"Jonathan, you are truly blessed. How many other sons are at home behind this one?"

"Two more: 13-year-old Symonds Epes and 11-year-old Amos. I also have four daughters, two young ladies and two youngsters."

"I met your fifer son, Samuel at Saratoga. We had a nice long chat. He said he wrote you once but didn't hear back from you."

"We got his letter just recently, although it was written before the battles at Saratoga. I wasn't sure how to send a reply. How is he? Was he in the battle?"

"He has been in several battles, even one on board a ship. He is such a fine young man. You must be very proud."

"I am, but my wife and I miss him terribly. We were aware of his involvement in the battle on the ship as he returned home briefly before starting a new enlistment. I hope he comes home next June when his year is up."

Francis changed the subject to another which he knew was important to Jonathan: "I would like to review plans for the Barker-Swan marriage we discussed. I may be able to be more involved than I had suspected. My friends in Acton tell me they have in mind to appoint me Justice of the Peace when the war is over. Can you agree to have Jon Barker and Nancy Swan come to Acton so that I can perform the marriage?"

"That would be just fine. I can almost guarantee you we can do it, even though Jon and Nancy will both be in Fryeburg when the time comes. I will write you when I have a date for the marriage."

"Excellent! We have a firm agreement.."

They shook hands, smiling broadly. "Now tell me what Samuel told you about the action he has seen."

They spoke for several minutes, until Francis realized he had better start his trip to Acton, lest he not make it home that day.

Jonathan and Jesse served less than four months, then were released on April 3rd, 1778. The prisoners were being put on ships and sent to Virginia. Abigail was relieved to see them at home so soon. She was also happy to hear all about Samuel's experiences, although she was still fearful about his well being, since he seemed always to be involved in battles.

Abigail had unwelcome news for Jonathan.

Jon, who had promised to stay on the farm, had a change of heart and enlisted for one year in January 1778. He joined Captain Whittier's Company, which marched to join Samuel Johnson's 4th Essex Regiment at Fishkill, New York. He was hoping to meet up with Samuel, who was serving nearby.

"Abigail, we must learn to accept these separations. We are fighting for independence and it is not a part-time war. We are fortunate to have daughters who are always here, helping, and most of our sons are here almost all the time."

Jon served his full year at Fishkill, without major engagements. He was stationed at General Washington's largest supply depot in the northeast and was responsible for guarding against enemy incursions.

The depot supplied materials to the armies that fought at Saratoga, and in later engagements. The worst part of Jon's service there was enduring the harsh winter of 1779-80, albeit in much better circumstances than his younger brother, Samuel, at Morristown.

A month after Jonathan's and Jesse's return home in the spring of 1778, a long letter arrived from Samuel.

May 10, 1778

Dear Mother and Father,

I expect you have heard about my war experience from Major Faulkner by now. About one month after that, we received orders to march south with General Learned's Brigade. We are to help strengthen General Washington's army setting up winter quarters in Valley Forge – a few miles west of Philadelphia. When we got that news, I was excited to again serve closely under General Washington. However, these last few months have been the worst of all my time in the army.

We marched many days, even as the weather got colder and it snowed quite often. My shoes wore out and I tied the soles on with leather straps, but they wore out, too. I marched the last few miles in stockings, and there were holes in my last pair when we arrived at Valley Forge.

None of us had shoes when we arrived, and some had no stockings. Some died from disease on the way, and others deserted. Even after we arrived, sickness spread among us and many more died.

They built barracks first for those who arrived before us, so we didn't get our own until most of the winter was over. We were also the last to get clean clothes, because they had to come from Newburyport, Beverly, and Marblehead, and those people were also suffering from the recession caused by the war.

As bad as these things were, it got worse.

A new leader arrived who would become our commanding officer – to teach us to be better soldiers. He was Baron von Stoybin, who was hired by Benjamin Franklin in France and sent to General Washington, who liked him.

He spoke no English – he speaks a little now. He had a translator, who repeated some of his orders to us, when we didn't understand. Much of what he said to us in German was swear words, which we soon learned without translation. He called us "shise kopf," which means "shit head." The other words he used were numbers he shouted when we marched, "Ine, svy, ine, svy, ine, svy." He taught us to march in tighter formation.

Major General Friedrich Wilhelm Augustus Baron von Steuben

He also taught us to re-load our muskets much faster than I believed possible. He counted for each of the eight steps he taught us, "Ine, svy, dry, fear, funf, zex, zeben, ocht" and shouted at us if we were too slow or made a mistake."

At first we hated him and we thought he hated us. But after two or three weeks, we realized we were getting much better, so we didn't hate him so much. Finally, two weeks ago, he spoke to us in his broken English.

'I give you something special. Now you must give back. I make you soldiers. Don't waste it. You have a chance to have a free country, but you

Baron von Steuben at Valley Forge

must fight for it first. Not everyone can be soldier, but you are soldiers. Go fight for your country.'

After that, all of us signed up for another year. We want to be part of Washington's army when we win this war, and now we believe we can do it.

I miss all of you very much and I am sorry that my absence must cause you – especially mother – some sadness. I think about how much Amos and Symonds Epes must have grown while I have been away. I hope that they will remember me when I come home.

My love to everyone, Samuel

Samuel's letter was passed around to the Barker children. Each read it in their own time. They treasured it, almost as a replacement for the brother they had seen very little of during the last few years.

One month later, Washington broke camp with his army in pursuit of 10,000 British troops and their 12-mile-long supply train.

On June 28, 1778, in 100-degree heat, they engaged the British at Monmouth Court House. They fought all day, but it was a standoff. Von Steuben's training had paid off, as the Americans showed themselves equal to the professional British army. The heat caused most of the casualties on both sides.

The British abandoned Philadelphia and moved on to New York City, while Washington set up a new encampment at Morristown, New Jersey.

In July, a large French fleet with 4,000 troops arrived at Sandy Hook, New Jersey. There would be many important land/sea engagements between this fleet and the British in the next two years before victory would be achieved.

Samuel's service in Col. Wesson's 9th regiment continued without major engagements during the summer and fall of 1778. In September, they moved to Washington's new headquarters in Morristown. On the frontlines, in September of 1778, Samuel was fortunate to be in Morristown when the Tappan massacre took place nearby. It was the bayonet killing of 30 Americans by men of British officer Charles "No Flint" Grey. There were several small engagements by elements of Washington's army in this area, but this was one of the more gruesome. Unlike most British officers, Colonel Grey preferred surprise attacks at night. He had been very successful with one in Paoli, Pennsylvania one year earlier, when his men bayoneted over 400 American troops. He had ordered his men to remove the flints from their rifles to prevent them from shooting one another in the dark and in order to ensure the surprise attack.

In Methuen, Molly Barker was courted by Solomon Jennings, whose family owned a farm next to Jonathan's. The two families had been walking to Sunday meeting together for several years. On these walks they crossed the Spicket River, then through the Huse property to the church.

After Jonathan gave his blessing, Molly and Solomon married on May 11, 1779. Jonathan gave the couple several acres of his farm, bringing the size of the Jennings farm nearly equal to the Barker's.

In 1780 Molly gave birth to a son, named for Solomon's grandfather, Elijah. The following year, a second son was born, and Molly named him Jonathan Barker Jennings, after her father. Jonathan gave the young Jennings family an additional one hundred acres of unimproved land adjacent to their farm.

Many years later, Molly's ninth child was named Dorcas Huse Jennings, after the wife of her young brother, Amos. Molly had cared for Amos through his infancy, childhood, and young adulthood. They remained very close for decades.

The ensuing winter was the harshest on record, with heavy snows and continuous weeks of sub-freezing temperatures. As that winter began, Samuel's Company moved to Col. Michael Jackson's Regiment in West Point, New York on the Hudson River.

Meanwhile, in Methuen, Benjamin courted Lydia Foster of nearby Boxford. Benjamin had been attending afternoon meeting at Boxford with some of his friends and met Lydia there. The Boxford pastor was an excellent preacher and drew many visitors from nearby towns. Benjamin brought Lydia home to meet his parents, making it clear that he intended to marry her.

After this meeting, when Benjamin was alone with his father, Jonathan spoke seriously to him. He reflected that his own marriage to Abigail had gotten off to a difficult start, since it was nearly four years before their first child arrived. Jonathan said he believed the delay was caused by Abigail working so hard on the farm with him, detracting from her more feminine ways, including having children. He pointed out it is important for farm families to have children early in their marriage, in order to have their help as soon as possible. To avoid this problem, Jonathan suggested that Lydia should be pregnant before they were married.

On March 6, 1780, Benjamin married Lydia Foster, She was invited to stay on the Barker farm until they could arrange travel to Fryeburg, Maine to settle. This, however, was not a comfortable arrangement. Benjamin began making plans to travel to Maine as soon as possible.

In June 1780, General Washington issued a call for new enlistments, for an abbreviated term of three months, to be part of an assault he was convinced would re-take New York City.

Jesse Barker answered that call and enlisted on July 10, 1780 in Capt. John Abbott's Company. They marched to Great Barrington, Mass., where they joined Col. Nathaniel Wade's Regiment, and arrived at West Point in early August. The site sat high above the Hudson, where the colonials had strung a huge iron chain across the river, to prevent British ships from passing.

Washington expected major support from the French, but the British arrived with 10 ships, bottling up the French Fleet in Newport Harbor. Washington then abandoned the campaign to liberate New York City.

While at West Point, Jesse met his brother, Samuel. They had not seen each other for well over three years. Both of them had matured substantially. Jesse remarked how strong and muscular Samuel looked.

"You would not have said that when I was at Valley Forge. I nearly starved – I was nothing but skin and bones. You, Jesse, have really grown since I last saw you.

"You missed Molly's marriage a year ago, and Benjamin's this past March. Benjamin and his wife are staying on our farm, because they plan to move to Maine with Jon and me as soon as we can arrange it. Do you want to come there with us, Samuel?"

"I have been away from home for so long, I will want to stay in Methuen and get re-acquainted with my brothers, sisters and parents. They are all so important to me that I just can't go so far away again, without spending more time with them."

Jesse and Samuel were together at West Point for seven weeks. It was the scene of one more major incident of the war.

General Benedict Arnold commanded the fort. He was highly esteemed by his men, for many had seen his bravery at Bemis Heights and Saratoga.

Eight of Col. Wade's regiment were assigned to row General Arnold's personal barge, when called upon. On September 21st, Arnold raced up on horseback and jumped into the barge, ordering the men to row south. After

Major Andre

eighteen miles they reached the British ship, Vulture. Arnold grabbed the rope ladder and boarded.

Unwittingly, Wade's men had helped him escape being hanged. His treason had been discovered when British Major John Andre was arrested in civilian clothes with maps of West Point and details of its defenses were discovered in his stockings. The documents were brought to General Arnold's assistant, who was studying them when Arnold saw them and quickly left.

General Washington then expected an attack and put Col. Wade in charge of all troops at the fort. But the attack never came.

Major Andre was tried as a spy by a military court and found guilty. The Americans would much rather execute Benedict Arnold and tried to exchange Andre for him, but the British refused. Surgeon James Thatcher wrote of Andre: "during his confinement and trial he exhibited those proud and elevated sensibilities which designate greatness and dignity of mind."

On October 2nd, a solemn procession set out from the village of Tappan as Benjamin Abbott of Andover and Isaac Organ of Lynn tapped the death march on muffled drums while the cortège ascended to a makeshift gibbet. Jesse and Samuel Barker were in the large detachment of military marchers while an immense concourse of people assembled, including all the American officers except General Washington and his staff. Major Andre made the short walk from the stone house of his confinement to the gibbet, one officer on each arm. He stepped into the wagon and bandaged his own eyes with a white handkerchief. He affixed the rope to his neck while the executioner stood nervously by. Colonel Scammel asked for his last words, which were, "I pray you to bear me witness that I meet my fate like a brave man." The wagon was removed and he was suspended and quickly expired. He was dressed in his royal regiment and boots and his remains, in the same dress, were placed in an ordinary coffin and interred at the foot of the gallows.

Jesse and Samuel wept openly as did hundreds of other on-lookers. Samuel, who had witnessed the bravery of Benedict Arnold at the Battle of Saratoga, turning the tide of the war to the colonists' favor, would now remember him as the symbol of treason, as would everyone in America.

Jesse's three-month tour ended on October 31st and he headed home with his regiment. Samuel's final enlistment ended the last day of 1780. Soon, all the Barker family would be together at their Methuen farm. The fighting continued for nine more months, when General Cornwallis surrendered to General Washington at Yorktown. Negotiations finally yielded a peace treaty in September 1782.

CHAPTER TEN

THE BARKER PIONEERS

Jesse Barker arrived home to find that Benjamin had already left on his own for Fryeburg. He and Lydia had married in March as soon as they learned she was pregnant. Since Molly had already married and moved out, and Jesse and Samuel were away in the army, there was room for Lydia to move into the Barker house. However, there were awkward moments and they longed to have their own place.

Benjamin did not want to build a house on his father's land, since he wanted to move to Fryeburg soon. So, he and Lydia agreed he should go to Maine alone to build a house for them. Lydia would follow with her baby when Jesse and Jonathan went. Lydia's baby, Elijah, was born a few weeks after Benjamin left.

Samuel Barker finally arrived home on January 8th, 1781, exhausted and hungry. It was cause for celebration at the Barker household. Elaborate preparations were made for a feast, to be attended by their extended family and friends.

Molly came with her husband, Solomon and their 10-month-old baby, Elijah, and two of Solomon's brothers. Benjamin's wife, Lydia and her 3-month-old son, Elijah, returned from a visit to Lydia's parents home, bringing her sister, Hannah. They roasted a pig on the spit in the fireplace and Abigail, Molly and Hannah prepared pea soup, roasted root vegetables, beans, johnnycakes, pickled beets and carrot pudding.

When Lydia and Hannah arrived, they approached Samuel. "Welcome home, Samuel, do you remember us?"

"I remember going with Benjamin to meeting at Boxford and how you both exchanged glances from across the aisle."

Hannah took Samuel's hand, with a smile asking, "Do you remember me, Samuel?"

"We were just children then, but I do remember you. I believe you smiled at me, too."

"I did, and so did you, but you also blushed. I really liked you for that."

Lydia moved away, leaving Samuel and Hannah to talk.

"Benjamin told me that you were a hero at Saratoga."

"My brother exaggerates. Benedict Arnold was the hero; he led the charge between enemy lines and took two balls in his leg. He was in the hospital for six months. General Learned was close behind Arnold and the rest of the brigade followed him. I just ran like hell, and when we reached our goal, we had closed the escape route for Burgoyne's troops."

"It was a major victory for our side. Everyone was talking about it. I bet you did more than you say."

"Probably my biggest contribution was playing my fife on the long march from Saratoga to Valley Forge. A few died on the way, and I thought at times I might not make it. When I felt that way, I saw most could barely summon strength to take each step. They held up their collars to fight off the bitter cold.

I decided more was expected of me. I held my hand to my mouth and blew to unfreeze my lips, which I wet with my tongue. I pulled out my fife and with a lot of effort played a happy marching tune.

At Valley Forge, three of the men said I saved their lives. They thought that "if that kid can play a lively tune at a time like this, an older man like me should have the strength to march."

Hannah looked at Samuel adoringly. "Benjamin was right, you were a hero."

"I suppose a hero can be an ordinary person just doing what he is supposed to do."

Benjamin packed a large sack for his trip to Fryeburg. He brought an axe, a hatchet, a knife, winter and summer clothes, and a good supply of dried food.

He arranged passage on a schooner at the Methuen dock and loaded a small canoe on board. From Saco, he voyaged four days up the Saco River in his canoe. The trip was challenging to one who had not had a lot of canoeing experience, especially on waters that were sometimes rapid and shallow, continually filled with rocks which presented small dangers. On the afternoon of the first day on the river, he saw rapids ahead and had to maneuver his boat to shore, so that he could ford past the falls. He observed a few settlers at a new village near the falls. He encountered falls each of the next two days and followed the same process.

Benjamin arrived at Fryeburg in late September and located Caleb Swan's house. There he learned James Swan had moved his family to Sudbury Canada, a small settlement begun just two years earlier. The land had been granted to a man from Sudbury, Massachusetts for his service against the French. Being so far north, the settlement thus gained its name. Caleb was very helpful.

"James said if the Barkers arrive, tell them Fryeburg was getting too crowded for me. He said he wanted to sail and explore a wider river before he was too old. At Sudbury Canada, the Androscoggin was ideal for him. He also wanted his sons to have an opportunity to own more land. It's about 30 miles to his new house. If you get an early start and walk quickly, you can make it in one day."

Benjamin arose early the next morning and set out north bearing a back-pack following a well-marked old Indian trail through the forest. Late the next evening, Benjamin arrived in Sudbury-Canada and was directed to James Swan's house, where James greeted him. "Are you one of Jonathan Barker's sons?"

"Yes sir, my name is Benjamin."

"Where are Jon and Jonathan?"

"Jon and Jesse will come next spring. I came early because my wife was pregnant when I left and I wanted to have a house built when she arrived."

"You will need help. Do you know my sons, Joseph Greeley and James, Junior?", nodding towards two rangy men standing beside him."

"Nice to meet you both. I heard all about you from Jon, back when he crewed with you on the schooner and on the Merrimac ferry. It would be great if you can help me."

"Their sister is pledged to Jon, so they are obliged to help. I will find a spot for you to lay your mat for the night and tomorrow I will show you an unsettled area ideal for you and your brothers. I will take you there in the small sloop I built this summer. If you like the area, we can all start building right away."

The next morning, James, his two sons, and Benjamin loaded the tools and supplies they needed and sailed up the Androscoggin to its junction with an unnamed river which flowed south. They tied up the sloop and walked along its banks. James pointed ahead to a mountain on their left.

"We should look for a clearing at the base of that mountain and next to the river. The mountain will provide protection from the winter wind. You should be able to acquire a lot of land here at very little cost. It is at the outer edge of Sudbury Canada but has not been laid out or assigned. I believe the land is quite fertile and suitable for farming. If you decide to settle here, you can name them 'Barker River' and 'Barker Mountain.'

"Since you know this area quite well, I could do no better than to follow your advice, Mr. Swan. I am anxious to find a good spot and get started building a cabin."

When they arrived at a clearing near the mountain, James appeared quite pleased.

"I believe we have arrived at the new Barker property. Let's get started."

They set about cutting trees for the cabin. A one-room cabin went up for Benjamin and his family, then an extension was added for Jon and Jesse. By first snow, they were well prepared for winter and arrival of more of the Barkers in the spring. Benjamin missed Lydia very much and counted the days until she would arrive with their first child, born a month after Benjamin left Methuen. He was sad he had missed the first months of its life and tried to picture what he or she would look like when Lydia finally arrived.

Back in Methuen, Lydia was very busy with her infant son, whom she and Benjamin had agreed to name Elijah. She longed to be with Benjamin and kept noting to Jon and Jesse how mild the winter was, and that they should soon be able to travel.

In early March a full week of warm weather melted nearly all the snow. They began packing for their new home. They had not heard from Benjamin since he left, so they assumed they would be settling in Fryeburg, and much of what they needed was available there.

By mid-March they were on a schooner heading up the coast of Maine to the Saco River. They continued the journey on the river by canoe. Rowing was difficult, as the river current was hard against them, due to the melting snow upstream. At times, they wished they had come without the canoe, for movement by foot seemed faster than by the river.

At dusk of the second day of the river trip, they arrived at Steep Falls and noted a settlement on the west side of the River. As they pulled their canoe ashore, two settlers approached them, offering assistance. The settlers told them they were at Ossipee Plantation, named for the river that flowed into the Saco, just above the falls. This village would later be incorporated as Limington, and a smaller settlement on the east side would become the village of Standish. The travelers set up a camp for the night, saving the trek around the falls until morning.

At sunrise, they were able to catch trout, and cooked a tasty breakfast of it. They then cleared their camp and continued the journey. As they progressed inland on the Saco, the temperature dropped, and they encountered deeper snow. They were happy when they finally reached Fryeburg and Lydia excitedly looked for Benjamin.

They met Caleb and Dorothy Swan, who told them Benjamin had gone to Sudbury Canada, where James Swan had moved his family more than a year earlier. Dorothy helped Lydia and her six-month-old son to settle for the night, and Caleb helped Jon and Jesse. They were told the journey to Sudbury Canada would be a difficult two-day trek for Jon and Jesse in snowshoes.

There was still nearly a foot of snow on the ground so Dorothy strongly advised Lydia to stay with her for a few days. Jon and Jesse could borrow their sled to carry heavy cooking pails and other items they would need. Benjamin could bring it back and use it to bring his wife and son to Sudbury Canada. Lydia was disappointed at the delay, but accepted the plan.

Jon and Jesse started their 30-mile trek at dawn. Jon drew the heavy-laden sled most of the time, with short periods of assistance from Jesse. Jon's five-foot, ten-inch 175-pound frame was more suited to the task. Jesse was much smaller and could barely draw the sled twenty feet before having to rest. Jon lost patience with Jesse.

"We'll never make it in two days at this rate. You can fill your pack with as much as you can, and I will pull the sled with the rest."

"I only wanted to do my part, but I guess you are right," apologized Jesse.

At sundown, they found fallen branches for a fire and set up camp for the night. After eating nuts, cheese and corn meal, they collapsed on their mats and slept soundly until daybreak.

Another long day brought them at last to Sudbury Canada, where they soon found James Swan's house. They were too exhausted to travel the final two miles to the Barker cabin in the dark, so they stayed the night.

The next morning, Joseph Greeley Swan led them to Benjamin and the cabin he had helped him build. Benjamin was happy to see them, but his first thoughts were of his wife and baby.

"Where is Lydia and my baby? Are they all right? Didn't they come with you?"

Jesse understood his concern. "They are both fine. They are staying with Caleb and Dorothy Swan, waiting for you to get them. It would have been too much for them to make the trip in the snow without help. We borrowed this sled from Caleb, so you can return it to him."

Despite his six-month absence and all that had occurred during that time, Benjamin had no patience for a long and friendly reunion with his brothers. "I must get started immediately. I can't wait to see Lydia and my baby."

"Your son is six months old, a rather large baby at this point," offered Jesse.

Benjamin drew the empty sled at a rapid pace and didn't stop until he reached Caleb's house after midnight. He knocked, rousing most of the family. Lydia awoke as well, hoping that it would be Benjamin. As Caleb opened the door, she was peering from her room and rushed to Benjamin's arms as he appeared.

"She sobbed as she opened her heart to him. "Oh, Ben, this long separation has been so painful. Please don't ever let us be apart again." He brought his gear inside and into the room to see, for the first time, his six-month-old son, Elijah.

The next morning, Dorothy cooked a hearty breakfast for the Barkers to send them on their way to their new home. Caleb invited them to stay until the snow melted completely, but they were anxious to settle for good. The Swan's gave them a small sled they could use to pull Elijah, for they had no children left to use it. Soon they were on their way, stopping to camp one night on the way.

The next few months were busy for the three Barker brothers. They found an area they could clear and prepare for planting of corn, tomatoes, potatoes, and beans. They ate a lot of fish they caught in the Barker and Androscoggin

Rivers.

Joseph Greeley, Nancy, and ten-year-old Naamah Swan would visit them occasionally, bringing gifts from their father to help the new pioneers. Jon was becoming enamored of his intended bride, Nancy, as the teenager's body matured. She, in turn, still admired Jon's tall, manly appearance.

Just as their lives began to become more routine and comfortable, they were harshly disrupted by the totally unexpected.

The Barkers met some Indians who lived in the area and often seen canoeing on the Alder River. They were friendly and occasionally traded with the Barkers. However, on August 3rd, 1781, six Indians in war paint arrived at their door, demanding food, clothing and money. They carried tomahawks and made it clear they would be satisfied or they would kill.

Benjamin spoke, "We have very little, for we have just arrived from the south to settle. We have no money and just enough food to last until our first crops come in. Take what you want, but leave us in peace."

They accepted the offer and took all of the food they could find, as well as some boots and shirts. They asked, "Where you hide rum?"

Benjamin told them that they did not drink rum, so had none. The Indians left but warned Jesse and Benjamin to stay in house all this day, or be killed."

They huddled together in the house for several hours, to settle their nerves and be sure the Indians were out of sight.

A few days later, James Swan arrived to hear their story and to tell them what had happened in Sudbury Canada, which was much worse.

"The raiding Indians came from Quebec at the orders of the English troops who still held that territory. Their mission was to collect skins, whiskey, and food, as well as scalps and captives, for which the English would pay them. They killed and scalped your cousin, James Pettengill of Methuen and Peter Poor of Andover, and another. Joseph Greeley and another settler buried them. They captured Jonathan Clark and Nathaniel Segar and took them back to Canada, even though one of the Indians, Tomhegan, knew Segar and had even stayed at his house."

James also asked Benjamin to accompany him and help build two garrison houses and fort to defend against any additional attacks. James served four days at the fort and Benjamin six and one-half days.

The next week, James received orders from the selectmen at Fryeburg to serve in a small detachment under Lieutenant Nathaniel Hutchings, to cruise the Androscoggin and guard against incursions by Indians from Canada. He served three months. Then the group disbanded, since there had been no new threats.

As James Swan completed his first service, word came of Washington's defeat of British General Cornwallis at Yorktown, Virginia, on Chesapeake Bay, with the help of the French fleet under Count de Grasse in October 1781. Victory now appeared inevitable, yet skirmishes continued throughout the colonies. Thus, the Fryeburg selectmen decided that service on the Androscoggin should continue until the war was finally finished. James Swan was called on again in July of 1782 until Nov. 21, 1782 for the same service.

By mid-December, word came of a preliminary peace treaty signed in Paris to end the war. All British troops would soon leave America. An air of jubilation flowed through the Sudbury Canada area.

On June 17, 1782, Lydia gave birth to a second son they named for Benjamin's brother, Samuel. This was the first settler's child born in what would a few years later become the town of Newry. He was born one month before the first white child, Peregrine Dustin, was born in Sudbury Canada.

One by one, the brothers began to buy livestock from residents of Sudbury Canada or Fryeburg. In the spring of 1782 they expanded their planting fields, so they could become self-sufficient with that fall's harvest.

One day, as Jon was fishing on the Alder River, three local Indians approached him. Jon had seen them before and knew that they meant no harm to him. One of them had seen Jon wrestle on occasion with Benjamin, and they soon made it clear to Jon that they also wanted to wrestle him.

The smallest approached Jon and he quickly swung him over his thigh and laid him flat on his back. The next approached Jon and this one struggled a bit but also lost quickly. Then, the third approached. He was about as big as Jon. The two struggled for several minutes, but finally, Jon was able to throw him to the ground on his back.

The Indian jumped up, saying, "You all mattahondou" which means "you all devil." Jon shook hands with all three of the Abenaki Indians and they made the peace sign to him.

CHAPTER ELEVEN

A HAPPY MARRIAGE AND THREE TRAGIC YEARS

In mid-July 1784, a surprise visitor arrived at the Barker houses in Maine. It was Abner Foster, father of Benjamin's wife. "I came as the postman from Methuen – but I also wanted to see my grandchildren and their parents."

Lydia greeted him with a hug., "What letter do you bring, daddy?"

I believe it is an invitation to attend the marriage of your sister, Hannah, to Benjamin's brother, Samuel. Hannah is with child, and they want to wed as soon as we return together. I see you are also pregnant and I wonder if you are able to make the trip."

Lydia was giddy with excitement. "I would not miss it. Benjamin will take good care of me and you can help Benjamin with the luggage and canoe."

Lydia unfolded the letter and read it to Benjamin. "We must prepare to leave immediately. You are less than two months from giving birth; we have no time to waste. We will have to ask Mr. Swan to help us. Lydia is in no condition to make the 30 mile walk to Fryeburg."

Benjamin hoped James Swan could take them down the Androscoggin to the sea, but they soon learned that what appeared to be a quiet, wide and navigable river in Sudbury Canada quickly changed downstream. There were many steep falls, making it a very difficult if not impossible journey. The best Mr. Swan could offer was his horse for Lydia to ride. James would send Joseph Greeley with them to Fryeburg so he could ride the horse back.

Benjamin then talked privately with Jon. "Jon, I would like you to live in my house while my family and I are away. We will likely not return until next year, so you will have a lot of private time while we are away. You should use this to seriously court Nancy Swan so your marriage can take place in Acton next year.

"Perhaps we will all wait there for you, so we can be present at your wedding. We all know this is father's great goal in life, for you and Nancy Swan to be married by Francis Faulkner.

"We have become good friends with James Swan, but this is not sufficient to reconcile the charge of witchcraft against William Barker by Timothy Swan back in 1692, just as our great grandfather's friendship with Francis Faulkner's grandfather was insufficient.

"Our whole family is counting on you, and I believe Nancy is ready for you; she will soon be nineteen. I hope that she may become pregnant while we are away."

"Nancy has been very nice to me lately. I think you are right, that this may be the time. Thank you for the use of your house."

Benjamin lifted Lydia onto the horse and then put Elijah in front of her, to his great delight. He was not yet four years old, but he was a bright and happy boy.

Benjamin carried two-year-old Samuel most of the time, so they did well to make the trip in two days. Abner carried Samuel part way, to relieve Benjamin. For brief periods, they put Samuel on the horse with Lydia, and Elijah walked. This did not work well as Elijah tired of walking and Samuel was afraid to be on the horse.

They spent the second night at Caleb Swan's house in Fryeburg and then took his largest canoe down the Saco River to the coast, where they put it on a schooner that took them to Methuen. Lydia was exhausted when they arrived, but still in good health. Her baby was born August 29, 1784. She and Benjamin named him Ely.

Samuel and Hannah waited another month to be married. They all walked together to the Methuen church, where Ely was baptized just before the marriage ceremony.

Hannah was overjoyed to have her sister back in Methuen after more than two years, and she was especially pleased to have her attend her marriage. After the service at the Methuen church, Hannah embraced her sister.

"Lydia, I have missed you so much since you have been in Maine. It would be great if you, Benjamin, Elijah and Eli could stay until next spring so you can be here for the birth of my first child.

"I would love to spend the fall and winter here and to see your new baby. I will ask Benjamin, telling him how important it is to me." Benjamin readily agreed.

Samuel had built a house for himself and his new wife and baby, on his father's land. He had become the primary worker on his father's farm and had not yet decided when he would move to Sudbury Canada.

Despite Jon, Benjamin, and Jesse having left the farm, it was still very productive, since Symonds Epes was now twenty and Amos was eighteen. The youngest of Jonathan and Abigail's children, Abigail and Alice, were teen-agers and handled the livestock and the kitchen work quite well. The older married daughters, Molly and Hannah, often visited on Sundays with their husbands and children.

Samuel and Hannah's first child, named Dudley, was born March 3, 1785. The joy of his birth was short-lived.

In June, Elijah fell under a strange sickness. Healthy color faded from his face and a bluish pallor took over. His nose ran nearly constantly, occasionally mixed with blood. After two days, he had difficulty breathing; a few days later, he shook with chills and a deep barking cough. Lydia and Benjamin did all they could to comfort him, but his condition only worsened.

Jonathan was observing Elijah's symptoms, which seemed strangely familiar. Finally, it struck him. These were the same he had seen in his baby sister and his father when he was a little boy, more than fifty years earlier. The disease was called 'the Strangling Angel of Children' and it had killed most of the children in Methuen and Andover in 1735-40.

Jonathan visited the local physician and asked him to visit his house. The doctor asked Jonathan to describe the symptoms, which he did.

"The disease you describe is very contagious. If I came to your house, I would likely carry it to other families. The disease is 'breathing distemper.' (Many years later, it would become known as diphtheria.) You must isolate the patient from everyone in the house, especially children, who are most vulnerable."

To partially isolate the disease, Benjamin and Lydia moved into Samuel's house with Elijah. Lydia had to bring Ely with her, as well, since she was nursing him. Samuel and Hannah and their baby moved into Jonathan and Abigail's house, in a room of their own.

Elijah's condition worsened. His nose filled with a dark lining which obstructed his breathing. He kept his mouth open to breathe but it soon became coated as well. Benjamin and Lydia watched their four-year-old Elijah die a slow and painful death on July 8, 1785. Lydia cried almost constantly for several days.

"How ironic we gave him a biblical name like Elijah when it seems that God has forsaken him. He gave us such joy every day of his brief life, yet we could do nothing for him."

Barely a month after Elijah's death, baby Ely began to show the same symptoms. They started very slowly and Lydia hoped he simply had a runny nose or cold, but gradually the other symptoms appeared. Ely died November 23rd.

Fear was gripping the entire Methuen Barker farmstead. While Ely's condition was deteriorating, Samuel and Hannah feared their baby would also contract the disease, though they kept him away in Jonathan's house.

"Ben, Hannah and I are fearful for our baby's life. I recall the stories you told us about a marvelous physician in Maine, an Indian woman named Molly Ockett. The local settlers said she knew more about herbal remedies than any Massachusetts physician. She knew where to find them and how to prepare them. Moreover, she knew which remedies would cure which illnesses. Perhaps she can help us at this critical time."

They decided to travel to Sudbury Canada where they felt Dudley would be safe. They left quickly in order to arrive before the winter set in. Hannah and Lydia's father, Abner Foster, who decided to settle on Barker River with the Barkers, accompanied them.

Lydia became so depressed she stopped eating and began losing weight. She became weak and bedridden. Her sister's departure added to her depression; nothing Benjamin did or said would help. She died on May 7, 1786, leaving Benjamin with one healthy son, Samuel, now four years old.

Molly Ockett

At Barker River, a few days after Benjamin left him, Jon summoned courage to visit Nancy and speak privately to her.

"Before my brother returned to Methuen, he spoke to me about our parents' expectations for our marriage. I think my father is becoming impatient; Benjamin encouraged me to court you more fervently, so that we may be married next year in Acton."

"I hear this from my father, as well, Jon. I believe that we will marry, but I would like to get to know you, first. You men are all so busy, clearing fields, plowing, fishing, hunting, and the like. I never get to see or talk to you.

"You have lived an exciting life, compared to mine. You have been in the war; have seen big towns like Concord, Lexington, Cambridge, and Boston. I have only vague memories of Methuen and Andover and then I grew up in Fryeburg when it was a wilderness. Just when it was becoming more interesting, we moved here, back to the wilderness. I don't hate my life, but I would like you to tell me about yours."

"You are right, I have not been as concerned about you as I ought. You see my life as more exciting, but my view is different. I have always done what was expected of me, and I thought I should continue to do that. That includes marrying you and raising a family here. I will come to visit you and talk about all of these things.

"You can ask about the places I have seen and things I have done. Perhaps my remembering them and telling you will help to make my life more interesting. Benjamin told me to move into his house so I can court you privately there. I can see you are not ready for that, so I will continue to visit you in Sudbury. When you are ready, you can surprise me with a visit to Benjamin's house at

Barker River."

Tragedy continued for the extended Barker family.   Samuel's trip to Sudbury Canada kept their baby son from contracting the dreaded breathing disease, but he had been weak from birth. He was barely a year old when he died in Sudbury Canada in June 1786.

Hannah was saddened that the long trip had not helped and now she was separated from her sister, as well. She asked Samuel to take her back to Methuen right away, which he did. When they arrived, she got the tragic news that her sister had died less than a month before her baby Dudley died in Maine.

One Sunday, after the extended family attended meeting together, they came to Jonathan and Abigail's house for Sunday dinner. Towards the end of the meal, Jonathan rose to address the gathering.

"We have all felt the sadness of the loss of Elijah, Ely, Lydia, and Dudley in these last few months. Understandably, Lydia felt that God had forsaken Elijah, Ely, Benjamin, and herself. It is a normal reaction in our time. But I want to remind you of a former time, that of my grandfather Benjamin's.

"In those days, the Puritans often spoke of God's providence, which brought bad things as well as good. Grandpa Benjamin told me it was God's providence that took my father from me so I could grow up in his home and learn about early Andover and the Barkers' role in the events of 1692.

"I became a person of history, a link between his generation and yours, and I received the task of reconciling the Barker, Swan, and Faulkner families. It has been the great mission of my life, and I began to instruct all of you about it as soon as you were old enough to understand.

"Now, God's providence has awakened us to that mission. We must encourage Jon to get on with his plan to marry Nancy Swan."

"Before I left Jon in Maine last year," added Benjamin, "I reminded him of his pledge to marry Nancy. I asked him to move into my house and to court Nancy during my absence. We need to see him again to learn how that is going."

Jonathan added, "I must also help my sons to establish their ownership of the lands they have staked out in Maine. When Abner returned from his visit there he brought a message for me from James Swan. James is concerned that the land near Barker River has yet to be surveyed or assigned to any town. A resolution in the General Court is needed for that to happen.

"He suggests I travel to Caleb Swan's house in Fryeburg with all my sons who have settled in Sudbury Canada or plan to.

"Caleb was educated at Harvard College, so he is capable of preparing the petition. After all the residents or potential residents of the new area have signed it, Caleb will get Fryeburg's representative to the General Court to bring the petition to Boston."

"Then I will certainly go with you to help with the petition and to see Jon," replied Benjamin.

"Abner also told me what James Swan said about you, Benjamin. He wanted me to know that Benjamin is highly respected by everyone in Sudbury Canada. They see that he works very hard, is quick to offer assistance to anyone who asks or needs it, and is very pleasant to all.

"Benjamin has suffered great losses, not only two of his sons, but of his wife, Lydia, whom he loved very deeply. He needs time to grieve and to recover those virtues for which he has been known. Then, he needs to take a new wife and return to his home in Maine."

"Those are kind words and I appreciate your understanding, father. I agree that it is too soon for me to return to Maine permanently, but I will make this trip with you."

Samuel spoke next. "Hannah and I are not yet ready to make a permanent move to Maine. However, I want to be part of this petition, since I believe we will eventually settle there."

Symonds Epes had been waiting for a chance to speak. "I have not seen Jon or Jesse for four years. I believe I will also settle in Maine one day, so I would like to go along on this trip."

"Well, we will have quite a few signatures on our petition. I expect we may find a few others near the Barker River when we arrive."

"I can assure you there will be two or three, in addition to Abner Foster," concluded Benjamin.

Jonathan's sons and daughters applied themselves to the work on their father's farm for the rest of the summer and fall of 1786. During the winter, they planned a spring trip to Maine.

The extended Barker family grew still larger, before the big trip to Maine. Molly and Solomon Jennings' fifth child was born in February 1787. It was their third daughter, following two sons. On March 6th, Samuel's wife,

Hannah, gave birth to a daughter, named Hannah.

In the early spring of 1787, the family worked together to prepare and plant the fields so that they could be tended by Amos, who had just celebrated his 21st birthday, and his younger sisters, Elcy and Abigail.

In early May, they assembled all they needed for the trip by Jonathan, Benjamin, Samuel, Symonds Epes and Abner Foster.

They loaded a large canoe and several backpacks with provisions onto the schooner at the Methuen dock.

In two days, they arrived in Saco and began the trek up the river to Fryeburg. It was the easiest and fastest trip up the river by any of the Barkers, since there were so many strong hands to carry the canoe around the falls and to set up and clear overnight camps.

When they arrived at Caleb Swan's house in Fryeburg, Jonathan greeted him first, introducing himself and thanking him for all the kindness shown to his sons.

"I heard so many fine things about you, Jonathan, and I am happy to finally meet you.

"I agreed to my brother's suggestion to write a petition to the General Court for the settlers at Barker River. Do all of you want your lands formally registered?"

"Yes, that is the purpose of our visit, and I have brought all my sons who plan to settle there. Also with us is Abner Foster, father of two of my sons' wives."

Caleb shook Abner's hand. "I met you some time ago, when you brought a letter from one of your daughters to Benjamin's wife. I was saddened to hear she died."

"It was a shock to all of us", added Jonathan.

"We are all looking forward to a visit to Barker River to see Jon and Jesse. It has been several years since I last saw them."

"I have already prepared the petition, so you can leave for Barker River in the morning and take it with you, and have all the settlers sign it there.

"I have two suggestions for you. You should be the first to sign, and when Jon signs he should use his formal name, Jonathan, adding Jr. to show he is your son. That will be required on all legal documents."

The five men started early the next morning and arrived at Sudbury at sundown. They stayed the night at James Swan's house.

The next day, James and his sons walked the two miles to Barker River with them, laden with provisions for a reunion feast. Jonathan Barker and his six sons would be together there for the first time since before the war. This happy occasion would be enhanced by the presence of James Swan and his sons, Joseph Greeley and James Jr.

Jon and Jesse were working their small fields and saw their siblings, father, and friends coming. They greeted each one with a vigorous handshake. Jesse spoke first.

"I am very surprised to see you here, father, but I am happy you chose to come, and to bring all my brothers. I would not have recognized Symonds Epes – he was but a boy when I saw him last – but, as I look at him more closely Isee that he has our mother's eyes."

"We have come to help all of the Barkers gain ownership to the land they have been working. You probably know that Mr. Swan suggested we get his brother to prepare a petition for the General Court, which he has done. I have it with me and we all need to sign it. We also need the signatures of any other settlers in this area."

"Jon pointed to the north. "There are three others upriver - Nathaniel Spofford, Benjamin Sleeper, and Joseph Jackson. We can get them to sign the petition as well."

All of the Barkers set about preparing the reunion feast. They built a fire to cook the salmon the Swan boys had caught in the Androscoggin and set out blankets. They unpacked the other food they had broght from James' house: Johnny cakes, apples, and cider.

Soon, they were joined by Nancy and Naamah Swan, who had walked separately from Sudbury. Jon and Jesse stepped out to greet and to introduce them to the others. As they all sat to eat, Jesse announced that Naamah had just celebrated her sixteenth birthday. Naamah smiled blushingly; she had grown to the full meaning of her name, 'the beautiful.' Jesse was clearly very fond of her, much as were Nancy and Jon.

After a while, their many conversations and the smell of salmon cooking attracted the other residents, who had cabins further up the river, to join them. After they had eaten, Jonathan retrieved the petition and each of the assemblage signed it. It read:

To the Honourable Senate and House of Representatives in General Court assembled in Boston, May 30th, 1787.

The Petition of Jonathan Barker and others, Honorably Sheweth, that whereas there is certain tract of unappropriated land lying between the mountains northerly of a township granted to Josiah Richardson and others, lying on Androscoggin river and joining to a Grant laid out joining to said township. Said unappropriated land contains eight hundred acres and lyeth on a small river that comes off the mountains and is surrounded with mountains on every side except that end that joins to the Grant aforesaid, so that it cannot be convenient to be joined to any Township except it be that, that was laid out on Androscoggin river as aforesaid, and as your Petitioners are inhabitants of said tract of land and have done much labour thereon for seven years last past they conceives it would be reasonable that they should have a Grant of the same. Your Petitioners therefore prays that your Honors would grant the said tract of unappropriated lands to them, so that they may have a lawful claim to the same, either by way of purchase or some other way, as you in your great wisdom shall see fit and as in duty bound prays your Petitioners.

(Signed)	*Jonathan Barker*	*Jonathan Barker, Jr.*
	Benjamin Barker	*Benjamin Sleeper*
	Samuel Barker	*Joseph Jackson*
	Nathaniel Spofford	*Jesse Barker*
	Abner Foster	*Simon Epes Barker*

Later that afternoon, Jonathan signaled to Jon that he would like to speak privately, and the two walked along the river.

"You have been here several years, Jon. Have you and Nancy set a date for your marriage?"

"I am quite certain it will be next year, father. Nancy and I have talked about it several times, and I must confess I am responsible for the long delay. When Benjamin left and suggested that I move into his house so I could court Nancy privately, I talked to her about it. That bold suggestion caused her to finally erupt about how I had ignored her and simply assumed that she would agree to marry me whenever I wished.

"Only then did I learn what courting really meant. Since then, we have spent many hours talking and walking together so we could get to know each other. She told me after we had done that, she would visit me at Benjamin's house. I am sure this will be the summer she does that. I can't predict when she will be pregnant, but I am confident it will be no later than early next year."

"I am relieved to learn there has been no change in the plan for you two to marry. I understand and believe you are doing well by Nancy. Take your time, but get a message to me as soon as you know when you will come home for the marriage."

"You can count on that, father."

The next morning, Jonathan, Benjamin, Samuel, Symonds Epes and Abner Foster walked the long way to Fryeburg and gave the petition to Caleb Swan. It was presented to the General Court during their next session.

While the Barkers were meeting in Maine, a convention was convening in Philadelphia to draft a constitution for the new country. Most of the states sent representatives and there were many disagreements about what form the government would take. During the war, they had operated under the Articles of Confederation, which loosely bound thirteen independent states in a common cause.

Many believed this would be the foundation for the constitution. This was not the case, however, as a new, federal union, was developed, which would grant major powers to the central government.

Finally, on September 17, 1787, thirty-nine delegates voted to approve the final draft of the new constitution. Adoption of the constitution required approval by nine of the thirteen states. It would be several months before this was achieved. Many of those which at first rejected it agreed to sign when the Bill of Rights was added.

All the Barkers returned to Methuen to see that Amos had tilled and planted several acres of fields. They were growing rapidly as were the weeds. The older brothers got to work to clean, water and otherwise care for the crops.

Lydia's sister, Hannah, was caring for Benjamin's son, Samuel, while he was away or in the fields. They were getting quite attached to one another, which was cause for concern to Benjamin and Jonathan. He reminded Benjamin that Samuel needed a new mother, fairly soon.

This was a problem for Benjamin, who knew he would never love another woman as he had Lydia. He recalled telling his father when he was quite young that he wanted to choose his own wife, and he had done that. He had courted Lydia, attending afternoon meeting in Boxford just to see her each week.

He knew he needed a wife to care for Samuel and bear other sons to work his farm in Maine. He could not put his heart into the search, however. Now he needed his father's help to arrange this marriage.

Jonathan surveyed the families which had intermarried with Barkers in the past, and learned that there was a Stevens girl in Methuen of suitable age. It was Dorcas Stevens, daughter of Joseph Stevens who had recently moved to Methuen from Andover. Jonathan contacted Joseph and made the necessary arrangements. Benjamin courted Dorcas for several days until both were satisfied with the match. They were married in Methuen on December 27, 1787.

CHAPTER TWELVE

A MARRIAGE OF RECONCILIATION

After most of the Barkers returned to Methuen, leaving only Jesse and Jon at Barker River, Jon spent more time in Sudbury with Nancy Swan. They took frequent long walks, talking about everything they remembered from their childhood, through the war, and the pioneering years.

The discussions were good for each of them, as both were normally shy. Jon was able to look into himself and draw out his feelings. All of Jon's simple stories were interesting tales to Nancy and she became more enamored of Jon for revealing them.

As summer turned to fall, Nancy considered Jon's request that she visit his cabin when she felt comfortable about it. Jon himself thwarted her from doing so. Just when she would think about making the walk to Barker River, Jon would appear at her door, so it didn't happen.

As cold weather arrived Nancy took up the idea more seriously. One day in late November, as the snow fell heavily, Nancy packed clothes for several weeks and set out on the six-mile trip to Jon's cabin. When she arrived, there was four inches of snow on the ground. Jon was inside, with a fire going.

Nancy's announcement said it all. "It's time, Jon."

They embraced as Jon replied, "I do believe you are right. Come in, warm yourself by the fire."

Faulkner House

Jon and Nancy spent the winter together, as man and wife. When the thaw began in April, it was clear Nancy was pregnant. It was time to prepare for the trip to Methuen. Jon left Nancy at his house and walked the mile to give James and Mary Swan the news and invite them to make the trip as well.

James and Mary were pleased. Mary spoke.

"You should go, James. The Swan name is part of this reconciliation. You can represent Timothy Swan and his treachery against William Barker better than Nancy or I. Perhaps you can convince Jonathan and Abigail to meet us in Fryeburg when Jesse and Naamah marry this fall."

"Alright then. Give me the evening to pack and say my goodbyes, Jon. We will meet at your cabin in the morning"

Jon walked back to Barker River. He and Nancy packed that evening. Early next morning they all walked to Fryeburg. Part way was clear and dry, but parts were muddy from melting snow.

James Swan was sixty-six and not so agile as Jon and Nancy, especially with the muddy going. At sunset, they camped for the night. At dawn, they cooked eggs and ham on the fire, then continued to Fryeburg. Arriving at Caleb's house in mid-afternoon they banged on his door.

Caleb answered. "What a rare pleasure to have a visit from my brother and his daughter. Is there a purpose for your visit?"

James shook hands with his brother. "Nancy is with child, and we are on our way to Methuen, then Acton for the long-awaited marriage of reconciliation. We would like to impose on your hospitality once more and stay the night, before we start down the river tomorrow"

"You will need one of my canoes. Get it back to me on your return trip."

"That's exactly my plan. I hope more of the Barkers may be with me on the return, to attend the marriage of Naamah to Jesse here in Fryeburg. Naamah insists she must be married in the presence of her godmother, your wife, Dorothy."

"That will be a happy day for all of us. Jesse is a fine young man and, of course, Naamah is our favorite."

The three set out down the Saco River, swollen with melting snow. The torrent made the trip faster than usual.

Sixty-six-year-old James, a life-long sailor, took the fore paddle and deftly guided the canoe past rocks and into the less shallow stream. When they neared the first falls, James directed the vessel to shore and grabbed a low-hanging branch to pull the canoe onto land.

Jon helped Nancy disembark. He and James lifted the canoe out of the water. Jon hoisted the canoe over head and carried it past the falls, where they resumed their journey.

At dusk, they set up camp where many had obviously done so before. Stones were arranged for seating and to enclose a fire. It took some time to gather broken branches for the fire, but then they cooked two trout they had caught along the way. They laid out their blankets and slept until dawn.

This process was repeated smoothly for three days, until they arrived in Saco. After a few hours wait, they boarded a schooner for Methuen.

When they arrived at the Barker homestead, Abigail was excited to see their eldest son, Jon, whom she had not seen in nearly seven years. Jon introduced Nancy to his mother, announced she was pregnant and they wished to wed as soon as the ceremony could be arranged with Francis Faulkner in Acton.

Jonathan smiled broadly, seeing his life-long mission of family reconciliation was finally to be achieved. "I will send a letter to Mr. Faulkner and post it in the morning. We will have to wait for him to tell us the date when he can perform the ceremony."

Abigail's

Jones Tavern

thoughts were closer to her own family. "Too bad you could not have come a bit sooner. Your younger brother, Symonds Epes, married last week to neighbor Olive Morse. She is the younger sister of Hannah's husband, Daniel Morse. It would have been nice to have both marriages at the same time."

Nancy spoke for the first time. "My sister, Naamah, and your son, Jesse, plan to wed this fall in Fryeburg. It is important to Naamah that the ceremony be held there in the presence of her godmother, Dorothy Swan, who was the midwife at her birth. However, she and Jesse, as well as Caleb and Dorothy, hope all of you will come to Fryeburg for that marriage ceremony.

Jonathan watched Abigail for her reaction. He could see she struggled to suppress her excitement at the prospect of visiting the new homes of her sons in Maine, but she looked to her husband for his decision.

"Abigail and I will certainly be there. We will make the trip when most of the harvesting is done. Let me get started on the letter to Francis Faulkner.

"I also need to arrange transportation for all of us. Jon and Nancy can use our small carriage, and they can use it for a honeymoon trip after the wedding. The rest will need to reserve a stagecoach, for there will be several of us: mother and I, Benjamin and Dorcas, Samuel and Hannah, Symonds Epes and Olive and Amos.

"I will have to get Mr. Faulkner's approval for this many to come to his home for the marriage. Oh, and forgive me, I have neglected my friend and Nancy's father, James Swan, in all of this excitement.

"Welcome to our home, and I am sure you will join us on the trip to Acton. I believe the coach holds only eight and one on top with the driver, so one of the people I mentioned will have to ride on my other horse."

Symonds Epes' new wife, Olive, spoke. "Since I am the newest member of this family and know neither Jon nor Nancy, I should stay behind so that the rest of you can go together." After a brief discussion, all agreed with this plan.

Jonathan posted his letter the next morning. One week later he received a reply, setting the date for June 18th. Francis stated his reply was delayed because he wanted to arrange for his cousin, Paul Faulkner Jr. to attend. Paul, he explained, was the son of the brother of Francis' father, Ammi Ruhammah Faulkner. His presence, Francis wrote, would be important to Jonathan, and he would understand why when they all gathered on June 18th.

When the important day arrived, all was prepared. Jonathan harnessed his horse to the small carriage and Jon and Nancy boarded. They headed to the ferry while the others followed on foot.

In Andover, they were met by the stagecoach. The four couples took seats in the carriage and Amos climbed on top with the coachman. They set out towards Acton, following the same road that Jonathan, Jon, and Samuel had taken for part of the way on April 19, 1775. Jonathan told the other passengers what he had experienced that day, at the Battle of Lexington and Concord. The twenty-five mile trip took about an hour and a quarter.

As the carriage and stagecoach drove up the hill to the entrance of the Faulkner mansion, Francis Faulkner emerged to welcome them.

"I must say, this is the largest assemblage for any marriage ceremony I have yet performed. On the other hand, I guess it is deservedly so, for this may be one of the more important ceremonies I have ever conducted, at least for our three families."

Jonathan introduced each of his children, their spouses and Nancy Swan to Francis Faulkner, who welcomed each in turn. As these introductions were made, a man and boy emerged from the mansion, walking down the step to stand beside Francis Faulkner, who introduced them to the assemblage.

"This is my cousin, Paul Faulkner, from Bolton, and his five-year-old son, Lovel. Paul has agreed to meet all of you and to consider arranging the future marriage of Lovell to the next daughter born to one of the pregnant wives here. I see that Nancy is with child. Are there others here?"

"Other than Nancy, only Hannah may soon be with child," answered Samuel.

"Well, with two chances for a girl, we have a fair possibility of developing a match. We shall look to God's providence. Would all of you follow me into the courtroom so that we can proceed with the marriage service?"

All of the Barkers marveled at the fine house they had entered. They were seated in the main room, which was larger than the cabins the boys had built in Maine. It was about twenty feet by eighteen feet.

Once all had assembled, Jon and Nancy stood before Francis as he read the brief legal service from his book.

It was concluded quite quickly for such an auspicious occasion decades in the making.

However, it did not appear so to Jonathan. As he stood behind Nancy and Jon, facing one man – the vision changed to two old men, the original Francis

Faulkner and his grandfather, Benjamin Barker. The two peacemakers were completing their work, healing the wounds between these families cleft ages ago. Francis saw Jonathan's mind drifting, and brought him back to the moment, speaking to Jon.

Francis Faulkner reminded Jon to sign the marriage certificate with his full legal name. Jon was happy to do as instructed.

"I will, and from this time on, I will use my full name, since I will be living apart from my father and have my own family." Francis gave the certificate to Jon and turned to the others.

"I have alerted the innkeeper at Jones Tavern across the road to have a noon repast prepared for us. If you will follow me, I will lead you there, where I can continue my discussion with Jonathan and my cousin Paul."

It was a short walk down the hill and across the road to the tavern. They entered and took seats, except Francis, who pulled Jonathan and his cousin aside for a quiet conversation.

"Paul is a man of little means. He has but one grown son to help on his farm, and is unable to support himself, his wife and daughters and his mother, who lives with him. His house there is a simple shack. His one other asset is a piece of land in Andover where he was born, but the house there is idle and decayed; it needs to be torn down.

My hope is that, when one of your granddaughters is of age, and Lovel is accepting of a marriage to her, you can provide some assistance to the couple to build a house for them in Andover, and livestock to begin a farm. Then, at last, there would be a Faulkner-Barker marriage."

"I believe I can pledge the labor of the father of the Barker girl to that marriage as well as one or more of his brothers, so they could build the house. I can provide the cost of the materials and the livestock. I am not sure I will still be alive when that time comes, but I can make sure that all is in place if I am gone."

"Let us join the others and drink to a future Faulkner-Barker marriage."

The festivities continued for an hour. The coachman, who had been invited to join them, reminded Jonathan he had an afternoon schedule to keep, and they should be heading back to Andover.

The party walked back to the Faulkner house together. Jonathan thanked Francis for his important role in this event, which has been a major goal of his life. Francis said his goodbyes to the Barkers and watched nine of them board the coach. Jon and Nancy climbed into the carriage which headed north to the Concord road.

Longfellow House

Jon had promised Nancy she would see all of the places he had seen during the Battles of Lexington and Concord, Bunker Hill, and more.

They visited Concord Bridge where the Acton militiamen had outfought the English Regulars and started them on their retreat to Boston. Nancy's attention was turned to a fine house nearby. "I have never seen such a fine house as that one in Maine or Methuen."

"I believe it is owned by the Merriam family, who are very successful farmers."

They rode through the Concord town center, where Nancy marveled at many more beautiful houses. "I am really impressed with this town. There must be many wealthy people living here."

When they arrived in Lexington, Nancy's excitement grew. "Let's stop here for awhile, Jon. This is such a beautiful town green, with several fine homes around it. I would like to spend some time to drink it all in, as something I will remember."

Buckman Tavern

Jon tied up the carriage at Buckman Tavern and they walked around the green for nearly an hour. Jon had some knowledge of the buildings from things that Major Faulkner told him and his father as they chased the

British to Cambridge. "There is another fine tavern, Munroe, I believe. British General Percy used it when he brought 1,000 reinforcements to counter the offensive of the Minutemen. Across the way is John Hancock's fine house. The British thought they would surprise him there and take them captive, but Paul Revere had warned him and he had left before they arrived."

Nancy could barely contain her joy to be spending time here with her new husband. "What a wonderful scene for this historic place. These two towns are where the war of independence began. They are beautiful in themselves, but the historic importance gives them museum status."

They returned to Buckman Tavern for supper. Nancy felt very privileged to be dining in such sumptuous surroundings. "This dining room is fitting for a governor or royalty. It makes me feel that I am one of them."

Jon checked with the tavern keeper, learning there was a room available for the night. They decided to stay and enjoy more of this luxurious atmosphere.

In the morning, they had breakfast and continued their journey east through Menotomy (which later became Arlington) and then into Cambridge. Nancy was further impressed as they rode past the mansion which served as George Washington's headquarters during the Siege of Boston in 1775. It would later be occupied by Henry Wadsworth Longfellow.

Soon, they arrived at Harvard College with its many ivy-covered brick walls. They rode along the Charles River to Dorchester Heights, where thirty canon had been mounted in one night, facing Boston and forcing the English to leave on March 17, 1776. They continued on Dorchester Neck into Boston. They visited the Old South Church and the State House, where many important meetings had taken place. It was here John Adams defended the English officer charged with the murder of civilians at the Boston Massacre. Here also, were meetings of Massachusetts legislators who voted to protest to the king about unfair taxes, and of their attack on militiamen at Lexington and Concord, who took only a defensive position.

Jon drove his carriage to the wharf and stopped, pointing out towards the harbor.

"When I was but fourteen years old, I crewed on your father's schooner, along with your brother, Joseph Greeley. We would travel out the Merrimack River from Methuen and down the coast to this harbor, where we would load goods ordered by Methuen businesses.

"On one of those trips, a British officer stopped us and put us on his ship, to force us into service. Joseph and I over-powered his seamen and your father sailed the boat back into the harbor. We returned to our vessel and fled back to Methuen. The next day, you and your whole family fled to Fryeburg."

"Father has told us the story several times, but I remembered little of it from the time. Now I have a picture of the scene to help me remember."

"When we got back to Methuen, and sailed up the coast to Saco, I put you on the canoe to start the trip up the Saco River, you hugged me and said you would marry me when I came to Fryeburg."

"Did I really? I must have been impressed with your size and strength." Nancy chuckled from the teasing way she was responding to Jon.

The next day, they put their carriage on a ferry to cross the Mystic River to Charlestown. Jon pointed out Breed's Hill and Bunker Hill, where he had served with his father and brother Samuel. Jon described the horrible fighting and many who died.

"I must confess to you that I became so afraid of war from just watching that battle, that I vowed to steer clear of the war after that. Samuel was also afraid – he was just fifteen years old. Yet he served for three more years and was right in the middle of the decisive battle at Saratoga. I will always look up to him for his bravery and for his service to his country.

They continued up Charlestown Neck to North Cambridge. They passed Winter Hill where he had camped during the Siege of Boston and later, where Burgoyne's troops had been encamped and guarded by his father's company. They continued north through the town of Medford, then east through Malden and Lynn. They then turned north towards Marblehead.

On the way, Jon explained how more than two hundred Marblehead seamen had brought their small vessels down to New York and rescued 3,000 of General Washington's troops cornered on Long Island. All of this in one night, while the British slept. They awoke to find the Americans gone. When Jon and Nancy reached Marblehead Harbor, they saw dozens of fishing vessels docked there. "Jon, this scene will stay with me and help me understand the enormity of what those fishermen did during the war."

A more important reason for this visit to Marblehead was that it was the birthplace of Jon's grandmother, Mary Abbott. Her grandfather was John Devereaux, the wealthiest man in Marblehead. He owned a large tract of land along the beach, which Jon hoped to find. They were able to find a park next to the beach and a sign for "Seaside Park, given to the town by John Devereaux".

Jon and Nancy left Marblehead and drove a short distance up the road to Salem, the earliest city in Massachusetts. There were many impressive houses spaced tightly on its streets, and a fine harbor and wharf.

Jon explained to Nancy, the important fact about Salem was that it was the Essex County seat, where the jail and courthouse stood. All the innocent people from Andover charged with witchcraft were incarcerated here. "William Barker and his son, William Jr., plus his cousin, Mary Barker, whom William Jr. later married – all of them were imprisoned here."

"Were any of them tried here?"

"No. Had they been, they would have been hanged, for very few were found innocent after trial. Abigail Dane Faulkner was found guilty, but her pregnancy saved her. By the time her son was born, the governor had called a halt to all executions. Abigail was Francis Faulkner's grandmother, and the boy who saved her was Ammi Ruhammah, Francis' father. He never forgave the Barkers, since it was William Barker's testimony which convicted her."

"What happened between the Swans and Barkers?"

"Timothy Swan was dying from an unknown illness. The foolish girls from Danvers named several who were torturing Timothy with pins in a poppet. William was one of those they named. The authorities were then able to get William to testify against others to save himself."

"Now I remember. My father has always been pained by it. He said Timothy Swan's charge of witchcraft against William Barker was the cause of the enmity between the Faulkners and the Barkers. If Timothy had never named William Barker, Barker would not have named Abigail Faulkner."

"None of the Barkers ever felt that way, because Timothy did not actually charge William Barker. It was one of those silly girls from Danvers who said she saw William's specter sticking a pin in Timothy's poppet. They then put Timothy Swan's name down as William's accuser. Timothy was in great pain and dying. Father didn't believe he ever accused anyone."

Jon and Nancy stayed in a tavern in Salem that night, where they had a fine supper. The next day, they headed up the road to Ipswich. They were surprised to see so many fine homes, but of a much earlier period than most of the ones in Concord , Lexington, or even Salem. Here the homes were all sided with unpainted wood clapboards and leaded windows, like the ones they had seen in pictures of England. Jon studied several of the buildings.

"I can see evidence of the early wealth in this town.

"John Winthrop, Jr., Simon Bradstreet, Daniel Epes, William Symonds, and Governor Dudley all lived here before Andover was begun. They had education and wealth, unlike the founders of Andover.

"The plans for Andover came from people in this town, so there is a connection. There is another important one. The grandson of Daniel Epes and William Symonds was Symonds Epes, who befriended my great grandfather, Benjamin Barker, when they both served in the General Court in 1725. For this reason, my father named my younger brother Symonds Epes Barker.

They headed west along the Ipswich River to Topsfield. Nancy noticed an impressive house off to her side of the carriage. "Look at that house, Jon. It's quite impressive, sitting at the top of that little hill. It looks quite old, like one or two we saw in Ipswich and Salem."

"I believe it was Parson Capen's house; you are right – it is quite old, built before the witch hysteria."

They continued west to Boxford. On the common stood the twin chimneyed house built for Thomas Symmes in 1702. He was the first pastor there and a relative of the pastor of Andover's South Parish.

They continued northwesterly to West Boxford, passing the old cemetery, where Richard Barker's first son, John is buried. Richard was probably the first settler of Boxford, in 1639. His son, John was likely born here, before Richard and his wife moved further west to Andover.

As they continued on the road to Andover, they saw a small saltbox colonial, built by John Faulkner soon after the witch hysteria. Now they were passing Andover's First Parish Meetinghouse and the old cemetery, where most of the early Barker's are buried. They stopped there to sense the history of their forbears, perhaps for the last time in their lives.

"Sitting in this place brings back the stories my father repeated and that he first heard at the feet of his grandfather Benjamin. It gives me a chill, as I can almost see him as a little boy, hearing of our family's early history."

"This whole trip will provide wonderful memories for the rest of my life. Thank you, Jon, for taking me to these historic places. When our children are growing up, you and I can tell them about them and the history you have lived through there."

They continued up Osgood Street, past the oldest farm in Massachusetts, first tilled, seeded and harvested by William Barker, and now by his descendant, John Barker.

"Do you remember when you and I walked here during stops between ferry trips when you were a little girl? I often visited my cousin and friend, John Barker. He was a hero at the Battle of Bunker Hill. I watched him carry Lt. Isaac Abbott down the hill to safety."

"I'm sorry, Jon, I do not. I was just too young to remember."

They boarded the ferry and crossed the Merrimack River to Methuen and were very soon at the Barker homestead.

It was a warm sunny day and the extended family were congregating in front of the house. All welcomed the newlyweds and asked about their journey. Nancy excitedly reported all they had seen and that it had been such a great education for her.

Her father, James, smiled broadly at his daughter's enthusiasm, pleased she could, at last, have seen some of what he had experienced earlier in his life as a Methuen seaman.

Since Nancy was due in the fall, she and Jon decided to head back to Maine soon. Her father, James, also encouraged them in this decision. Before leaving, however, James took them back to Swan's Tavern to visit with relatives.

They then began their journey to Maine from the ferry dock nearby.

The remaining members of the extended family were larger than had ever assembled for several weeks at one place before.

There were not enough rooms to allow privacy to the four married couples plus twenty-two-year-old Amos and teen-agers, Abigail and Elcy. Olive took her new husband, Symonds Epes next door to the Morse farm, where her brother, Daniel, lived with his wife, Hannah, the sister of Symonds Epes. Benjamin and Dorcas stayed at the small house Samuel had built earlier on his father's farm. Samuel and Hannah spent most nights at the Foster home in Boxford.

The Barker farm was worked during the day by Jonathan, Benjamin and the three unmarried children. They were often assisted by Samuel and Symonds Epes, who would on most days arrive late in the morning.

Summer passed quickly, happily, and effortlessly, with so many hands to

help. As harvest season approached, they planned the trip to Fryeburg for Jesse's marriage to Naamah Swan.

It was clear that Samuel's wife, Hannah, was pregnant, so they decided not to make the trip. Symonds Epes decided not to go, as he was not planning to undertake a pioneering effort in Maine with his new bride – at least not for a year or two. He and Olive could live in the small house Samuel built on his father's farm, after Benjamin and Dorcas left for Maine.

Early in October, Jonathan, Abigail, Benjamin, Dorcas, and Benjamin's six-year-old son, Samuel, loaded a canoe on a schooner at Swan's Ferry and headed for Fryeburg. The trip went smoothly, and they soon arrived at Caleb Swan's house in Fryeburg. After a day of rest, Benjamin set out alone on the trek to Barker River to bring word to Jesse and Naamah that Jonathan and Abigail were waiting in Fryeburg for them to come and be married there. A few days later, he returned to Fryeburg with Jesse, Naamah, and Naamah's parents, James and Mary Swan.

On October 21, 1788, Jesse and Naamah were married by Fryeburg's Justice of the Peace. Caleb and Dorothy Swan were witnesses. Parents of both the bride and groom were present, as well as Jesse's brother, Benjamin and his wife, Dorcas.

Abigail would have liked to travel to Barker River to help with the birth of Nancy's first child. However, she was cautioned about the oncoming winter and the difficult travel back to Fryeburg in an early snow.

Jonathan celebrated his sixtieth birthday two days after Jesse's marriage, and he was beginning to feel his age. The three-day canoe trip down the Saco River would be tough enough for Jonathan, without adding severe cold and snow to the problem.

They took a small canoe, to allow an easier transit around the three falls. Jonathan was able to complete the journey with Abigail, albeit with great exertion. When they arrived back at their farm in Methuen, they knew they would not be able to travel to Maine again and that they would see their Maine children and grandchildren only when they visited Methuen. It was a bittersweet experience for Abigail and Jonathan. Their life's work was nearing completion, and their energy was depleted.

CHAPTER THIRTEEN

A NEW COUNTRY

When Jonathan and Abigail returned to Methuen, they found Samuel, Symonds Epes, Amos, Abigail and Elcy had completed the harvesting and were making preparations for winter.

Samuel's wife, Hannah, was several months into her pregnancy, and would soon give birth. Thankfully, it would be a girl – to eventually wed Lovel Faulkner – for they would soon learn that Naamah had given birth to a son, William, in November. Dorcas Barker was born to Hannah and Samuel Barker February 27, 1789.

Seventeen eighty-eight was a busy and important year for the Barker family, and it had been important to the new nation. On July 2, 1788, the President of the Congress announced the new Constitution was in effect, having been ratified by the required nine of thirteen states.

On December 15th, polls were set up for all white male adults to vote for presidential electors. Unlike most states, Massachusetts did not limit voting to property owners, so Jonathan and three of his sons voted the next month. Polls closed on January 10, 1789.

On February 4th, electors from all states which had ratified the constitution met in New York City to vote for president. On April 6th, those ballots were counted and it was announced that George Washington was the unanimous

Samuel Phillips, Jr.

choice of the electors, receiving 69 votes. John Adams was vice president with 34 votes. On April 30th, Washington was sworn in as president, on the balcony of New York's Federal Hall, the temporary capitol.

The Massachusetts General Court never acted on the Barker petition of 1797. However, a few years later, the land they had developed, as well as the surrounding area was surveyed. The surveyor ignored the name the Barkers had given to their river, and called it Sunday River. The other nearby stream was named Bear River. The peak, however, would always be known as Barker Mountain.

It was likely that 1789 would be the last year Jonathan Barker would be able to till, plant and harvest a large crop. He had three grown sons and two teen-aged daughters doing the yeoman's work, and some of them would soon depart.

As fall arrived, the family was excited to hear that George Washington would be touring Massachusetts.

A tentative schedule of towns he would visit was distributed by Samuel Phillips Jr. of Andover. Although Washington would not be passing through Methuen, he would visit nearby towns. He would be in Salem on October 30th, heading through Ipswich to Newburyport, Amesbury and Salisbury, before crossing the Merrimack and heading west.

It was not clear whether he would pass through nearby Haverhill, so the Barkers decided to go across the Merrimack River to Andover's South Parish, which was on Samuel Phillips' itinerary for Thursday, November 5th.

The extended Barker family all left their homes at dawn and boarded the first ferry to Andover. They walked towards First Parish Meetinghouse, passing the oldest house, first built for Pastor Thomas Barnard. Jonathan and Abigail paused at this fine house, which evoked memories of 1692 and later.

"I hope posterity will remember him as a man who helped to heal the town

HISTORIC SKETCH OF METHUEN

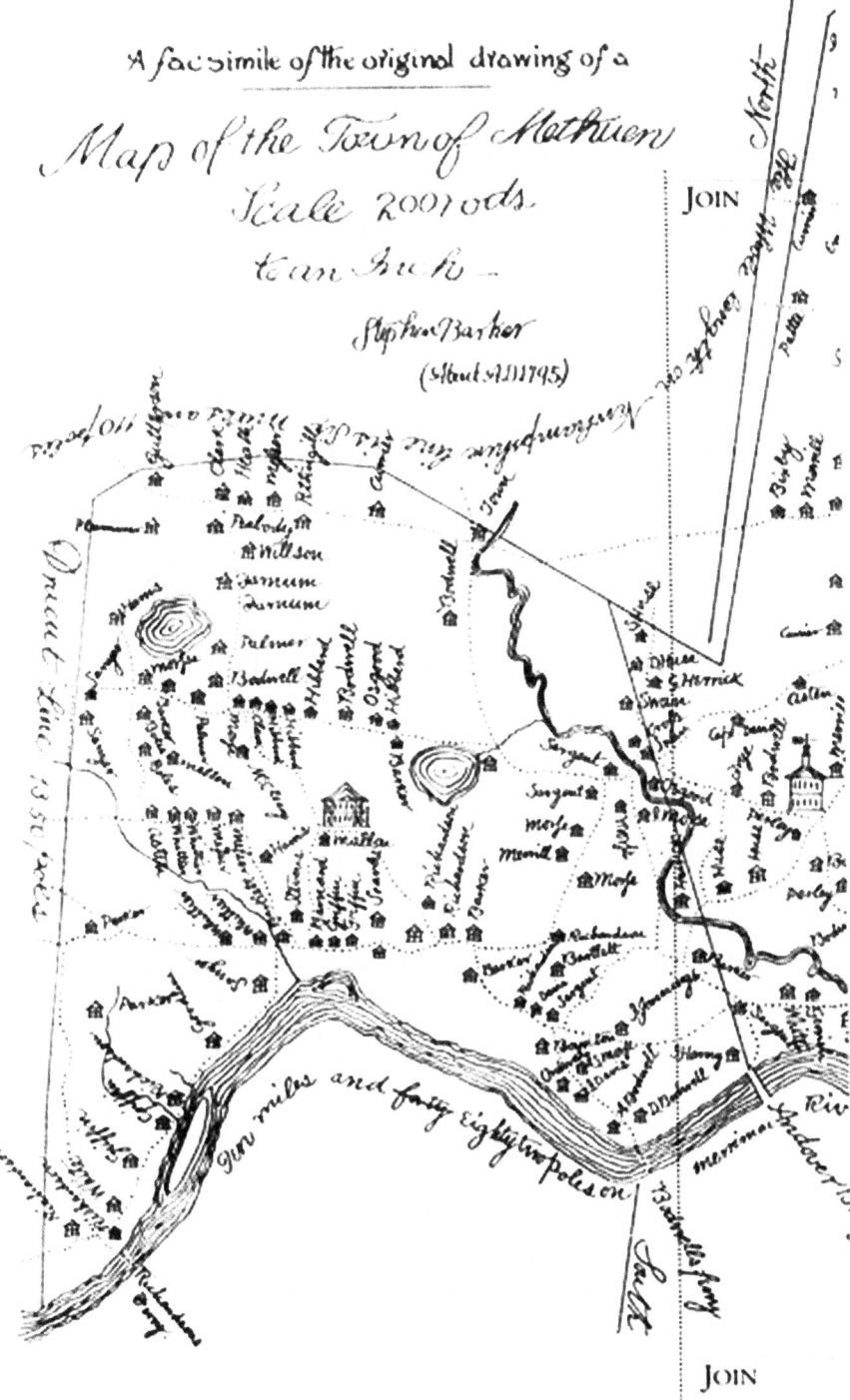

A fac simile of the original drawing of a

Map of the Town of Methuen
Scale 200 rods
to an Inch

Stephen Barker
(About AD 1795)

from the pain of the witchcraft hysteria. Although he was deceived by the devil and led by Cotton Mather to promote false witchcraft charges against many of his flock, he helped end it and worked very hard with Francis Faulkner and Benjamin Barker to bring peace back to Andover. Thomas Barnard was not the lone villain; he could not have succeeded without Richard Barker's support. In fact, he might never have come to Andover, had not Richard Barker turned against Pastor Francis Dane."

They continued past the old burial ground and the Meetinghouse and headed towards South Parish. As they continued on their way, they were joined by dozens of others, who also sought to see President Washington. When they came to the south village, they moved to the side as the president's entourage passed. All of them cheered as the president waved toward them. He stopped at Isaac Abbott's Tavern, where he entered to have a late breakfast.

The Barker family were all together in the crowd across the road. Jonathan noticed his cousin and son's friend, John Barker, near him, got his attention and smiled. Inside the tavern, Washington was seated at a small table and was served by a quickly moving man with an obvious limp. It was Lt. Isaac Abbott, the wounded officer John Barker carried off Breed's Hill in June 1775. Outside and across the road, John Barker stood as just another citizen in the crowd that was unaware of the irony of the scene.

Soon, Washington emerged from the tavern and boarded an open carriage with

Samuel Phillips Jr. which took them to his newly built mansion on School Street. They entered the house for a brief reception arranged by Phillips.

After a short time, the two left the house and mounted horses which they rode across the street to the training field where Phillips Academy students had assembled. President Washington addressed them before heading towards Lexington. Jonathan and his family had moved towards the Academy so they could listen to George Washington's message to the students.

As he watched, Jonathan recalled how his ancestor, Richard Barker, had prevented Old Andover from establishing a school, despite the guidelines of the General Court that suggested every town with 50 or more residents should have one. Richard was opposed to the teaching of the Latin language, which he considered 'the Pope's language'. Knowledge of Latin and Greek were a requirement for entering students at Harvard and Yale. Now, Old Andover had faded in importance, while the South Parish had emerged and became known to outsiders and President Washington as the 'real' Andover.

The crowd dispersed and the Barker family headed home. Jonathan and Abigail reflected on all that they had experienced during their life together. They raised ten children to adulthood. Seven were married with children (Symonds Epes' wife, Olive, had borne her first child, also named Olive, in June). Although all six of their sons had either moved to the mountains of western Maine or were planning to do so, their two eldest daughters, Molly and Hannah, lived on adjacent properties, and had provided nine grandchildren to entertain them at family get-togethers. Molly's second son, Jonathan Barker Jennings, was now eight years old and very proud to be named for his grandfather. He and his older brother, Elijah, worked on their father's farm and took care of their four younger sisters. Hannah's sons, named for her husband, Daniel, and her brother, Jesse, were just three and five years old.

Jonathan had once been the largest property owner in Methuen, with land on both sides of the Spicket River. In his later years, however, he gave much of it away, to Molly's and Hannah's husbands, Solomon Jennings and Daniel Morse. He also set aside land on the east side of the river for his two youngest daughters and his youngest son, Amos, should he choose to stay in Methuen.

In June 1790, Samuel, his wife, Hannah, and their children, Dudley, Hannah, and baby Dorcas, made their long delayed move to Sunday River, Maine. Samuel had been separated from his parents for most of the war, and felt the need to become re-acclimated to farm life in Methuen.

It was time to set out on his own. He and his family vacated the house he had built on his father's property, which became the home of Symonds Epes, his wife, Olive, and baby. Symonds Epes had also planned to move to Maine, but first wanted to take over his father's farm for him.

Prior to Samuel's departure, Jonathan and Abigail planned a large outdoor party with all of their extended family. There were more than twenty family members present, which delighted Jonathan and Abigail. They were kept very busy, taking turns holding the youngest grandchildren and participating in some of the games of the older ones. After Molly and Hannah and their husbands and families returned to their homes, Jonathan spoke to Samuel.

"I doubt your mother and I will be able to visit you in Maine, due to our declining health. We want you to know we will always love and think about you every day. You have been a fine son, serving your new country with distinction and working so hard on our farm. We especially appreciated your remaining here with your wife and new family for a few years, when you could have joined your brothers in Maine.

There is the chance that I may never see you again, after your departure. I must leave you with a reminder of your responsibility to complete the final part of my oath to my grandpa Benjamin, a Barker-Faulkner marriage. Your daughter, Dorcas, is pledged to Lovel Faulkner of Bolton. They must be wed as soon as both are of age. We have the promise of Lovel's father, Paul, made before you and me at Acton and before his cousin, Francis Faulkner."

"Hannah and I have enjoyed our time here. She needed time to mourn her sister's death and rebuild her strength before moving to the frontier in Maine. She appreciated your love and support and will miss you. Of course, I hope that, somehow, we can visit you in the future. If that does not occur, you can pass in peace, being sure the marriage will be completed, for I am committed to your promise to your grandfather just as you were."

As the months and years passed, Jonathan's health declined and he rarely ventured onto his farm. A smaller section was farmed by Symonds Epes, Amos, and the two younger girls, Abigail and Elcy. Soon, Elcy married and moved to her husband's family's farm, leaving only three to work the fields and tend the animals. Jonathan and Abigail encouraged each to wed and care for their own spouses and families.

Jonathan suffered from an unknown malady which caused him great discomfort. In March of 1794 he was confined to his bed, and was cared for by Abigail.

With great effort, he rose and was helped outside to his carriage, which Amos drove to the meetinghouse where Amos married his neighbor and childhood playmate, Dorcas Huse, on March 6, 1794. Jonathan returned to his bed, exhausted. He slept for hours, finally waking at noon the next day. As Abigail fed and nursed him, he became philosophical about all that had occurred during his life.

"Grandpa Benjamin lived a very long life – nearly ninety years. I feel I am approaching the end of mine at just sixty-five. He explained many things according to God's providence and that may explain this. He had yet much to do when his son, my father, died when he was 74. During the next fourteen years, he raised and imbued me with the history he had lived, so I would take up the mission he could not complete. Now I have completed that, my life's purpose is fulfilled and God's providence has left me to chance."

"Jonathan, you cannot leave this life when you and I are now left with only one another for our happiness. I cannot be so without you."

"Abigail, I have never considered happiness something I deserved or expected. It has come as a blessing as I completed my life's tasks."

"And what has the completion of those tasks brought to you, your children, or posterity, or your ancestors? Who among them are aware if it, and what value do they give to it?"

"These questions can only be answered by the Almighty. My mission was only to do, and not to understand why."

"Will you not say you have enjoyed your life with me and that we have shared a love above that shared by most others?"

"That I will certainly do, Abigail, and thank God for our love and the life we have enjoyed together. I especially cherish your love and care as I recall Grandpa Benjamin's last weeks. He was confined to his bed with no wife or children to care for him. I was pleased to put my life on hold and comfort him during his last days. I know you remember that because you ran our farm all by yourself until he died. Two days later we were married."

In late March 1794, Abigail sent letters to her sons in Maine, stating that Jonathan was confined to his bed. She feared he would soon die. Samuel made the trip as soon as the Maine winter allowed, but he arrived to see his father in a very weak state. Samuel sat by his bed for several hours each day until Jonathan spoke his last words, "Remember your promise."

Samuel held his hand, replying, "It is my sacred oath. History will record a Barker-Faulkner marriage in my lifetime, I guarantee it." Jonathan forced a slight smile, showing Samuel that he understood. He then breathed his last. Abigail sat on the other side of the bed and her head slumped onto Jonathan's chest. She wept uncontrollably for a long time until Samuel came around to comfort her. He lifted her by her shoulders, turning her to face him, and then hugged her as she continued to sob.

Finally, Abigail was able to speak. "He deserved a longer life, more restful years to enjoy the fruits of many years of hard work." Samuel nodded empathetically.

"I believe he lived the only life he knew – one of service and dedication. Having finished all he intended, his spirit declined. He never learned how to really enjoy life."

Samuel and Symonds Epes led the effort to bury Jonathan and erect a simple stone at the Methuen cemetery by the Merrimack River, showing the date of his death, April 29, 1794.

CHAPTER FOURTEEN

"A CURSE ON YOU"

Samuel stayed on for two more weeks, to comfort his mother. At first, his efforts were futile. Samuel thought, "What do I say to a mother who has lived for more than forty years with a man she loved so deeply? She had endured pain and sorrow with him but also joy and triumph at their many small successes".

Finally Samuel remembered back to the days when he was barely more than a child, when Jonathan told stories of the witchcraft hysteria in old Andover. They continued as the children grew older and more capable of understanding. These were pleasant memories for Samuel, and he often pictured the scene of Jonathan with Abigail at his side and all of the children seated on the floor around him.

"I'm sure those are pleasant memories for mother. I will get Essy to help me bring them back for mother. That should help to lift her spirit."

He spoke to Essy about this idea and he enthusiastically agreed. They would take turns telling of their personal memories of those days and evenings after supper. Abigail had been very quiet for a few days, unhappily reflecting on Jonathan's last days.

Samuel began, "Essy, do you remember those days and nights when father would gather us around him on the floor and tell those stories of the witchcraft hysteria in old Andover?" Abigail perked up and looked to Essy for his response.

"I was very young when he started, so I didn't follow the discussion for two or three years. But I remember the first gatherings vividly, because it was nice to be included with my older brothers and sisters. It is one of the nicest memories I have."

"Abigail smiled knowingly. "Do you remember those days, Amos?"

"At the beginning, I was just a baby, but my earliest memory is of being held by Molly as the whole family sat on the floor around father and you. I feel warm inside every time I think of it."

Samuel continued, "As the years passed, we grew older and more understanding of the complexities of those stories. Each year, we all looked forward to doing it again, hearing the stories repeated, or new parts added. Those were wonderful days and evenings. They will bring pleasure to me each time I think of them, throughout my life."

Abigail put one arm around Samuel. "You are such a good son. Thank you for lifting my spirit."

"I am enjoying these recollections as much as you, mother. There were other family discussions which were more important to me than most of my brothers and sisters. They were the times we sat together and read the booklets written by Thomas Paine. One was 'Common Sense' and the other, 'The Crisis.' What Mr. Paine wrote gave me my strong commitment to the revolution."

"I remember that all too well, Samuel. After Bunker Hill, I was hoping my boys would stay home for awhile, but you left while your father was away. You kept quoting from the booklet that referred to 'summer patriots' and 'sunshine soldiers,' saying you would not be one of those. I had great fear of losing you, until Jonathan returned to comfort me."

"I'm sorry to have caused you much distress, mother. Let's talk of the other family discussions – about the issues that led up to the war. I recall the event they now call 'the Boston Massacre' where British soldiers killed several men in Boston. At the supper table, Molly and Hannah argued in support of the British soldiers, saying the local men were just young ruffians who were throwing things at the soldiers and daring them to shoot. Jon and Benjamin argued more forcefully that there was no need for the British soldiers to be in Boston at all. Their mere presence was a strong provocation. I was just ten years old, but those discussions stayed and helped inspire me later to enlist."

Essy added, "I was just six years old, so I barely remember that discussion. But I recall clearly you and Jon and father marching off to Lexington and Concord. I remember as clearly the Battle of Bunker Hill because we could hear the sounds of canon and thousands of muskets firing all the way to Methuen. We all huddled around mother and prayed for your safe return."

"I was so relieved that Jonathan promised not to serve in any more battles. He enlisted in a regiment of guards, which was not a dangerous assignment". Abigail had calmly involved herself in the discussion, forgetting for the moment her grief at Jonathan's passing. Samuel continued.

"One of the happiest discussions our family had was when father brought home a copy of the Declaration of Independence. As we took turns reading from it, my spine tingled with pride, especially when we read the part that included – 'all men are created equal.' We all felt a special connection to that, since our ancestor, William Barker, had made a similar statement as part as his confession of witchcraft. He was a man ahead of his time. To the Puritans, those sentiments were evidence that the devil had taken over an otherwise good person.

Abigail nodded as they all recalled that family discussion. "I will enjoy the company of my three sons for a few more days, before Samuel and Essy return to Maine. Thank you for your love and support."

Symonds Epes spoke for the three sons, "We can never return the full measure of love and support you and father provided each of us. We can only try, especially now you are in greater need of it."

The remaining days of Samuel's visit passed quickly. It served its purpose of reorienting Abigail's thoughts to her children and away from her departed husband. Her daughters and their children were still visiting regularly, and Amos was close by.

On the eve of Samuel's departure, he spoke seriously to Abigail. "Mother, I will try to visit you again in two or three years. However, I know I will return when my daughter, Dorcas, weds Lovel Faulkner, as I promised dad. Father would want you to be at that wedding as much as I do. Please try to keep fit so we can all celebrate that day together."

"We must look to Providence and accept what He brings. If it were not so far away, I would be in excited anticipation, but my body tells me it has not the strength to endure so long."

"I will pray I may see your smiling face that day, mother."

Samuel embarked on his journey to Maine, and Abigail settled back to a quieter life. Symonds Epes and Amos continued to farm a small part of their deceased father's property with some help from his wife. They enjoyed meals together so that Abigail was seldom alone. On weekends, the house was full with visits from Molly, Hannah and their many children. In January 1795, Molly gave birth to her ninth child, whom she named Dorcas Huse Jennings, after the wife of her brother, Amos, whom she had helped to raise.

Symonds Epes and his wife, Olive's family was growing. In June 1797, their third child was born in Methuen. Olive had been pressing Essy about his plan to move to Maine. She said they should leave soon or else they would remain in Methuen permanently. Essy agreed to leave as soon as this child was born. They embarked on their journey when Lydia was just four weeks old. It was a very difficult trip for Olive, with a newborn baby plus two young girls, eight and five years old. She was exhausted when they reached Fryeburg on July 14th, where they rested just one night. The next day, they began the two day trek on foot to Bethel. As they reached the homes of Benjamin and Jon, Olive collapsed. Essy carried her into Ben's house and tried to nurse her, to little avail. After an uneasy night, she died the next morning.

In April 1800, Abigail was thrilled to receive a visit from her son, Benjamin and his wife, Dorcas Stevens Barker, their two sons 18-year-old Samuel, and 10-year-old Joseph Stevens. They stayed two weeks, delighting Abigail with stories about Jesse, his wife, Naamah, and their six daughters. They also spoke about Jon and Nancy, their five sons and daughter. They were blessed with more sons than any of the other Barker children, yet Jon's farm was not so successful as Benjamin's. Ben joked that Jon was never a very hard worker, and the Maine soil gave no allowance for such farmers.

When Abigail was in a good mood, Benjamin told her of Symonds Epes' travails. After Olive's death, Essy married Borough Bartlett, the daughter of another settler. After less than a year of marriage, she died, again leaving Essy alone with three young daughters. He married for a third time just this past November to Sally Barker, whose ancestors were from a different Barker line.

Benjamin's visit would pass all too quickly for Abigail. Molly and Hannah did their best to keep their mother from being lonely with almost daily visits with their youngest children. Molly's nineteen-year-old son, Jonathan Barker and seventeen-year-old daughter, Elizabeth, also visited on their own at least twice each week. Abigail was particularly proud of the grandson named for her husband, now that he was a young man. He became like another son to Abigail. Hannah's teenage sons, Daniel and Jesse, also visited regularly. Besides all of these, Molly and Hannah's entire families came at least one Sunday each month for a large gathering. They were joined by Amos and his wife, daughters Abigail and Elcy and their husbands. Abigail had little time alone to be sorrowful at her husband's early passing.

The years went by rather quickly for Abigail. In April 1804, on the tenth anniversary of Jonathan's death, Abigail asked Molly to accompany her to the cemetery to place flowers on his grave. She asked Molly to give her some time alone at the grave to visit with him. Molly could hear Abigail as she spoke softly to her husband, as if he were there to hear her. It was a peaceful visit, comforting to Abigail. She had long since passed the sobbing and sorrowful remembrance of her dear husband. Now, it was as if she was longing to join him in a quiet place where they could rest together.

In February 1806, Abigail suffered a stroke. She was partially paralyzed and unable to rise from her bed. Molly wrote to all of her siblings in Maine to tell them of their mother's condition. Maine winters were generally harsh, but Samuel felt the need to make the hazardous journey to see his mother one last time before her passing. He arrived the day after her death on February 15, 1806. As he had done with his father, he made arrangements for the funeral and burial.

There was another reason Samuel made the winter trip to Methuen. His daughter, Dorcas, had just celebrated her seventeenth birthday. It was time for Samuel to help Lovel Faulkner build a house on Lovel's land in Andover, where the two could live after their marriage in the coming year. He packed a lunch and set out on the twenty mile walk to the Bolton farm of Paul Faulkner and his son, Lovel.

Samuel found the Faulkner farm, but was troubled to see it in disarray. Very little of the land showed signs of the previous fall's harvest and there was no sign of pigs, goats or cows. He saw just a few chickens, no more. He knocked on the door of the house. Two women came to the door.

Samuel announced, "I am Samuel Barker of Methuen. Francis Faulkner, introduced me to Paul Faulkner at the marriage of my brother, Jonathan Barker in Acton eighteen years ago. At that time Paul pledged his son, Lovel, to wed my daughter, who was not yet born. I have come to plan to deliver the dowry for that marriage, by building a house for Lovel and my daughter, Dorcas on Faulkner property in Andover."

The women appeared flustered and their faces filled with a deep red blush.

"We are daughters of Paul Faulkner. I am Betty and this is my sister, Releaf. We are alone here. Lovel and our father are living in Andover now."

A frown grew on Samuel's brow. Many questions rotated in his mind, but he did not feel he could ask them of these strangers. He decided on just a basic request.

"Can you tell me how I can find them in Andover?"

They looked at each other for a moment with nervous embarrassment. "You will find them at the house of Mr. George Abbott there," replied Betty.

The women nervously backed away from the door, wanting to reveal no more. Samuel took their cue, and turned and left. He began the long walk home, but was at least comforted by the knowledge that Andover was on the way to his destination in Methuen.

This had been a very troubling and confusing experience. Samuel wondered about these two marriageable aged sisters of Lovel Faulkner. Why and how were they living alone on Paul Faulkner's farm? Was their obvious embarrassment due to their own circumstance or was there more bad news awaiting him in Andover? Why were Paul Faulkner and his son, Lovel, living in Andover? He knew Paul Faulkner had been warned out of Bolton and would have to return to Andover one day unless his fortunes increased, and they had obviously not done so. And who was George Abbott and why were the Faulkners living in his house? Had Abbott hired the Faulkners to work his farm to get back on their feet? Whatever the explanation, Samuel prayed that the marriage of his daughter to Lovel Faulkner could still take place within a year.

When he entered Andover's south parish area, he stopped at Lt. Isaac Abbot's Tavern for a quick supper. The proprietor was able to give Samuel directions to George Abbot's house. It was dusk as he walked the short distance to his destination. He knocked on the door and was greeted by a gentleman, asking Samuel's business.

"I am Samuel Barker of Methuen. I have come to see Paul Faulkner and his son, Lovel, who I understand now live here with you."

"Wait here and I will get Paul Faulkner for you."

As Paul approached him, Samuel spoke. "I am Samuel Barker of Bethel, Maine, formerly of Methuen. I hope that you remember me. Sixteen years ago, your cousin, Francis Faulkner of Acton, introduced us at my brother's marriage there. At that time, you pledged your son, Lovel, in marriage to my daughter, Dorcas, who was born a few months later."

"That was long ago. I have had a very difficult life these past few years. I fell into debt which I was unable to repay, and I had no money to buy seed for the farm. Last year, I traveled to Andover to apply for admission to the almshouse, because Bolton had notified me they would not be responsible for me. While I was at Andover, they introduced me to Mr. George Abbott. That man told me that he had a daughter of marriageable age, for whom he was seeking a husband. He offered to pay my debts and more if my son married his daughter. Lovel married his daughter last May, in Andover. This is my son, Lovel, and his wife, Martha."

Samuel was irate. "A curse on you, Paul Faulkner. You have abrogated your responsibility by reneging on your sacred oath. And a curse on your marriage, Lovel Faulkner. It was born in treachery and will achieve no good."

Paul and his son, Lovel, spoke almost in unison. "We are sorry. We had no choice."

Samuel turned on his heels and left quickly. He walked to the north Parish meeting house and camped on the green there. The last ferry to Methuen had already left. Samuel was unable to quiet the anger he had expressed to Paul and Lovel Faulkner. It was mixed with fear and desperation. He had made a promise to his father on his deathbed that there would be a Barker-Faulkner marriage in his lifetime. He was confident all was arranged for that marriage and now it was impossible. What could he do? Was there another young Faulkner available to wed his daughter? He spent a fitful night, unable to sleep.

He took the first ferry the next morning. Arriving at Methuen, Samuel told Molly and Hannah the distressing news. They were shocked and saddened by this turn of events. He also told his sisters about the curses he had pronounced on Paul Faulkner and his son, Lovel.

"Perhaps providence will act on those curses and free Lovel to marry my Dorcas. I don't particularly blame him for marrying Martha Abbott. He was only five years old when his father pledged him to my first daughter."

Samuel stayed in Methuen until a mid-March thaw promised an easier journey back to Bethel, Maine. When he arrived at his home there, he told his daughter, Dorcas, that her marriage would have to wait for new developments. He turned his attention to his own farm, working on it harder than he had done before. He also enlisted full effort from his three teen-aged daughters and twelve-year-old son, Samuel. All of them ardently contributed to the family effort. They were happy to have their father concentrating on the family farm, without the regular trips back to Methuen.

Samuel Barker's farm prospered for the next five years, as the children grew in age, size and capability. Finally, on June 1, 1811, a letter arrived from Lovel Faulkner.

Dear Mr. Barker,

The almighty has acted on the curses you pronounced on me and my father. After five years of marriage, my wife, Martha, finally gave birth to a baby boy on March 31, 1810. Martha suffered severe loss of blood during the birth and became bedridden and weak. She never recovered her strength and died August 19th last year.

Without Martha, we lost the support of her father. My father moved to the Andover almshouse. I just received a note from the almshouse telling me he died May 23rd.

I am now in desperate circumstances and have no right to ask anything of you. Most would not consider me an appropriate spouse for their daughter. Because of your pledge to your father, I am hoping you might accept me as your son-in-law. If you will help me build a house on my land in Frye's Mill, Andover, I promise you I will work very hard to be a successful farmer there. More than that, I promise to love your daughter as no other could.

Your humble servant,

Lovel Faulkner

Samuel's heart pounded as he read. His spirit surged between exhilaration, doubt, and indecisiveness at the decision thrust upon him. He put the letter in his pocket and tried to turn his mind to other things – to no avail. As he prepared to retire, he showed the letter to Hannah and asked what she would suggest.

"You will never forgive yourself if you fail to fulfill your pledge to your father. If you are concerned about what Dorcas wants, there is a simple solution. Take her to Andover to meet Lovel Faulkner. Give her some time to know him and let her decide. Show her the letter in the morning and ask if she will go with you to meet this young man."

"If we go, we may be there for some time. If Dorcas agrees to marry Lovel, I need to build their house in Andover right away. This will be a good test to see how hard he works on his own house, at my direction."

Dorcas did not hesitate to agree to her mother's suggestion. She was anxious to make the trip to Andover to meet Lovel Faulkner. She also looked forward to meeting her cousins in Methuen.

Samuel quickly penned a short letter to Lovel, explaining his and Dorcas' plan to meet him. He asked that Lovel give Dorcas a few days after their arrival to decide to accept him or not. He instructed him to go to the old Barker farm in Methuen, where he would find Hannah and Daniel Morse, his sister and brother-in-law. Samuel wrote he would start soon, and arrive shortly after his letter. He also wrote Molly, asking her to provide a bed for Lovel, and himself for a few days, as well as one for Dorcas for a few weeks. Samuel planned to camp at the house-site with Lovel as soon as Dorcas made her decision – until the house was completed. These plans, of course, would change if Dorcas decided not to marry Lovel. Dorcas' enthusiasm encouraged him to believe all would turn out well.

As Samuel and his daughter prepared for their trip, he worried things might not go well. What if Lovel turned out to be ugly and disagreeable? His letter suggested otherwise, but it could be disguising the true Lovel Faulkner. Samuel put these thoughts out of his mind and set himself to the tasks at hand. He, Dorcas, and Hannah had to decide what they needed to bring on the trip. They had to decide whether they could walk the thirty miles to Fryeburg, carrying all they needed, or to use Samuel's horse and count on one of Caleb Swan's sons to loan them a canoe. Hannah encouraged them to take the horse and leave it with Caleb's sons until Samuel returned, a few weeks later.

The day before they left, Hannah spoke for a long time with Dorcas, who was very excited about the trip. Hannah told Dorcas she would be staying in the house in which her father was born and grew up. It was also where Hannah and Samuel first met as adults, at a party celebrating his return from the war.

She told Dorcas about her brazen gesture of taking Samuel by the hand to engage him in conversation about his war experiences. Both of them laughed and blushed about this precocious move for a young woman.

After just a day of preparation, they both mounted the horse, laden with saddlebags. They left very early in the morning and arrived at the Swan's house before noon. Joseph Frye Swan happily agreed to accompany them down the Saco River in his canoe. When they arrived at Saco three days later, they were fortunate to find a schooner preparing to depart for Haverhill. Samuel arranged passage and they were soon underway.

In Haverhill, they had the task of carrying their luggage for three miles to the Barker farm on the west side of the Spicket River. This was particularly stressful after the long journey, but they were able to accomplish it, stopping several times to rest.

As they approached the Barker farm, they were greeted by Samuel's sister, Hannah, and her husband, Daniel. Samuel introduced Dorcas to them and they all walked to the house. Just inside the front door stood a handsome young man of slender build and a ruddy complexion. Hannah introduced him. "This is Lovel Faulkner. Lovel, I believe you have met my brother, Samuel, and this is his daughter, Dorcas."

Lovel shook Samuel's hand. "I am very pleased to meet you again, sir. Thank you for coming and bringing your daughter."

Dorcas stepped forward and offered her hand. Lovel hesitatingly shook her hand softly. "I am especially pleased to meet you, Miss Barker."

Dorcas held onto his hand and turned slightly, slipping her arm under his. "Come, walk with me, Lovel."

She led him out the door and down the path alongside the Spicket River. "Do you remember meeting my father the day my uncle was married at Colonel Faulkner's house in Acton?"

"I remember just two things about that day. One was the long walk from Bolton and how my father kept pushing me to walk faster. The other was Colonel Faulkner's house, which seemed like a mansion to me. We were so poor I couldn't imagine how we could have such a rich and important cousin."

Dorcas continued to engage Lovel in conversation as they walked to the Merrimack River and back to the Barker farm. As they neared the house, Dorcas surprised Lovel. "Shall we go to the Town Hall tomorrow to register our intentions to be wed?"

Lovel broke into a broad smile. "Nothing would please me more."

Dorcas cautioned that they could still change their minds in the next month or two, but assumed they would not. The two said nothing about this plan until the next morning when they left for the Methuen town hall.

The initial meeting had gone well. Dorcas was feeling comfortable about the prospect of marrying Lovel. Samuel cautioned his daughter to take her time. "Let us begin construction of the house in Andover and see how we get along there. You can come with us and watch. You can also prepare some food for our noon meal and eat with us."

That afternoon they walked to Frye's Mill in Andover and found the Faulkner land. They also ordered lumber they needed to begin construction. The next day they returned with Daniel Morse, Jr., Hannah and Daniel's son. He was a tall and muscular young man, who would be a great help in the work. Both Lovel and Dorcas bonded quickly with their cousin.

As the work progressed, the house was soon weather-proof, so that they could sleep there over-night. When the fireplace was completed and working properly, Samuel felt it was time for him to get back to his family and farm in Maine. Now was when he should give his final advice to Dorcas.

"My father always suggested we should choose our mate but wait until the wife was pregnant before formalizing the marriage. If you feel comfortable with that arrangement, I could leave you with Lovel here. You could take your time and wait for a romantic moment to consummate your relationship. If that moment never comes, you could return to your home in Maine."

"You needn't be concerned, father. I am feeling very close to Lovel now, so that tender moment could come very soon. I do not believe there is any likelihood of my returning to Maine alone."

Samuel returned to Maine and Dorcas and Lovel began living as man and wife. By January it was clear she was pregnant, and Dorcas happily wrote to her parents, announcing their plans to formalize the marriage on March 5, 1812. Their first child was a boy, and Dorcas insisted they name him Lovel. Barely nine months later they had a daughter, Mary, and a year after that, in July 1814, their second son was born. They named him Daniel, after Hannah's son who had helped them so much building their house and had continued to help them to start their farm.

In April 1816, Dorcas wrote an important letter to her parents.

Dear Father and Mother,

Lovel and I welcomed our third son March 25, 1816. We named him Samuel Foster, in honor of both of his grandparents. I want you both to know how happy I am to be your daughter and to have been the instrument to achieve the Faulkner-Barker reconciliation that my father and his father Jonathan and his grandfather Benjamin before them committed their life to achieving.

In Maine, I learned that the town of Lovel was named to honor a famous Indian fighter named Lovewell, so my Lovel is also shortened from Lovewell. He is very aptly named, for he loves me well, as he does his children. He also loves his Barker cousins as I love my Faulkner cousins. Each day, I realize that this Faulkner-Barker marriage is not simply a symbol of reconciliation. It has brought love between the two families, to replace the enmity that remained after the wrong done on Abigail Dane Faulkner by William Barker and his father, Richard Barker.

Lovel has been working very hard to be a good farmer. He works mostly by himself, spending long hours in the field and in the barn. I am little help to him, having to care for three young children. Lovel, Jr. is now five years old and is beginning to help a bit by collecting eggs each morning and feeding the chickens. We hope he will soon be able to milk the cow, to relieve his father of one more task. As our children grow, so should the production of our farm and our well-being.

My happiness has been dulled as we have not seen the sun during the last few days. It is as if a pall has been draped across the sky, denying us of the sun's warmth. I hope it will be lifted soon, so that we can have a good growing season.

Your loving daughter,
Dorcas

Dorcas Barker Faulkner died December 7, 1829 when her seventh child was born. She was just forty years old.

EPILOGUE

1816 was 'the year without a summer,' caused by a massive volcano eruption in Indonesia. The dust blanketed New England from May to September, causing heavy frost in May, snow and freezing rivers in July and August. Needless to say, there were no crops harvested in Maine and few in Massachusetts that year. Many were impoverished as a result.

Marriages were the primary means of reconciliation in the town of Andover, where nearly every family contained at least one accuser or accused during the 1692 witchcraft hysteria. Most of the provocateurs (the judges and pastors) never apologized. No monument was erected in (North) Andover to the memory of those unjustly hanged or imprisoned. In a sense, both accusers and accused were victims – victims of the superstition and ignorance represented by fundamentalist Puritanism. After 1693, this system unraveled rapidly. Andover split into north and south parishes, with the newer south parish populated mostly by families who preferred a more liberal and enlightened form of Christianity, represented by Pastor Phillips. The north clung to the old ways for a while, championed by Richard Barker and Thomas Barnard. But it faded in importance while the south grew, eventually buying the name of the town for $500.00, forcing Andover to change its name to North Andover.

The class at Phillips Andover Academy which was addressed by President

George Washington was its first. Dr. Phillips established it as the primary preparatory school for Yale, while Boston Latin had been the primary prep school for Harvard. Over the years, its students chose both Harvard and Yale, as well as the other Ivy League Schools, which were established later.

In 1796, the village of Sudbury Canada was incorporated as Bethel, Maine. In 1805, the nearby village of Sunday River was incorporated as Newry. In 1820, Maine was separated from Massachusetts and became a state. This was a part of the Missouri Compromise, which accepted Missouri as a slave state and Maine as a free state to maintain an equal balance.

Jon Barker never did become 'the Jonathan.' After raising five children in Newry, he became an alcoholic. His wife took their sixth and youngest child, Anne, and returned to Methuen where she worked as a housemaid and cook in Swan's Tavern. Jonathan Barker 3rd became an embarrassment to his children and grandchildren. After all had moved from his house, he burned it down in a drunken stupor.

Jonathan Barker 3rd is buried in an unmarked grave in the back of the Newry Cemetery. His brothers and co-founders of Newry, Benjamin and Jesse Barker and their wives, are buried on a rise at the front of the cemetery.

An example of the comparative industry and success of the Barker brothers may be illustrated by the 1807 tax report. Samuel got a much later start than the others and suffered from limited growing seasons due to his frequent trips to Methuen on family business.

1807 NEWRY TAX REPORT

	Bldg Value	ACRES OF LAND			Horses	Cows	Cattle	Swine
		Improved	Un-improved	Improvable				
Benjamin Barker	$75	6.5	25	0	0	1	5	2
Jesse Barker	$15	2	35	0	1	2	4	2
Jonathan Barker	0	3	60	10	1	0	0	0
Samuel Barker	0	1	30	4	1	1	0	0

One hundred years after the death of the three Barker brothers, people began to ski on the mountain opposite their original cabin on the Sunday River. They had named it Barker Mountain and it is well-known today as the principal mountain at the Sunday River Ski Resort.

The Village of Menotomy, where many fought and died in the aftermath of the Battle of Lexington and Concord, became West Cambridge, and later, Arlington. In 1842, the town of Somerville was created from land formerly known as Charlestown Neck, including Prospect Hill and the Powder House, plus part of Cambridge bordering the Mystic River (Winter Hill).

Swan's Tavern was torn down in 1963, but the Faulkner House (where Jon Barker and Nancy Swan were married) still stands at the corner of School and Main Streets in South Acton. It sits opposite Ericsson Grain Supply whose buildings include one which was part of Francis Faulkner's fulling mill operations. Faulkner House is owned by Iron Work Farm, Inc. and is open to the public on the last Sunday of each month, but closed November thru April. Across Main Street, Jones Tavern still survives, the place where the Barkers and Faulkners met and supped after the marriage of reconciliation.

One of Jonathan's granddaughters was my great grandmother, Marcia Barker Saunders. She became an active leader of the Women's Temperance Union in western Maine and became a close friend of Abraham Andrews Barker, a local representative who was instrumental in leading Maine to pass a law banning the sale of alcoholic beverages in the state. A.A. Barker was a direct descendant of the accused witch, William Barker. He was a successful merchant with political aspirations, so he moved to central Pennsylvania, where railroad construction was spurring growth that created a new congressional district. He brought Nathan and wife Marcia Barker Saunders with him, providing employment to Saunders. His primary focus in political life was anti-slavery, which soon resulted in a friendship with Abraham Lincoln. As a delegate to the Republican Convention, he supported Lincoln's nomination. A.A. Barker was then elected to the U.S. House of Representatives.

Marcia Barker Saunders' husband fought in the Civil War and was wounded, spending several months recovering in a Philadelphia hospital. Upon his return to civilian life, he took a job on the railroad, where he was killed in a tragic accident in 1870, at age 42. He left his wife with a house in Gallitzin and four children. Her oldest daughter, Carrie, married David Williamson and bought a house across the street from Marcia. Her oldest son, Charles, moved to Altoona and her youngest son, George, became a deaf-mute at age six. However, this did not deter him. He was a successful barber and photographer and lived in another house across the street from Marcia. His other daughter was my grandmother, Laura, who married John Hysong, a carpenter.

Marcia judged everyone by their position on Prohibition. The Williamsons and Hysongs did not support it, so they were not allowed in Marcia's house. Yet, John Hysong's wife Laura lived there and somehow, they managed to have four children. My mother, Margaret, grew up in that house with her mother and grandmother and two sisters and baby brother, and rarely saw her father, until Prohibition became law. John Hysong was then allowed to move in with his wife. However, by then, my mother was attending Pennsylvania Teachers College at State College – which later became Penn State University.

My wife, Gail Chadbourne Kaepplein, is a direct descendant of Humphrey Chadbourne, who arrived from England in 1631 on 'The Pied Cow' and reportedly built the Great House at Strawbery Banke (today's Portsmouth, NH). Six generations later, Samuel Chadbourne served with Jonathan Barker Sr. at Winter Hill in Cambridge as part of Col. Gerrish's Regiment of Guards, as they guarded General Burgoyne's captured troops.

APPENDIX

AUTHOR'S NOTE

Historians have often criticized works of historical fiction for playing loose with history to enrich the story. In this book I have only sought to learn the truth of what happened in Andover in 1692 which would explain the commitment of five generations of Barkers to arrange marriages of reconciliation among the Barker, Swan, and Faulkner families in 1788 and 1808. Unfortunately, the historical record of 17th century Andover is silent on several critical pieces of the story. Therefore, I have had to assume what I felt to be the most likely explanation.

To be clear, I offer this disclaimer. There is no historical record to support the following:

1. That Richard Barker held a commanding position in Andover's town council.
2. That Pastor Francis Dane's theology became more liberal, leading Richard Barker to criticize him and Dane to then reduce the amount of his preaching.
3. That Rev. Thomas Barnard was, in any way, the provocateur of the witchcraft hysteria in Andover.
4. That Abigail Dane Faulkner shunned John Faulkner's family because of his role in the Great Swamp Fight of 1675.
5. That there was an anti-educational attitude among the council members of Andover.

Having stated that, I believe that the story I have told about the 1692 Andover witchcraft hysteria is the most probable one, given all of the other facts I have uncovered.

This book is built on a solid framework of facts; from these facts I have not knowingly deviated, nor changed a date or circumstance. All of the characters are real, including the Indians, Sabatus and Mollyocket. My determination to present authentic history has necessitated a scrupulous adherence to the findings of research. I felt that Jonathan Barker Jr., with his passion, courage and perseverance, lived a life sufficiently dramatic without fortuitous inventions. Mine has been a job of re-creation and interpretation, "putting flesh on the bones."

Some historians familiar with the 1692 witchcraft hysteria in Andover may be surprised at some of my interpretations and conclusions, particularly about the roles of some of the characters in that historic event. I have arrived at those conclusions by following the evidence as I confronted one question after another about my ancestors.

Why did Jonathan Barker 3rd and his 4-month-pregnant fiancé, Nancy Swan, make an arduous six day journey from the mountains of western Maine to Acton, Massachusetts to be married in 1788? The Acton Historical Society provided a partial answer: the marriage was performed by Justice of the Peace Francis Faulkner, grandson of Abigail Dane Faulkner, who had been convicted and sentenced to be hanged for witchcraft in 1692, partially due to testimony against her by William Barker.

Who would have directed Jonathan Barker 3rd to do this – 96 years after the betrayal by a Barker on a Faulkner? The logical answer would be his father, Jonathan Barker Jr. How would he know the history well enough to be so driven? Documents at the North Andover Historical Society provide the answer. Jonathan Barker Jr.'s father (the first of three Jonathan Barkers) died when Jonathan Jr. was just eight years old, and he was raised by his grandfather, Benjamin Barker. Benjamin was the youngest son of Richard Barker and he lived and cared for Richard during the last years of his life.

Similarly, Jonathan Barker Jr., after re-establishing his father's farm in Methuen, returned to Benjamin's home in Andover to care for him during his final days. Two days after Benjamin's death, Jonathan Jr. returned to Methuen and married his fiancée, Abigail Mitchell, who had likely been caring for the farm during his absence.

Why didn't Benjamin repair the damage to the Barker-Faulkner relationship himself? Why did he have to pass it on to his grandson? Documents in the No. Andover Historical Society show that Benjamin did develop a relationship with Francis Faulkner. The two lived on opposite sides of the ferry road north of the town. When Francis Faulkner conveyed the deed of his property to his son, Ammi Ruhammah, the conveyance was witnessed by Benjamin Barker and his son, Joseph. More importantly, it appears that Francis helped to arrange the marriage of Benjamin's youngest son, Jonathan, to Mary Abbott. Mary's father had moved from Andover to Marblehead where he married Susan Devereaux, daughter of a prosperous businessman. He raised his family there, but as his daughters reached their teen years, he sent them back to Andover to escape the drunkenness and rape by seamen in Marblehead. Mary returned to Andover to live with her uncle, John Abbott. John Abbott was married to Hannah Chubb, orphaned daughter of Pasco Chubb and Hannah Faulkner Chubb who were both slaughtered by Indians. Francis and Abigail Dane Faulkner raised Hannah Chubb as their own daughter. When Francis' wife, Abigail, died, he moved in with Hannah and John Abbott. When Francis Faulkner died, the executor of his estate was John Abbott.

If Benjamin had achieved this level of friendship with Francis Faulkner, why was more needed? Apparently, what was needed was a Barker-Faulkner marriage, and I believe that it was Abigail Dane Faulkner who would not allow this by any of her children or grandchildren. Her son, Ammi Ruhammah would have been even more adamant. In his youth, he had suffered the taunts of other children as a "son of a witch" and he had seen his mother suffering from the conviction that hung over her head for ten years, before her petition was finally granted by the court. More importantly, Richard Barker's apology and sense of guilt was directed only to the Faulkners, since Edmund Faulkner had been a close friend of his for many years. Richard had apparently not felt any guilt about the Barker role against Abigail Dane Faulkner.

An important piece of history of the witchcraft hysteria in Andover is the confession of William Barker. No historian has offered an explanation for William's two long confessions. While most of the many accused of witchcraft in Andover confessed, their 'confessions' were generally simple assents to the words that the judges or pastors expressed for them. William, on the other hand, went into great detail about 'riding on a stick to Four Mile Pond and signing the black man's book.' He further stated that he had a large family and life went hard with him and that the devil promised to pay all his debts and that he would live an easy life. Then, profoundly, he stated that the devil said that when he ruled, 'all men would be equal and live bravely and there would be no punishment for sin.'

William Barker was a simple farmer, educated enough to read the Bible and write his confession, but probably not much more. He did not have access to the philosophy of John Locke, although Pastor Francis Dane might have. The words of his confession had to have come from some local source. I believe that source was Pastor Francis Dane, and his mention of those sentiments was his undoing with the Andover selectmen, in particular, Richard Barker.

Most writers have assumed that Pastor Dane had reduced his preaching due to his advanced age and possibly, some infirmity. Some have even stated that he stopped preaching entirely. There is no historical evidence for either of these assumptions. Eleven years after the arrival of Pastor Thomas Barnard to supplement Dane's preaching, Dane was extremely active, trying to douse the flames of the witchcraft hysteria alone. He wrote numerous letters to pastors of nearby towns and to the judges, objecting to the use of 'spectral evidence' and the 'touch test' to convict those charged with witchcraft. He could not disagree with the existence of witches since it was a Biblically- based belief held by all Puritans. All other attributions to witches were based on long believed legends and superstitions. Dane likely doubted all of them, but could not openly say so. However, the use of spectral evidence (a statement by an observer that she saw the specter of the accused attacking another in the room) to convict and execute an accused was, he argued, an affront to Christian principles.

Thus, I maintain that there was another reason that Pastor Dane reduced his preaching in 1781, and I believe it was because the selectmen, and in particular, Richard Barker, had soundly criticized his preaching, which had changed after the events of the Great Swamp Fight in 1675 and the subsequent Indian attack on Andover in 1676. William Barker's surprising attribution to the devil of 'all men shall be equal and live bravely' is the antithesis of Puritan beliefs. They held that most men were of a lower class than the leaders and the wealthy and that they must live humbly and respect those above them. Dane may have found the corollary in his analysis of the 'Prodigal Son' story from the gospels and he may have read an early version of John Locke's article, which was the basis for Thomas Jefferson's words in the Declaration of Independence.

Some have painted Pastor Dane as the hero of the Andover witchcraft hysteria and Pastor Barnard as the villain. This is a major distortion of the truth. Clearly, there was some animosity against Pastor Dane after the arrival of Thomas Barnard. Most likely, it was due to his appeal to the court and the court's order that the townspeople must fully support two pastors. On the surface, they felt that Dane was undeserving, since his reduced preaching had necessitated the hiring of Thomas Barnard. The animosity led to many charges of witchcraft to members of the Dane family – nearly a third of all those charged in Andover.

On the other hand, there is no evidence of any animosity among the townspeople against Thomas Barnard, whatever his role had been in the witchcraft affair. The evidence suggests that he was involved in the questioning of some of the accused, and possibly counseling some of them to confess. When you consider the universal belief in witchcraft and the fact that many of the accused were strongly counseled to confess by their spouses or parents, his actions were entirely acceptable. More importantly, after the witchcraft hysteria had ended, Thomas Barnard continued to serve as pastor for several more years, until his death. At that point the town called his son, John Barnard to succeed him. The people of Andover, clearly, held Thomas Barnard in high esteem.

There is one minor entry in John Barnard's journal concerning his father's sermons, which suggests that one or more early historians may have found some issue in them for criticism. John Barnard wrote that "I have read all of my father's sermons and found them all to be in accordance with proper theology of the day." This raises the question: why did he then destroy all of them? If he did not, why did he not ensure the preservation of at least one of them? Unfortunately, we are left without a single sermon of Francis Dane's thousands, or John Barnard's hundreds.

CHRONOLOGY

HISTORICAL EVENTS AFFECTING THE BARKER-FAULKNER RELATIONSHIP

October 1675	Francis Faulkner married Abigail Dane
May 1689	Hannah Faulkner (sister to Francis) married Pasco Chubb
August 1692	Timothy Swan accuses William Barker of witchcraft. William Barker confesses and names Abigail Dane Faulkner his recruiter
August 1692	William Barker, Jr. testifies against Abigail Dane Faulkner
November 1692	Abigail Dane Faulkner convicted of witchcraft and sentenced to hang. Since she was pregnant, the sentence was delayed until the birth.
December 1692	Francis Faulkner and John Barker provide bail for the release of William Barker Jr. and Mary Barker.
January 1693	Gov. Phipps orders a halt to witchcraft trials and executions
March 1693	Richard Barker dies, leaves his house and land aside the road to Swan's Ferry plus land in Methuen, to his youngest

son, Benjamin.

February 22, 1698 Capt. Pasco Chubb, commander of Fort Pemmaquid, has his men attempt to kill Penobscot leaders during a peace parley. They escape and return with large contingent of Indians and French soldiers and surround the fort. Chubb abandons the fort to them and escapes, sailing south to Boston, where he is imprisoned for abandoning his responsibility. He is released to return to his Andover home, on appeal by Simon Bradstreet.

March 4, 1698 Indians invade the home of Pasco Chubb, killing him and wife Hannah. Seven-year-old daughter Hannah is spared. She is then raised by Francis and Abigail Faulkner.

November 28, 1708 Abigail and Francis Faulkner arrange the marriage of their daughter, Dorothy, to Samuel Nurse, nephew of convicted and hanged witch, Rebecca Nurse of Salem Village (Danvers).

April 11, 1710 Francis Faulkner arranges the marriage of Hannah Chubb to John Abbott

January 1725 Benjamin Barker elected Andover Representative to General Court

June 1726 Ammi Ruhammah Faulkner, son of Francis & Abigail, married Hannah Ingalls, great niece of Abigail's mother.

April 1727 Mary Abbott leaves her parents and siblings in Marblehead and moves to her uncle John's home in Andover.

January 26, 1728 Francis Faulkner arranges the marriage of Mary Abbott to Jonathan Barker

June 1728 Francis Faulkner deeds to his son, Ammi Ruhammah, his house and land on the road to Swan's Ferry (across the road from Benjamin Barker's). The deed is witnessed by Benjamin Barker and his son, Joseph Barker.

February 5, 1729 Abigail Dane Faulkner died. Her husband, Francis, moved to town to the home of his adopted daughter, Hannah, and her husband, John Abbott.

January 20, 1737 Jonathan Barker, age 28, died in Methuen, leaving his wife, Mary, son Jonathan Jr. and three young daughters. Mary returns to her uncle John's house in Andover with the three girls, two of which die within two years. Jonathan moves in with his grandfather, Benjamin, who raises him until he can return to Methuen to run his father's farm.

Jonathan Barker Jr. (1728-1794) was the son of Jonathan Barker and Mary

Abbott. Mary was the granddaughter of Thomas Abbott, who came to Andover around 1660 from Rowley. Her father, Joseph Abbott, was born in Andover in 1674, but he moved to Marblehead around 1694. He married Sarah Devereaux there. Mary Abbott was born in Marblehead in 1709 and she had two brothers and three sisters there. She moved to Andover to stay with her uncle about 1726 and married Jonathan Barker two years later.

Mary's uncle, John Abbott, was the husband of Hannah Chubb, who, as an infant, was orphaned when Indians killed her parents, Pasco Chubb and Hannah Faulkner Chubb, in 1698, in retribution for Chubb's betrayal at Fort Pemmaquid. Hannah was raised by Abigail Dane Faulkner and Francis Faulkner. When Abigail died in 1729, Francis moved in with Hannah and John Abbott. When Francis died in 1731, John Abbott was the executor of his estate. By this time, his son Ammi Ruhammah Faulkner and baby son Francis Faulkner, were living in Acton.

THE ANDOVER CONFESSIONS

How would innocent people know what to say in their confessions? For the most part, the examiners gave them the words. Did you sign the devil's book with blood? Did you ride on a stick to Three Mile Pond to be baptized by the devil? Did Abigail Faulkner and Elizabeth Johnson go with you? The person being questioned would simply agree and the detailed confession would be written up for their signature.

William Barker's confessions were quite different. Some statements did follow the standard pattern, but Barker included much material which was totally his own. His confessions were long and extraordinary. The full text of his first confession, written after his examination, plus his second confession, written while he was in jail, follow.

WILLIAM BARKER'S CONFESSION OF WITCHCRAFT

"He confesses he has been in The snare of the Devil three years. That the Devil first appeared to him like a black man and perceived he had a cloven foot. That the Devil demanded of him to give up himself soul & body unto him, which he promised to do. He said he had a great family, the world went hard with him and was willing to pay every man his owne. And the Devil told him he would pay all his debts and he should live comfortably. He confesses he has afflicted Sprague, Foster and Martin. his three accusers That he did sign the Devil's book with blood brought to him in a thing like an inkhorn. That he dipped his fingers therein and made a blot in the book, which was a confirmation of the covenant with the Devil

"He confesses he was at a meeting of witches at Salem Village where he judges there was about a hundred of them That the meeting was upon a green piece of ground near the minister's house. He said they met there to destroy that place by reason of the peoples being divided and their differing with their ministers.

"Satan's design was to set up his own worship, abolish all the churches in the land, to fall next upon Salem and so go through the country. He says the Devil promised that all his people should live bravely, that all persons should be equal; that there should be no day of resurrection or of judgment, and neither punishment nor shame for sin. He says there was a sacrament at that meeting, there was also bread & wine. Mr Burse[1] as a ringleader in that meeting. It was proposed at the meeting to make as many witches as they could. And they were all by Mr Burse and the black man exhorted to pull down the kingdom of Christ and set up the kingdom of the Devil. He said he knew Mr. Burroughs and Goody Howe to be such persons .And that he heard a trumpet sounded at the meeting and thinks it was Burse that did it. The sound is heard many miles off and then they all come one after another

"In the spring of the year the witches came from Connecticut to afflict at Salem Village, but now they have left it off. And that he has been informed by some of the grandees that there are about 307 witches in the country. He says the witches are much disturbed with the afflicted persons because they are discovered by them. They curse the judges because their society is brought under. They would have the afflicted persons counted as witches but he thinks the afflicted persons are innocent & that they do God good service. And that he has not known or heard of one innocent person taken up & put in prison. He says he is heartily sorry for what he has done and for hurting the afflicted persons, his accusers: prays their forgiveness, desires prayers for

---

1   The Rev. John Burse (or Buss), about 50, lived in Durham, New Hampshire, so was not subject to Massachusetts authority. His wife, Elizabeth, was the daughter of the imprisoned Mary (Perkins) Bradbury and her husband, Thomas. A physician and an unordained minister, John Burse at one time had been minister at Wells, Maine. His friend, the Rev. George Burroughs, became minister at Wells in 1690.

himself, promises to renounce the Devil and all his works And then he could take them [the afflicted persons] all by the hand without any harm by his eye or any otherwise. 5 September 1692 The above said is the truth as witness my hand. William Barker "Barker's two major claims of promises by the devil are extraordinary. That there should be no punishment for sin referred to the shameful public confession that was required when a Tithing man found one had violated the Sabbath. This practice had become unpopular with many Andover residents by the 1680's because there are records of people elected as Tithing men refusing to serve. Probably the practice had been discontinued in several other, more liberal, towns.

The most extraordinary statement was that "all men will be equal and live bravely" i.e. proudly. The last clause referred to the Puritan requirement for the lower classes to behave humbly. The major clause would appear to envision the Declaration of Independence, which would be written eighty-four years later. The real explanation is that William Barker, who was born in Andover just a year after its founding, had grown up in and lived in this oppressive orthodox Puritan climate for 46 years and had had enough. He was speaking for all of his generation in Andover who dared not speak. William Barker had the opportunity to speak and to ascribe his statements to the devil. His statement would signal the beginning of the unraveling of the Puritan theocracy in Massachusetts.

THE SECOND CONFESSION

From "Salem Witchcraft and Hawthorne's House of Seven Gables"
by Enders A. Robinson, with permission

A few days after his first confession, William Barker, Sr., produced a second confession from prison. "God having called me to confess my sin and apostasy in that fall in giving the Devil advantage over me, appearing to me like a black man in the evening to set my hand to his book, as I have owned to my shame. He told me that I should not want, so doing. At Salem Village, there being a little off the meetinghouse, about a hundred five blades, some with rapiers by their side, which was called, and might be more for ought I know, by Burse and Burroughs, and the trumpet sounded, and bread and wine which they called the sacrament, but I had none, being carried all over on a stick, never being at any other meeting. I being at cart a Saturday last, all the day, of hay and English corn, the Devil brought my shape to Salem, and did afflict Martha Sprague and Rose Foster by clinching my hand; and a Sabbath day my shape afflicted Abigail Martin, Jr. and, at night, afflicted Martha Sprague and Abigail Martin, Jr., Elizabeth (Dane) Johnson[2], and Abigail (Dane) Faulkner have been my enticers to this great abomination, as one has owned and charged her to her sister with the same. And the design was to destroy Salem Village, and to begin at the ministers house, and to destroy the church of God, and to set up Satan's kingdom, and then all will be well. And now I hope God in some measure has made me something sensible of my sin and apostasy, begging pardon of God, and of the honorable magistrates and all God's people, hoping and promising by the help of God, to set to my heart and hand to do what in me lies to destroy such wicked worship, humbly begging the prayers of all God's people for me, I may walk humbly under this great affliction and that I may procure to myself the sure mercies of David, and the blessing of Abraham."

Most of the imprisoned Andover people confessed that they joined the Devil's church. Their descriptions of this hellish church—its forms, ceremonies and sacraments—are the imaginings of clerical minds. The thoughts of the ministers shine through in the words of the confessors. The confessions were extorted by persistent importunities; sometimes threats were used, and even torture. Certain fanatic clergymen were first and foremost in the efforts to extort confessions. These ministers molded the persecution into a religious shape and form. The ministers then quoted the works of their own minds (the confessions that they zealously elicited) as proof of the Devil's plot, which they themselves claimed to dread. Cotton Mather, chief of this class, was the most forward in molding the affair of 1692 into a shape acceptable to his own illusions. The fabricated confessions revealed the whole scope of his superstitions and fanaticism. Cotton Mather used the confessions, especially references to Satan's plan to abolish all the churches and to the existence of hundreds of witches in the country, as proof of his own fantasies.

On September 16 William Barker, Sr. admitted to his confession before the Court of Oyer and Terminer at Salem. Sometime afterwards he made his escape from prison. On the back of his indictment for practicing witchcraft against Abigail Martin, Jr., it is written, "fled, persons fled." His cattle were

---

2   Elizabeth (Dane) Johnson in her confession taken on August 30 stated that she was carried to the witch meeting at the Village on a pole and her sister Faulkner was there and William Barker.

immediately seized, but were redeemed by his brother, Lieut. John Barker, who paid £2. 10s. to the deputy sheriff. About October 10 Lieut. John Barker and Francis Faulkner posted bonds for the release on bail of Mary Barker and William Barker, Jr. After six-weeks imprisonment the children were free, awaiting trial.

On January 3, 1693, the grand jury at the Superior Court of Judicature at Salem indicted both William Barker, Jr. and Mary Barker. However the two Barker children were not brought to trial at that time. A new bail bond had to be posted for the children to stay free. On January 13, 1693, Mary's father, Lieut. John Barker, together with Captain John Osgood posted "the sum of one hundred pounds to be levied on their or either of their lands & tenements, goods & chattels for the use of our said sovereign Lord & Lady, the King and Queen, on condition that William Barker, Jr. and Mary Barker having stood committed for suspicion of witchcraft shall make their personal appearance at the next Court of Assizes and General Jail Delivery to be holden for the County of Essex." At the May 10, 1693, meeting of the Superior Court of Judicature the two children made their appearance; each was tried by jury and found not guilty. Eleven years later, in 1704, Mary Barker and William Barker, Jr., first cousins, were married. Small wonder that these two, who had suffered hideous interrogation and imprisonment, should choose one another. They had eight children. He died in 1745, aged 66, and she died in 1752, aged 72. William Barker, Sr. died in 1718, aged 72; his wife, Mary, died in 1744, aged 88. The four graves may still be found in the old cemetery in North Andover.

ACKNOWLEDGMENTS

This book could not have come to fruition without the valuable assistance of several people. Carol Majahad, long-time director of the North Andover Historical Society, read an early manuscript. Because of my claim of historical accuracy, she diligently marked every paragraph dealing with 17th century Andover, noting the lack of original source material for my interpretation. An Email dialogue continued until I added disclaimers to my Author's Note to allow that such material did not exist, but that I had deduced a likely history for parts of my story.

Dan Gagnon, Director of the Merrimack Historical Commission and former Park Ranger on the Freedom Trail also reviewed an entire manuscript. He provided several corrections to my Revolutionary War detail.

Randy Bennett, former director and curator for the Bethel Historical Society, provided details of life in early Bethel, Newry, and Freiburg. He critiqued my descriptions of travel between Bethel and Freiburg and particularly, down the Saco River, fording three falls.

Historian Emerson "Tad" Baker apprised me of a most useful foundry of 17th century source material: *Siddeley's Harvard Graduates*, available in Google Books. There I found evidence of Pastor Thomas Barnard's close relationship with Cotton Mather at Harvard, where they were in successive classes. Tad also provided insight into Puritan life and practice.

Genealogist Melinda Lutz Byrne, A.S.G., offered valuable suggestions within and outside her high level of expertise. Her suggestion helped me to construct a better scene of the Battle of Bunker Hill.

Enders Robinson was an early collaborator and critic. As a Barker descendant and fellow M.I.T. alumnus, we shared a similar understanding of the Andover witchcraft debacle. He provided me with all of his research material and copies of his books on a disk, to get me started.

Kay McGinnis Ritter's many gifts and talents all contributed substantially to convert an assemblage of excerpts into a publishable book. I will be forever grateful to her.

Anthropologist Elinor Abbot met with me and my wife at Michael's Harborside in Newburyport to discuss her book, *Our Company Increases Apace* about early Andover residents.

Several other readers offered suggestions and support: Dianne Mather, Anita Dodson, Kitty Chadbourne, Anne Himmelberger, Evelyn Bonander, Chris Carlsmith, Elaine Donoghue, Claudette Sweeney, and Anne Forbes.

Last, but not least, my wife, Gail, for her forbearance with this long personal project of mine. Many years ago, she introduced me to the great historical novel, *The Winthrop Woman* by Anya Seton. It was praised by the N.E.H.G.S. for historical accuracy.

Mitch Barker has been far more than my esteemed editor. Before there was an idea of a book, he flew in from his home in New Mexico to research our common Barker ancestors with me. We went to the New England Historical and Genealogical Society headquarters in Boston. We visited with Dan Gagnon in Methuen. We met with Carol Majahad at the North Andover Historical Society and got copies of Barker ancestry data. We visited Salem, Ipswich, and Bethel and Newry, Maine and met with Randy Bennett. When I began to write and send snippets of my prose to him, he encouraged me to take a writing course at the Acton High School evening program. As I felt more comfortable, I began writing in earnest and he held back criticism, offering encouragement. I sent him a chapter at a time and he once commented, I can't wait to read what will happen next. I replied, "Neither can I," as I was learning more about the Barker boys' war service as I wrote. When I thought I had finished the book, he began his editing task in earnest, helping to mold my work into a readable story.

Finally, I must mention some of my sources of American history. Ronald Tagney's book, *The World Turned Upside Down: Essex County During America's Turbulent Years, 1763-1790* provided more applicable information to me than all of the books I read by great historians: McCulloch, Hackett-Fischer, Ferling, Ketchum and others. Tagney provides details of the Revolutionary War service of every officer from Essex County, Massachusetts. The service records of my Barker ancestors provides their dates of service and the officers they served under. This allowed me to construct the battle records of my Barker ancestors.

Insight into Puritan life came from *Every Day Life in the Massachusetts Bay Colony* by George Francis Dow, *Puritan Family Life* by Judith S. Graham, *The Wordy Shipmates* by Sarah Vowel, *The Winthrop Woman*, and several others.

ABOUT THE AUTHOR

Howard Kaepplein, 1933-2014, B.S. 1959 Sloan School, Massachusetts Institute of Technology. In his professional life he spent twenty-five years as an international sales and marketing professional, thirteen years in engineering management at Digital Equipment Corporation, and was a founder and President of Galaxy Power Corporation, 1994-2004.

Howard had a avid interest in genealogy. He researched his and his wife's genealogy, involving him with North Andover and South Berwick Maine historical societies, and served as president of the Chadbourne Family Association. He located distant German relatives and initiated a family reunion for 100 US and German Kaeppleins, held in Waghäusel, Germany. This work is based on his New England ancestors' role in the Salem witch trials.

He died of pulmonary fibrosis in September, 2014, when this book was in final production.

www.ingramcontent.com/pod-product-compliance
Lightning Source LLC
Chambersburg PA
CBHW072100170626
46813CB00004B/1417